# The Big Silence

# The Big Silence

**Bernard Schopen**

Foreword by William W. Savage, Jr.

University of Nevada Press :: Reno Las Vegas London

In memory of
Leah Storsve Schopen
1941–1971

**Western Literature Series**
Series Editor: John H. Irsfeld
A list of books in the series appears at the end of this volume.

*The Big Silence: A Mystery Novel* by Bernard Schopen was originally
published by The Mysterious Press of New York in 1989. The 1994
University of Nevada Press edition reproduces the original except for the
addition of a foreword and an afterword, a new cover design, and the
modification of the front matter to reflect the new publisher.

The paper used in this book meets the requirements of American National
Standard for Information Sciences—Permanence of Paper for Printed
Library Materials, ANSI Z39.48-1984. Binding materials were selected for
strength and durability.

**Library of Congress Cataloging-in-Publication Data**
Schopen, Bernard.
The big silence / Bernard Schopen ; foreword by William W. Savage, Jr.
p. cm. — (Western literature series)
ISBN 0-87417-254-3 (pbk. : alk paper)
I. Title. II. Series.
PS3569.C52814B5   1994
813'.54—dc20       9433718
CIP

University of Nevada Press, Reno, Nevada 89557 USA
Cover design by Heather Goulding
Printed in the United States of America

2 4 6 8 9 7 5 3 1

## FOREWORD TO THE NEW EDITION

When I was a youngster, my parents read a great many Agatha Christie novels—"mysteries," my mother called them. I was in a protracted Edgar Rice Burroughs phase, myself; but I was eventually persuaded to try Dame Agatha, not by my parents (who believed in letting kids read whatever they wanted, as long as it wasn't some lurid comic book) but by a magazine piece in which some since-forgotten sage observed that people with any brains at all naturally read mystery fiction in preference to any other form of the stuff. Anyway, I picked up one of her Hercule Poirot novels and proceeded to have a ghastly reading experience, from which I emerged feeling literarily retarded. I took to reading westerns, like Ike, who was, after all, the president of the United States.

Once Kennedy was elected in 1960, the papers were full of the new man's admiration for Ian Fleming's James Bond books. My father tried them and wound up liking them a whole lot more than he liked Camelot and its trappings. I deduced from the paperback covers that the Bond books were "campy crap" with "naked babes," but weren't the president and my father known intellectuals? What the hell, I thought, and gave Fleming a try. Alas, I couldn't get past all the brand names on the first page of the first novel I opened. My self-esteem ebbed.

In college I encountered a journalism professor (with a Ph.D. in English) who contended that Mickey Spillane was America's most imaginative creator of metaphor and simile, so I went after a few more paperbacks, the titles of which I now prefer to recall as *Kiss Me Quickly* or *My Gun is Dead*, because the parts were all interchangeable anyway. The racist, sexist, anti-commie thuggery practiced by Spillane's Mike Hammer was at the time in keeping with the racist, sexist, anti-commie thuggery practiced by, say, the F.B.I., but I thought it all rather pointless; and besides, I was having a hard time getting to the imaginative similes and metaphors, encased, as they were, in such vast quantities of abominable prose.

I came to Raymond Chandler in graduate school (for lack, I am tempted to say, of anything better to do), drawn to him as opposed to some other writer by nothing more than the Gothic-deco cover Ballantine Books had put on its paperback reprint of *The Little Sister*. Well, thank goodness for the folks in the art department. I devoured his work, read something academic about detective fiction, and went after, in rapid succession, Dashiell Hammett, Ross Macdonald, and John D. MacDonald. Thereafter, it was catch-as-catch-can, with prayers for serendipity tossed in for good measure. There was plenty to be caught, and I found my prayers answered with some regularity. My first James Crumley novel came from a supermarket, Ralph Dennis's priceless (to me, anyway) Hardman series from a variety store, Mark Smith's *The Death of the Detective* from a discount emporium that had it in the "true crime" section. One way or another, I have averaged a couple of hundred detective novels a year for the last twenty years, which doesn't make me an expert, but I can claim to have rolled up my sleeves and gone through the trash. In strange cities and towns, my young son has been heard to groan, "Not another bookstore," and wish aloud that he had gone shopping with his mother—although he well knows that she reads the damn things too, just as soon as I am finished with them.

I first found Bernard Schopen's *The Big Silence* in a small Dallas bookstore in the summer of 1992. It was one of two dozen books I bought that day, none of which were familiar to me. I was fishing again, to see what I could catch. I got around to reading *The Big Silence* that fall. When I finished it, I sat for awhile and stared out the window. When I gave the book to my wife, I said, "This is special." When she gave it back, she said, "Yes, it is." I would have passed it around to acquaintances, but I had only the one copy, and beyond your spouse, who can you really trust these days?

If God knows why the University of Nevada Press asked me to write this piece, that makes one of us. I am by trade a historian, but it seems to me the job wants a "lit critter," a dispassionate type for close analysis of form and substance, someone able to spot a symbol at a thousand yards in fog, not the commentary of an enthusiastic fan of a man and his genre. "Find someone who like the book less than I do, or somebody who knows Bernard Schopen," I said, "and get yourself something sensible." You see the result of an appeal to reason. My recourse has been to candor because I have no other choice—not unlike the private eyes who narrate the best stories, come to think of it.

What I know about Bernard Schopen is this: He teaches English. He has made an academic study of the detective novel. He has written a book about Ross Macdonald. He knows about Nevada. He has created a Reno detective named Jack Ross. Beyond that, whatever I say about Schopen is mere speculation. Perhaps he is like Jack Ross, or perhaps not. Perhaps he only wishes he could be like Jack Ross. Well, so do I. Maybe we both think there's a Jack Ross inside every one of us, a Jack Ross that can't come out because of all the sham and pretense and corruption and amorality and callousness and inhumanity we've shoveled in on top of him. Maybe that is why I read detective stories, to see done what I cannot do, and to see it done well, so that when I have finished reading, I can suppose there is indeed moral order in the universe—even if we must work hard to keep it in place one day at a time, and only then on the printed page. Maybe that is why anybody reads detective stories. But I am only guessing.

It pleases me to announce that Jack Ross conforms to the criteria for the private eye advanced by Raymond Chandler in his seminal and deservedly famous essay, "The Simple Art of Murder," which all interested parties should read, and sooner rather than later. If I had read it before that first meeting with Agatha Christie, I would have gone a-trysting elsewhere, for, as Chandler said, "The English may not always be the best writers in the world, but they are incomparably the best dull writers." Thanks to the laws of copyright, I cannot recite the whole thing here, but suffice it to say that Chandler wrote of heroes and of redemption, and how, to redeem himself or anybody else, a hero must have honor and be a good man and be a man of the people. He will be lonely, and he will be proud, and he will do what needs doing in order to find the truth, no matter what it may cost him, and the world will be a better place for his having been in it. Yes, I am happy to say, that describes Jack Ross.

It will perhaps displease Nevadans to read Jack Ross's perceptions of their place. As a historian, I have to say that there are no startling revelations. Desert dwelling promotes aberrant behavior, if not downright lunacy. Walter Prescott Webb said that (and several other things) about Nevada and its environs in an article he wrote for *Harper's* in 1957, and the outraged response he received allowed him to write an article in 1958 on what might be called "desert denial," because crackpots never know it, and if you want to argue with Webb or me or Jack Ross, go first and read your Bible and then a week's worth of your local newspaper. A detective needs a place to operate.

More to the point is the fact that, nowadays, the detective story traffics in social criticism. Schopen's Ross is, in this regard, an activist wading in the mainstream. What people are prone to do to each other is the issue, but they cannot do it outside the context of their environment, nor can they do it without leaving fresh prints on the earth. Increasingly, the American detective novel belongs to the literature of region, because it deals with a place and a time (and the time will often be a span of years), because one thing leads to another, and that is life. Why were we there? What did we do? What essential thing have we forgotten about the world? About ourselves? Hammett, Chandler, Macdonald—all the masters—knew that time is a place of ambush, and that none of us is too goddamn smart or cagey or tough to escape the crossfire. They knew we'll all meet up eventually with the consequences of our actions, in Nevada or anywhere else.

Schopen knows it, too. He writes detective stories. Go ahead and read this one. It is special.

*William W. Savage, Jr.*

There are many reasons why people go to the desert, some of which are not easily explained.

Sessions Wheeler
*The Black Rock Desert*

# 1

In Nevada, anything is possible.

In Nevada, nothing is as it seems.

In Nevada, nothing abounds, nothing signifies, anything is possible.

Even, in the Reno Hilton at nearly three o'clock in the morning, a hooker got up as a skin-flick witch and packing a beat-up old brown leather briefcase.

I was at the bar, drunk, but not enough. As I listened to the babble of voices and the ring and rattle of the slots, as I watched the eyes and the faces, like the Snowman I saw the nothing that was not there and the nothing that was. Seeing nothing was better than seeing hanging heads. . . .

Then I saw the hooker, and felt the psychic temblors that rumbled through the room. The eyes of pit bosses hardened. The backs of security men stiffened. The expressions of dealers and bartenders vanished behind their faces like vermin behind rocks before a silent swooping shadow.

All eyes were on the hooker.

She wore a high-collared black cape, a strapless bit of black brocade cut to the navel and trailing gossamer and sheen to the knees, high-spiked black heels. Her hair was black and short, her mouth wide and red, her eyes dark and shadowed with a dark and glittery swoop under brows plucked to arch in imperiously provocative inquiry.

She was fantasy sex, high-roller action at two bills a pop,

1

and, in the Hilton at three in the morning, as incongruous as the battered brown briefcase she clung to as if it were stuffed with money or the secret of life.

Standing before a gaudy bank of twenty-one machines, she searched the room. Then she moved quickly toward the poker pit. At the rail she stopped to stare at Haskell Dan.

Haskell Dan did not stir. His faintly melancholy old Shoshone eyes, as dark as hers, didn't waver. His handsome old Shoshone face didn't change. But after a moment he pushed two cards away, rose, moved through the pit, through the gate, and rested a hand on the hooker's arm.

The pit bosses turned away, inward, to tend private patches of 3 A.M. care. The security men slumped back into sore-footed somnolence. The hooker wasn't working.

She was talking.

Haskell Dan listened, his lean body attentive in neatly pressed jeans and a clean, faded plaid shirt. He looked over her shoulder at me. Then he shifted his hand to her elbow and led her to the bar.

She was, obviously, kin—his granddaughter, probably. She was half a head taller but her profile was a smaller, more finely-boned version of his own. Her skin was lighter, but dusted with his darkness.

I hadn't known that Haskell Dan had family. Playing cards, his talk was almost always about fishing. I knew that he left his trailer park most mornings at two to walk downtown, hide his flyrod and tackle under the Arlington Street bridge, walk to the Hilton and play $1-$3 seven card stud till sunrise, retrieve his fishing gear and work the ripples and pools of the Truckee River upstream until he had a meal, walk back to his tiny trailer and cook and eat his fish and watch television and go to bed. That was all I knew.

The hooker took a stool. Laying the briefcase on the bar, she enclosed it within a protective arm. Then she swiveled to face Haskell Dan and began again to talk.

I couldn't hear her words, but the tone was importunate—

that pleading irreverence, full of simple certainties, of the child secure in the knowledge that it is deeply loved.

Haskell Dan stood beside her, saying nothing. His eyes, meeting mine again, seemed even more melancholy.

The hooker stopped talking, pulled the briefcase closer to her body. Haskell Dan looked at her. Then he stepped away from the bar, walked its length, and sat down beside me.

"You aren't playing tonight, Ross."

I raised my glass. "Tonight I'm drinking, Haskell."

"Yes," he said. "Are you talking?"

"Must be," I said. "I could drink at home."

"Can you see your way clear to talk to my friend Glory?"

Friend? If Haskell Dan and the hooker weren't blood-bound, I was going to have to find another line of work. I was going to have to find another line of work anyway.

"I could, but I don't really want to."

"I know."

His eyes told me that he really did know.

"What does your friend Glory want to talk about?"

"Her grandfather. She wants you to find him."

My grip on reality, not so firm recently, slackened even more. A seventy-year-old Shoshone wanted me to help a hooker who was almost certainly his grandchild find her grandfather. I flashed the bartender the thirsty sign.

"Why does she want to find her grandfather?"

"She thinks he's alive."

A still chill lurked beneath the syllables. "He isn't?"

"The man she looks for has been dead forty years."

"Haskell," I said wearily, "I don't need this, not now."

"I know."

He was an old man. He was a good man. He was a friend. I drank, sighed. "What do you want me to do?"

He clasped his brown, battered hands and laid them on the bar and looked at them, and at the band of silver and turquoise he wore on the left ring finger.

"When I was a boy I heard the old people say, *The world began when I was born and will die when I die.* They saw with their visions and not with their eyes. The girl is like the old people. She does not see what is. She does not hear those who do. She hears only the voices in her dreams. I have told her that the man she looks for is dead. The voices in her dreams tell her that she must find him. She will try."

Haskell had always spoken simply, in phrases as spare and sometimes as beautiful as desert flora, but I had never heard this, the solemn cadences of the old-one chant.

"Haskell, what do you want me to do?"

He couldn't quite tell me. He stared at his hands. "As a boy, I could not see visions. I saw only with my eyes. I thought the visions were the dreams of weakness and whiskey. So I left my people and went to the people who saw as I did. I worked for the parents of the girl's father, and they became my people. I saw the blood of her father's birth, heard his birth-cry. I saw the blood of his death, too, and of the woman in his marriage bed, and I took the little girl from her bed so that she would not see the blood, and I carried her in my arms to her grandmother. I did not go back to the desert. I have tried to protect her. But I am old now."

Birth and blood and death, litanies of woe. I couldn't escape them. Hanging heads. . . .

I was growing sober, and colder. "Do you have visions now, Haskell?"

"No," he said, "I see only what is. Old things, things I have seen before."

"Why do you come to me?"

"You give a man your eyes, Ross," he said, and he gave me his.

So here I am in the Reno Hilton at three in the morning talking to an old Shoshone about visions and blood and a hooker who's dressed like something from a sick dream and hanging on to a briefcase for dear life. Little wonder that I said what I found myself saying:

"I carry death these days, Haskell."

"No, Ross, it isn't you. You don't kill them."

"That doesn't matter."

"I know," he said.

He also knew that I was going to talk to the hooker.

"You were sure I'd be here tonight."

"You are always here these nights, Ross."

That, I recognized, was true. I'd been cold a long time.

"You want me to find a dead man?"

"I want you to help her."

"To protect her? Doesn't she have a . . . *man* for that?"

"She has no one but me."

"What does she need protection from?"

"The past."

I sighed. "Just tell me what you want, Haskell."

"Show her that he is dead."

"How am I supposed to do that?"

"Go to the desert."

"I . . . is she in danger, Haskell?"

"I don't know. Maybe. But she needs help."

I looked down the bar at her. She was all slim limb and garish makeup and silly costume. To ward off stares, she'd made her face a carapace of street-wise disdain.

"She doesn't seem to need much help from anybody."

"She is not what she seems."

Catching my eyes in the mirror, the hooker turned, and I saw then as in a vision of my own that she was not Haskell's granddaughter. The warriors in her genes had ridden not ponies but ships, curve-bowed Nordic craft. The antishadow of pale skin between the exposed tops of her breasts said that her darkness came from the desert sun. The darkness of her eyes, her hair, might have come from anywhere.

Nor, suddenly, was I sure she was a hooker. Not when she smiled. Her smile quivered with intimations of childish delight, transforming her sleazy get-up into the gaily-worn appurtenances of a game of pretend.

Stunned, I turned to the old man. "I'll talk to her."

"Yes, and help her," he said. "It will help you too, the desert. So you will not sit and drink and remember."

"But not now." I rose from my stool and drained my drink. "Tell her to come see me. I'll do what I can."

"Thank you."

"You're welcome. Good night. And good fishing."

"Too much water to catch fish."

"Then just . . . good night."

I turned and walked through the bright hard chill of the casino out into the soft, starry chill of the desert night.

# 2

Virginia Street at three-thirty in the morning: the detritus of the day in the gutter, the detritus of the night—glazed-eyed drunks, crazed-eyed derelicts, empty-eyed tourists—on the sidewalk and in the streets, shuffling nowhere. I fit right in.

My Wagoneer was in the Cal-Neva parking garage. I left it there, shuffled down Second Street and up onto the bridge.

Haskell Dan was right—no fish would be caught in that wild water. The river ran high and fast, slapping at the bank, sucking at the concrete bridge supports. Thanks to a long wet spring and the melt of the winter's big snows in the Sierra, the Truckee was, for now, a real river.

Six weeks before I'd been hired by a divorced waitress who was certain that her missing six-year-old daughter had been stolen by the little girl's father. While I was in Vegas tracking him down, the real river gave up the child's small, battered, bloated body.

No escape.

I walked on, past the Reno Police Station, to my building. A faint light cast shadows in the office of Sierra Bail Bonds. Opening the main door, I stopped in the hall to collect the day's mail, then climbed the stairs to my office. I tossed the mail onto the pile—ten days high—on my desk and opened the door to my apartment.

I'd lived in these rooms most of my life. Through the alchemy of time and death, they'd changed from my grand-

7

parents' home into mine. Now my home seemed not mine at all, seemed the setting of a half-remembered dream.

I showered and slipped into an old robe. I was tired—I was exhausted—but I knew I would not sleep. Once my eyes closed I'd confront again the grisly image that for ten days I'd been trying to sear from my brain with alcohol.

In the living room I popped in a tape of Julian Bream and Bach and sank into my chair and picked up the new biography of Will James I'd started eleven days before. I read a sentence and put it down. I wasn't up to more of that Nevada Gatsby, the writer and artist whose only significant creation—himself— turned on its creator and killed him.

In Nevada, anything is possible.

In Nevada, nothing is as it seems.

Bach wasn't working. I changed tapes, let Linda Ronstadt sing those songs my mother, they say, had loved to dance to.

I looked at the liquor cabinet. The last thing I needed was more booze eating at my gut. I got up and poured half a tumbler of vodka.

I sat, closed my eyes, and warded off grim visions by conjuring the image of the person I most loved. My daughter, smiling, smiling—

"You don't look that old."

My eyes flew open so fast that my daughter's smile for a moment spread the hooker's wide red lips. Then the ghost image faded and the smile became the hooker's own. She stood in the doorway in the same high-sleeze outfit; the same beat-up briefcase brushed the hem of her black dress.

"That's blue hair stuff." Her smile slid into a stiff seriousness. "Although Ronstadt is certainly a fine artist."

"How'd you get in?"

"Your front door is so flimsy you should be arrested. The other door was open." She stepped inside. "What a nice, old-fashioned room. How old are you, anyhow?"

Angry, I struggled to get up. "Look, Miss—"

"Oh, please don't rise on my account." Easing with studied grace onto the couch across a low table from my chair, she crossed her legs demurely and slid her stiletto-heeled feet back beside the briefcase on the floor. With a flourish she tossed the cape back from her bare shoulders. Perched primly on the edge of the cushion, she smiled. "Now, about my grandfather."

The performance killed my anger. I was just tired. "I don't talk business in my living room, Miss. . . ."

"Dahlman. But please, call me Glory."

"And I especially don't do business in my living room at four in the morning. When I told Haskell I'd talk to you, I didn't mean—"

"Oh, I knew you were a night person, as I am. And there's no point wasting what's left of this one, is there?"

"You're not getting the message, Miss Dahlman. I'm not about to—"

"Please. I do appreciate your manners. One encounters real courtesy so rarely these days. Uncle Haskell said you were nice. But call me Glory. I'll call you Jack, if I may."

"Glory's your professional name? As in Glory Hole?"

It was as nasty as I could make it. She was oblivious.

"My mother named me Gloria, but my grandmother called me Glory, after the flower. All her girls are flowers."

Haskell was right. She was not what she seemed. She was illusion overlaid on mirage. She might have been twenty. She was made up to look five years older but instead looked five years younger, a handsome girl who should have scrubbed her face and scurried off to class. Her eyes—blue, surprisingly, the dark blue of the near-night sky—reminded me of an old song: *I've got the blues so blue they're black.*

"Haskell Dan is your uncle?"

"Only by affection. He was a dear friend of my father. He has always been kind to me. And he speaks very highly of you, Jack." Her mind skipped to a different groove. "What were you contemplating so deeply when I came in?"

"The mysteries of the universe."

"What mysteries? But then everything is probably a mystery to you. You're a private investigator, a detective. You probably see deep, dark secrets everywhere you look."

To not think about what I'd been seeing everywhere I looked, I said, "How about the mystery of the briefcase?"

"It's no mystery." She pulled it onto the table. "It's my legacy from my grandfather. It's art."

She showed me, fanning over the table perhaps two dozen sketches, their corners curled and bent and folded, edges browned, surfaces yellowed by age. "Aren't they wonderful?"

They were of two sorts: desertscapes—sage, twisted trees, gap-spoked wagon wheels jutting from sand dunes—or studies of a rather spectacularly constructed young woman in various stages of undress. The drawings were neatly initialed "L. P." in stiff block letters. They weren't wonderful.

Her eyes widened in expectancy. I didn't fulfill it. "So?"

"So he's alive." And now she was a different Glory Dahlman—not the witch-hooker, not the junior-leaguer, just a silly young girl. "He's a famous artist, and these are worth plenty. That's why I carry them with me, so no more of them will get ripped off."

"Somebody stole some of these? Who?"

"A gentleman I was foolish enough to show them to."

"What gentleman?"

"Just a gentleman."

"A john?"

She looked at me as if I'd said nothing.

"A man stole some of these sketches, so that means your grandfather is alive?"

"Of course."

"Haskell told me your grandfather died forty years ago."

"Uncle Haskell is sweet, but he's not always right." Her smile was serene. "He can be wrong, sometimes. He's wrong about this. He did agree that you were the man to see about finding my grandfather. I hope he was right about that."

I had no choice. I could have shown Miss Glory Dahlman and personae and costume and briefcase to the door. I wanted to. But that would have forced me to return to myself.

And I had given Haskell Dan my eyes, and my word.

"Okay. Tell me about it."

# 3

"**A**ll my life they told me he was dead, that the desert got him after he killed that guy. But the desert didn't kill him, he survived and became a famous artist. And he's not too old, only sixty or so. So he's alive. I know it."

The unhappiness in Haskell Dan's eyes took on meaning. "Your grandfather killed a man?"

"In Winnemucca. The son of a rich rancher. They fought over my grandmother, and my grandfather killed him. He killed for her." She picked up a sketch. "Wasn't she magnificent?"

She showed me, swift crude lines suggesting a voluptuous female figure, the face a blur of eagerness—a fantasy woman as adolescent as Glory's fantasy outfit.

"He killed for her. For love. My mother and father killed themselves for love, too." Her voice trilled with the thrill of high romance. "Doomed by love. Me too, probably."

It would have been hard to take anytime. At four in the morning, after ten nightmare days and surreal nights, it was too much. I invoked reality, ugly as it might be.

"For a prostitute, that's highly unlikely."

Reality couldn't touch her.

"Prostitute," she echoed airily. "It's just a word—words don't mean anything." She rose and stepped to the wall that was mostly bookcase beside my chair, so close I could feel the heat of her haunch, smell her scent. "Don't you read these books? They all tell us that real meaning comes from inside. Yeats, there—what was he but a man who made his life a poem, who

**11**

loved that Maud Gonne and made her into what he wanted her to be, in his poems, and then lived his real life in his verses. I do the same thing. I'm an artist, like my grandfather. I write poems—*heart bleeds*, I call them. And I'm an artist in love, I create dramas of love, entertain, give pleasure, just like any performing artist."

As Haskell said, Glory saw what she envisioned, listened to dream-creatures. One of whom was a man dead forty years.

"Your grandfather. What was his name?"

"Lawrence Parker. See the L. P. on these? Of course, he changed it. There isn't any famous artist Lawrence Parker."

"Why do you want to find him? Because he's famous?"

"No. I mean, I don't want anything from him, not money, if that's what you think. I just want to talk to him."

"Why?"

"Because he's my grandfather."

She seemed, for a moment, simply a grandchild.

She settled back on the couch, her breasts shifting under the cloth that couldn't cover them. Her legs crossed, her black high-heeled shoe danced on the end of her foot.

"Let's see if I've got this straight," I said. "Your grandfather, Lawrence Parker, killed a man in—"

"Not a man, really. A boy. He was still in high school. My grandfather was only seventeen himself."

"—in Winnemucca. Forty-plus years ago. What was the other boy's name?"

"Lotz. Daryl Lotz."

"They fought over your grandmother, and he . . . how old was she?"

"Thirteen." She smiled proudly.

"So your grandparents weren't married? I take it there's no question who your grandfather is?"

"My grandmother says Lawrence Parker. She's never been wrong about that, not with any of them."

I didn't quite get that, but I let it pass. "She's still living?"

"Right here, in the Valley."

Sun Valley—the main bane of the Sheriff's Office, the main drain on the Welfare Department—dust and violence, dereliction and dope and mayhem, bikers and red-necks and Texas two-stepping sluts and ADC mommas and kids like animals not ignored only when they were being brutalized. I began to understand Glory's refusal to address reality.

She anticipated my next question. "Flora Baker. She was Flora Magnusson then."

Dahlman, Magnusson, there were plenty of Vikings in her blood. I could see them in her squarish handsome face. Yet I couldn't shake the feeling that quite different blood had darkened her blue eyes, shaped her smooth-boned flesh.

"Right. So he escaped into the desert. He is, has been, presumed dead. Until a man walked off with some of Parker's sketches. You got them from your grandmother?"

"She kept them with my parents' things—my father's knife and belt buckle and ring, my mother's jewelry."

"Why with your parents' stuff? Weren't they your grandmother's?"

"No. My father's."

"Where did he get them?"

"From Uncle Haskell."

I must have looked as bewildered as I felt.

"It's really quite simple," she said. "Uncle Haskell found them in the Black Rock Desert. He gave them to my paternal grandmother, Dolores Dahlman. She gave them to her son, my father, Stuart Dahlman. My father brought them to my maternal grandmother. That's when he met my mother."

"But if Haskell found the sketches in the Black Rock, how do they prove that Parker didn't die out there?"

"They don't. Not the sketches." She held up the briefcase. "This. He never let it out of his sight. He had it when he ran after he killed Daryl Lotz. Haskell found it six weeks later, a hundred miles away from there."

I took a long pull from my glass. "But he obviously didn't have the briefcase when Haskell found it."

"Yes he did, Jack. Haskell found him too."

"Haskell told you that?"

"He told me that he killed him."

"Glory, this is. . . ."

"I know. Ridiculous. Haskell couldn't kill a flea. Don't you see? Haskell told me he killed my grandfather. But you and I both know that can't be true. The only logical explanation is that he's protecting him."

"From what?"

"From the Winnemucca sheriff. My grandfather is wanted for murder. Haskell obviously gave his word that he wouldn't reveal his new identity."

"Even to you?"

"That's what I said. But you know Uncle Haskell." She smiled, her dark eyes full of play-pique and affection. "He just goes Indian on you, gives you that look like he's ten million years old, and you can't get anything out of him."

The Ronstadt tape ended. I popped it out and popped in Merle Haggard. Glory smiled. "You like that cowboy stuff?"

"Country," I corrected her. "Yes."

She shook her head. Her breasts shivered. She noticed my noticing and smiled. "So how are you going to find him?"

"I'm not."

"But I thought—you told Uncle Haskell—"

"That I'd talk to you. I have. But Haskell says your grandfather is dead. Nothing you've said proves he isn't."

"That's what *you're* supposed to do, prove it! That's what you do. You're a private investigator!"

"You're a hooker, Glory, but we aren't fucking."

"Goddam you, Uncle Haskell said you would! He said you'd help me! He—" She bit it off, but it stayed in her dark eyes. Now she was just a spoiled little snot.

"Look, Glory," I said wearily, "if you're convinced that Lawrence Parker is alive, find him yourself. Track down the john who stole the sketches. If your theory is correct, then he knows who your grandfather is. Find out from him."

She sagged back onto the couch. "I can't."

"Where'd you meet him?"

"At a party at Cal Blass's." Cal Blass, originally Cal Blascovitch, on the street, the Sierra Snowman.

"How can you hook with all the coke-whores around?"

"Talent." She stared at me. Then her eyes changed. She gave

her arched brows a Groucho wiggle and began to laugh. I nearly laughed too.

"How did you meet him? Did somebody introduce you?"

"No. I was looking at this photograph and he came over and started talking about it and I told him I had a drawing of the same scene and he said he'd like to see it."

"What kind of photograph?"

"Of the desert. It was big, poster-sized. It was night, there was this little canyon kind of disappearing between these hills in the desert, that's all."

"What else can you remember about this guy?"

She twisted uncomfortably, briefly exposing most of a smooth breast, now not noticing my noticing.

"He was just a guy. I mean, I can't remember all the—"

"Try."

Her lashes, furry with mascara, her glistening dark lids, dropped. "He wasn't old. Dark hair. He was strong."

"Big?"

Lids still lowered, she shook her head. "Just strong. Solid. I remember I was leery about letting him take me to my apartment, but he was nice, a real gentleman; he was polite, and he wanted to see the sketches, so. . . ."

"He drove you to your place? You usually do that?"

"No, but he wanted to see the drawings. He knew a lot about art. I thought he might be able to. . . ."

"Tell you what your grandfather's new name was?"

She nodded.

"What was he driving?"

"One of those little sports cars, I don't know what color— blue, maybe."

"When you showed him the sketches, what did he say?"

"He—he just looked at them. He said they were good."

"And he never told you his name?"

"No. I don't let them."

"What would you guess he did for a living?"

"I—dope, maybe. He had the gold chains and all that thug-stuff. I don't know. He could've been a dentist."

"What else did he say?"

Her eyes rose, became street eyes. "He said he wanted me to sit on his face."

My eyes closed.

"Okay," she said, "I'm sorry. But it was three weeks ago. Ever since I found out he swiped them, I've been trying to remember him. I even asked Cal, but you know how that is."

I did. "Did he talk to anybody else at the party?"

"A couple of other chicks. And Cal—they seemed tight. He joked that I was going to show him my etchings."

"I don't suppose you'll tell me who else was there?"

"I . . . can't."

I understood why. It could be dangerous.

I sat and sipped my drink and listened to Merle Haggard.

When I looked at her, Glory was smiling a different smile— warm, sweet. "You're going to find him, aren't you? I knew you would. It was like fate, when I found out Uncle Haskell was your friend."

"You asked Haskell to talk to me?"

"I read about . . . it in the papers. I knew if you could find . . . well, you could find my grandfather. I called you. You didn't answer."

I hadn't answered for ten days.

"But now you're going to help me. Uncle Haskell said you would."

"I thought he didn't have visions."

She laughed. "Everybody has visions, Jack."

I didn't know about that, but I was having something like a vision of my own. I saw the desert, its shapes and colors, its emptiness. I heard its big silence.

Her laugh softened, deepened. She rearranged her limbs and her smile. "Now, about your fee."

"Don't worry about it."

"Is that the way you usually do business?"

"This isn't business. It's a favor."

"We could, uhm, trade favors."

"The favor isn't for you. It's for Haskell."

Her smile widened. "Are you telling me you're not interested in me? If you are, you're lying."

"You're attractive, Glory—or would be if you'd wash the clown stuff off your face. But I've never been interested in fantasy sex, especially the kind you're peddling."

She laughed again. "Jack, you know all sex is fantasy. And love. Love's just a story some medieval poet made up to explain to himself why he couldn't sleep with the queen."

I couldn't take much more. "Look, Glory, you don't owe me anything. Your grandfather's dead. I'm going to go prowl in the desert, and if I get lucky I may be able to confirm his death. But I'm really doing this for myself, to be doing something. To be going into the desert."

"But you . . . you really will try to find him?"

"Yes."

"Then you admit it's possible—that he's alive, I mean."

"In Nevada, anything is possible. Even you."

She took that as a compliment. Smiling, she rose. From a slit in her dress she pulled a small sheet of black paper, folded once. Inside, in white ink, in fat oval letters, was a phone number. "Call me as soon as you find him."

I stood and slipped the black paper into my pocket. She handed me the briefcase. "You might need these."

Her cape had fallen over her shoulder. With another flourish she swept it back. "Are you sure there's nothing I can do for you?"

"Very sure."

She smiled. "If you're going to play that cowboy stuff, Jack, at least you ought to listen to it."

I did listen.

It wasn't love, Merle pointed out, but it wasn't bad.

For the first time in ten days, I laughed.

I went with her to the top of the stairs. She stopped, put her hand on my arm. "You'll really try?"

"I'll really try."

Quickly she leaned to plant a brief soft chaste kiss on my cheek. Then she turned and, in her spiked heels and black hooker's costume, hopped happily down the stairs.

In Nevada, nothing is as it seems.

# 4

I slept until the dreams came. Then I got up, made the bed, showered, shaved, dressed in a tan light-weight twill suit of subtle Western cut, a pale green shirt, a chocolate tie with thin red and green stripes, gleaming brown boots.

I made coffee and took it into my office, ignored my mail and the red blink of my answering machine, and got on the phone.

After an hour, I knew one thing for certain: Humboldt County held an outstanding—forty years outstanding—murder warrant for one Lawrence Parker. So at least that part of Glory Dahlman's goofy tale was rooted in reality.

I stashed Glory's briefcase and left. At the Cal-Neva I retrieved my rig, then hit the interstate and headed east toward the Truckee River Canyon and what lay beyond it.

The drive to Winnemucca took four hours. It seemed less. The desert—so implacably harsh and forbidding to those who trudged over it a hundred years ago, so unutterably boring to those who race across it now—was beautiful.

Snow still spattered the tops of nearby ranges, and beyond them distant ranges rose in the hazy May light like ghostly bluish shadows of each another. Pale green and purple grasses pasteled their flanks. In the long valleys, sage spaced itself toward the horizon in a natural pointillism.

I followed the Truckee to Fernley. Then, in the Forty Mile Desert, what should have been blistering sand was shimmering lake, a mirage that wasn't; the Carson Sink in this wet year was a few feet of Sierra-born water spreading over the flat earth. Above it, on the brown hills, wave marks from long-gone Lahontan, a real lake that in the Pleistocene era had covered most of the state. Less than a quarter-mile from the end of the Carson Sink, the beginning of the Humboldt Sink; then the Humboldt River, for seventy miles hatched sun-silver and shade-brown like a fat rattler.

I drove and enjoyed the desert and thought of nothing.

Winnemucca stretched not very far along the south bank of the Humboldt. The main artery through town was clogged with plastic cholesterol—fast-food joints, mini-markets, souvenir shops, bars, gas stations—the casinos stamping "Nevada" on it all. The rest was small frame houses and metal trailers, front porch swings, struggling patches of lawn, old cars, bicycles in the shade of scraggly trees.

The Humboldt County Court House sat on a sunny corner two blocks up a side street. I bypassed it for the moment. Instead I parked in front of the library and went inside.

A stooped septuagenarian led me with a stove-up cowboy shuffle through the stacks to the old newspaper section, a dusty room not much larger than a toilet stall. The year I wanted squeezed like a green cardboard coffin into a long row of dead years.

My guide watched me open the volume at the tiny desk. "Lookin' for anythin' special?"

"I'm interested in unsolved murder cases in the state." That was more-or-less accurate. "I understand you had a nice one around here forty years ago or so. Lotz?"

"Wasn't unsolved. Young fella named Parker broke the neck of Pete Lotz's boy. Never did catch up with him."

"Know the boys, did you?"

"Some," he allowed. "Used to do a piece of work for Lotz. One registered son of a bitch. His kid had all the makin's himself. Seen the Parker boy around. Artist fella."

"Any good?"

The stoop of his shoulders resulted from something other than age. He had to shrug them in reverse, drawing his head down like a furtive vulture. "I ain't no expert. Looked okay to me, what I saw—desert, mountains, that stuff. And them he did of the Magnusson girl." His leer was awkward and unpracticed, an expression he hadn't called upon in years.

I flipped the bound papers, paged casually. "What happened to the Magnusson girl afterwards?"

" 'Bout what you'd figure with a heifer like that. A while after the fracas she dropped a kid, an' her daddy tossed her off the place. Come into town and fooled around an' finally got married right before she dropped another kid. Couple months later she was just gone."

"Who fathered her children?"

"Don't know. Do know it wasn't me." It seemed a matter of long regret. "Pretty thing, an' shaped so's many a hand gunked up his line-shack bunk dreamin' about her."

The vein I'd uncovered in the old man seemed pretty rich. I nodded at the chair. "Why don't you sit down for a minute, if you're not too busy, Mr. . . ."

"White." He drew the chair back and eased onto it. "Folks call me Spoon, on account of bein' bent over from a mule kick in the spine when I was a kid."

"Jack Ross," I said. "You strike me as a man who's spent more time with critters than with books, Spoon."

"Buckarooed some, till I got too banged up," he said. "Volunteerin' around here. They need help, an' I always did like to read. Ain't much else to do in a line shack."

"Except dream about Flora Magnusson?"

"Confess to some of that," he grinned. "But books help keep a man's mind off that. Specially detective books."

I leaned back in my chair. His laconic drawl fit with his worked-out body and weather-worn face. It didn't fit with his eyes, which were bright with amusement.

"Putting me on a bit, Spoon?"

His face slid into a yellow grin. "Some, maybe."

"You know who I am?"

"Read the Reno papers too."

I said nothing for a moment. Then I tapped the bound book. "What am I going to find in here?"

"What Pete Lotz wanted in there."

"What should be there?"

"What there was."

I waited. Not long. His eyes looked beyond me and the present, back. He rubbed his battered old hands together as if before a campfire.

"She always had it, Flora, that ready-to-rut look, even when she was just a kid. Had half the county pawin' dirt, waitin' for her to get legal. Didn't have a momma to tell her what to do with it, an' her ol' man, Jens, he sure didn't know. Worked all day in that little hay patch he had out north of the dunes, sat around all night sippin' schnapps. But it all started with him. He kinda pushed his girl and the Lotz boy together—not that young Lotz needed much pushin'. But Jens figgered bein' in-laws with Pete Lotz would fix what was ailin' him, get him more hay sold, maybe more land and water. Probly would of. Anyhow, Flora and Daryl Lotz took up together, an' none of the other young studs around was gonna do much on account of Pete. Except when young Parker drifted in—what'd he know about Pete Lotz. Once he got a gander at Flora, that was all she wrote."

"She dumped the Lotz boy for Parker?"

"Kept 'em both. Daryl 'cause of her daddy, an' Parker . . . well, she liked him enough, I guess."

"How long was Parker in town before the killing?"

The yellow skin of his forehead bunched up. "Wandered in about first cuttin', I think. Four, maybe five months."

"When was Flora's first child born?"

"Yeah," he nodded, "everybody counted. Next spring, April, May. So it coulda been either one of 'em. 'Cept that Pete said it wasn't a Lotz."

"Why'd he say that?"

"It didn't have balls."

I waited.

"Pete just had the one boy. Figgered he needed another, keep the name goin', all that stuff. Story is he made a deal with Jens, if Flora's kid was a boy Pete'd claim it."

"The girl, Flora, she went along with this?"

"Didn't have any say in it one way or the other."

That didn't seem to be taking me anywhere. I dug in a different direction.

"Did all Parker's sketches end up with the Sheriff?"

"Half the folks in town had 'em. He used to trade 'em for shirt-stitching an' such."

"The Lotz family—any of them still around?"

"Ol' Pete's out on the Circle Lazy L in Paradise Valley, livin' with the oldest daughter and her husband. Still meaner 'n a sheddin' snake. One registered son of a bitch."

I glanced down at the yellowed newspaper, then back at the yellowed old buckaroo. "What happened, Spoon?"

"The girl and Parker was in the dunes this Sunday afternoon. He was drawin' her, she said. Some say the doc said they was up to more'n that. Anyhow, young Lotz comes ridin' up and catches 'em. Him an' Parker get to arguin' an' Daryl puts a rifle bullet past his ear an' Parker grabs him and gives him a few shakes and snap!—there goes Daryl."

"He broke his neck?"

"An' then lit out."

"Why couldn't they find him?"

"Big snow fouled up the search. Probly fouled him up too. He's out there."

"Where?"

His neck dropped into a shrug. "Sink hole, lion den, earthquake rip, hot springs—the desert can get you a dozen ways. It don't leave much of anything when it's finished."

I knew that. "It doesn't sound like the clearest case for murder I ever heard, Spoon."

"It was to Pete Lotz."

"I see," I said, and might have been beginning to. "I suppose I'd better read through this stuff anyway."

The old man rose and shuffled off. I turned to the newspapers, immersed myself in sententious prose.

The story of the Lotz killing had competed with World War II for front page space in the local weekly for a month, but most was speculation, alleged expressions of community outrage, stentorian cries for justice.

The search had been spurred by a five-thousand-dollar reward offered by Pete Lotz, but after a week the Sheriff was talking about finding a body rather than a man—no mention was made of the fact that Parker himself was a boy. The desert, the Sheriff said, would exact its terrible tribute, and the taxpayers of Humboldt County would save a bundle.

As Spoon had indicated, it said more about the influence of Peter Lotz than about the facts of the case.

I found Spoon behind the counter doing a stiff two-step with a rolling rack of books. "Any help?"

"Not as much as you've been."

He grinned. Then the grin faded. "Got to ask you this. That fella, the one in Reno . . . how crazy was he?"

"Completely."

"Used to have them kind in the desert—Bristlecone and guys like that. Still a few out there. Sort of expect it in the desert. Never figgered it in the city."

"A city's just a different kind of desert."

He looked at me and said nothing. I left.

# 5

I stood for a moment in the now windy heat. The Court House looked busy enough that I might be able to lose myself in the shuffle. Wind stirred the dust on the street into delicate swirls as I crossed.

An hour later I'd gotten what there was to get.

The father of Flora Magnusson's first child, Rose, was listed as "unknown." Flora had married a James Baker. Two months after the marriage Flora gave birth to a second girl, Anemone. A month later, Jens Magnusson had eaten his shotgun. Six months after that, James Baker had sued for divorce on the grounds of desertion.

I walked back to the Wagoneer and sat making mental notes, marginalia to the rough draft of the story of Lawrence Parker and Flora Magnusson that Glory Dahlman had told me.

Then I headed north.

The Humboldt River churned high and brown past the youngsters collected on its banks to watch. I crossed the bridge, arched up into the sage. And then the sand.

The dunes lay parallel to the river, shaped by the wind that funneled through the Bloody Run Hills and created them. I followed the highway through the long, gray-white, green-tufted lumps, wondering vaguely where that sand was stained with forty-year-old blood.

North of the dunes, where the Little Humboldt River met them and died, pumps sucked water from the sink and piped it to rolling sprinklers that turned the desert into feed for stock. Somewhere down there Jens Magnusson had worked his hay field, sipped his schnapps, and eaten his shotgun.

The Little Humboldt tracked back into Paradise Valley. When I came to the turnoff, so did I.

The sageland swelled upward. Old cottonwoods marked the creeks and drainages down which water emptied from the craggy Santa Rosa Mountains to the north and from the Hot Springs Range to the south. Ranch buildings sat like fortresses within dark green hay and alfalfa fields; windbreaks of tightly-planted poplars protected them.

At the turnoff to the Circle Lazy L, a huge brand hung from a heavy chain stretched between tall posts. The mail box beside one of the posts bore the names Lotz and Harkness.

I followed the dirt road toward the base of the hills. A quarter-mile from the ranch buildings, a freshly-painted white fence blocked the road. I stopped, got out, opened the gate, got back in and drove through, got back out and closed the gate. The last part of this ritual took place under the scrutiny of a rider who had appeared from a sandy wash astride a big buckskin gelding.

I walked around to the front of the car. "Afternoon."

The brim of the rider's sweat-stained hat dipped. From within its shadow, eyes examined my rig, suit, face. "You state or federal?"

My Wagoneer was plain and white. That meant it looked like a government vehicle, at least to folks on the lookout for them. I smiled. "Neither, I, uh. . . ."

Long and hard-looking, the body hid under a plaid shirt and jeans stiff with dirt; the boots and gloves were a shade darker than the shaded face. But although the greeting hadn't been warm, the voice had a warmth, a softness, somewhere inside it. I took a chance. "Mrs. Harkness?"

She—I hoped—didn't answer.

"My name is Jack Ross. And I don't work for any agency—county, state, or federal."

Saddle leather creaked, the buckskin shivered, the wind

caught a sweet horse smell. A gloved hand nudged the hat brim up, releasing long stray strands of graying brown hair.

"I guess not. You had sense enough to shut the gate. I'm Janet Harkness. What can I do for you?"

"I'm a private investigator, Mrs. Harkness, and I'd like to talk to you, and to your father—"

"Get off our property!"

"Mrs. Harkness, I—"

"Leave him alone. He's an old man, he doesn't even know where he is half the time. I don't know how he managed to dig you up, but you better scurry right back into your hole." One hand shoved the hat down over her hair; the other jerked the reins and the nodding horse's attention.

"I mean your family no harm, Mrs. Harkness. I—"

"You're on private property. I've got an ought-six back at the house. I might not be able to hit you from there, but I can put enough holes in that machine. If it's on this side of the fence when I get there, I sure as hell will."

She gave the reins another jerk, the gelding a heelthump in the ribs. The buckskin wheeled and galloped down the road, throwing dust and the flash of shoes to the wind.

I moved my Wagoneer to the other side of the fence, got out and leaned against the front fender and waited.

A small activity stirred at the house, but no bullet holes appeared in my rig. She wasn't going to shoot at me. They didn't in this country anymore, even though they still might want to, even though sometimes they had good reason.

Finally a figure stepped from the house and mounted the buckskin. Horse and dust bore another body clad in plaid and denim. But the hat was a baseball cap, the head under it large and round, the face as lumpy and indented as the potatoes that grew in the valley. The hands reining in the buckskin were large and thick and would be formidable fists.

He climbed heavily off the horse, tossed the reins into a snarl of buckbrush, opened the gate and stepped through it, closed the gate, turned.

The hand that came at me wasn't a fist. "Jess Harkness. You

wanted to talk?" His handshake was heavy, but there was no threat in it, nor in his eyes. They were brown, calm, quietly aware.

"Jack Ross, Mr. Harkness. I'm sorry if I upset your wife. As I told her, I'm a private investigator. I'd like to talk to you folks a bit, and to your father-in-law."

He spat over his hard-looking belly into the dust, scraped the spot with the edge of worn boot. "What about?"

"A small part of the investigation I'm conducting concerns the death of your wife's brother, Daryl."

He turned, joined me in leaning back against the fender. I listened to the wind until he said: "Pete been in touch?"

"I've never communicated with him in any way."

He turned his head to study my face. I studied his. The intelligence in his eyes made his ugliness comforting, playful, a rubber mask a child might delight in wearing.

"Why should we talk to you?" he asked reasonably.

"Neighborliness?"

His eyes smiled. He pushed away from the fender. "All right, Mr. Ross. I'll talk to you. So will the wife, if she doesn't get too riled. I can't speak for Pete. Bring your outfit up and we'll find some shade."

I followed him to the house. In the ranch yard he pointed a thick finger at a new Ford Bronco sitting in a splash of cottonwood shade, and I parked beside it. "Get comfortable there on the porch. Got to see to the horse."

The porch was shaded, sturdy, bordered by a bed of daffodils and a small lawn inside a white picket fence. I sat in an old leather rocker and examined the place.

The Circle Lazy L looked prosperous—looked made and kept that way by hard work. A neat U of outbuildings and a white barn circled the house, a single-story frame structure, old but sturdy, painted the same white as the barn and the fence. The green trim matched the quilt-like squares of alfalfa, nearly matched the block of pasture beyond the barn.

Harkness came out of it and over to the porch. Sinking into the chair beside me, he took a pack of Kools from his shirt pocket. I shook my head at his offer, watched him light up. Smoke drifted away on the wind. "You probably got something that says you are who you say you are."

I showed him my I.D. and gave him a business card. He studied the card. "Lawyer too, huh?"

"I've got a piece of paper that says so. I only use it to impress people who don't know any better."

Jess Harkness obviously wasn't one of them. "Other lawyers, I bet." He dropped the card on the table between us. "Why don't we get right to it. Are you after the reward?"

"The only reward I know about is the five thousand Pete Lotz put up for the capture of Lawrence Parker. Are you telling me it's still good?"

He sucked up more smoke. "Make a difference?"

"No."

"It's still good. Pete. . . ." He looked out at the Santa Rosas, massive, dark, beginning to cast small shadows.

"We've had to deal with detectives before. Bounty hunters, most of them, con men. They heard about the reward and wanted to make a deal with Pete, usually half the money against expenses, the other half when they found Parker. Bad as Pete got sometimes, he only went for it once."

"But he thinks Parker is still alive?"

He flipped his cigarette over the flower bed and lawn and fence onto the hard-packed dirt of the ranch yard. "It's hard to tell what Pete thinks anymore."

"What do you think, Mr. Harkness?"

"I think you might be the Jack Ross in the Reno paper a few days back. What's it like, seeing something like that?"

I saw it again, shuddered. "I don't think I can tell you that, Mr. Harkness."

"Suppose not," he said. He seemed to be waiting for something. I gave him what I had.

"Early this morning I ran into a girl who told me a story about a man named Lawrence Parker and showed me some sketches and claimed that Parker was alive and asked me to find him. I told her I'd check it out."

"This girl, she'd be . . . ?"

"The daughter of Flora Magnusson's first daughter, Rose. Flora told her that Parker was her grandfather."

"Flora ought to know. And the girl may be right."

"Lawrence Parker is alive?"

"I don't know about that," he said slowly. "But I don't think the desert got him."

# 6

Jess Harkness looked out again at the mountains.

"Twenty years ago, a couple fellows came by, a soldier and an Indian. The soldier had some drawings too. He wanted to sell them to Pete. They were of Flora."

"Did Pete buy them?"

"A couple. They're inside, in his scrapbook." He shook his head. "Pete thought the soldier knew where Parker was. I had a hell of a time keeping him from busting him up. The guy said he'd track him down, if the reward still stood. By the time he left he'd talked Pete out of a couple hundred for expenses. Pete's been waiting for him ever since."

"This soldier—he had a name?"

"Dahlman. Stuart Dahlman."

"And the Indian was Haskell Dan?"

Harkness gave me a long slow look.

"Stuart Dahlman is the father of the girl I'm working for. Haskell Dan is the one who asked me to help her."

He dug for another cigarette. "Sort of fits, huh?"

"Where did he get the drawings?"

"From his mother's stuff. He showed up just after she died. On bereavement leave, he said."

"You knew Mrs. Dahlman?"

"Her place was only a hundred miles west."

Not quite next door, even in this sprawling, large-spaced land. "How would you guess she got them?"

"Parker was always trading drawings for meals, a washed shirt."

"You didn't go to the authorities?"

"Pete did. Didn't come to anything."

"Who else knows what you do, Mr. Harkness?"

"Hard to say. All I really know is that Lawrence Parker somehow got to the other side of the Black Rock."

"Spoon White says nobody could make it across."

"Good man, Spoon. Doesn't mean he's always right."

"Haskell Dan told me that Parker was dead."

Harkness looked at me. "Could be. Or he might have a reason to tell you that. It—"

The screen door swung open under the force of Janet Harkness's hip. She carried a pitcher of iced tea and a pair of glasses on a tray. I rose from the rocker. She set the tray on the table. "I thought you men could use a dust cutter." Her hands fluttered. She controlled them by pouring tea.

Janet Harkness wore the same plaid shirt and soiled jeans, but her greying hair was brushed and smooth, her face freshly scrubbed. It must once have been almost pretty; now it was worn, haggard, apprehensive.

She waved a nervous hand at me. "Please. Sit." She eased down to the porch and leaned back against a post.

"How is he?" her husband asked.

"Awake. Sort of." She took a deep breath. "I'm sorry about that stuff at the gate, Mr. . . . Ross, was it? It's just the idea of him getting all worked up again, especially now, when he's . . . like he is."

"How is that?"

"Senile," her husband said. "You're never sure where he is. It's like eighty years is one big picture in his mind and he'll just look at a piece of it and he's twenty and then the next minute he looks somewhere else and he's fifty. And he gets mean. Always was."

His wife glowered. "He can't even keep himself clean."

The iced tea was good. "I don't want to cause you any trouble with him, Mrs. Harkness."

"You can't imagine his kind of trouble." Her mouth twisted bitterly. "He killed my mother, wore her into the grave, at her all the time about having a son. My sisters he drove off the place. He ran off every beau I ever had, till Jess finally planted himself and wouldn't budge."

"But," I said to her, "you stayed."

She hugged her knees tightly to her chest. "At first I was taking care of my mother. Then I had the little girls to take care of. Then I had Jess. And there was nowhere to go. Besides, I'm as much a Lotz as he is. And he's going to die before I do, and I want to be there."

"I . . . may be able to get by without talking to him. Your husband says the old man has a scrapbook. Any chance I can get a look at it?"

"I—if he goes back to sleep, maybe." With a thumbnail she began to pick absently at the paint of the wooden porch. "Maybe if you could just tell us what it is you need to know, we could tell you and you wouldn't have to."

Jess Harkness shifted in his chair. "He's trying to track down Lawrence Parker, hon."

Her shoulders stiffened. "You think he's alive?"

I answered carefully. "There's never been any evidence that he isn't. If he's dead, I'd like to prove it."

"Why do you think we could tell you anything?"

"Your father has been trying to find him for years," I said. "He's probably traced a lot of false leads. If I could look at his scrapbook it might save me a few pointless chases. There also might be something in there that means nothing to him but might mean something to me."

"Lots of mights in there, Jack," Jess Harkness said.

"At this point, that's what I've got most of."

He lit a cigarette, his wife scraped the wood porch, I sipped iced tea. The wind soughed around the corner of the house. Dust drifted up from the valley floor into the sunlight. Shadows stretched down the mountains.

"I'll see about the scrapbook," she said finally.

When she was inside, Harkness refilled my glass. "You're trying to make things easier for her. I appreciate it. It's been hard on her. What she told you is just the outside. The inside stuff's been even worse."

Janet Harkness returned with a hand-tooled leather scrapbook in her hands. "There isn't all that much."

The first pages held photographs carefully fastened with corner clips: snapshots of a tall, broad-shouldered, proud-grinning man with a faceless bundle of blankets crooked in his long arm, and then several of a baby who gradually became a five-year-old, complete with a cowlick and a crooked grin. Through the pages the snapshot quality improved, the cowlick came under control, the grin grew more crooked. The final photograph was a formal school portrait of a young man who stared at the camera as if to suggest that only the official occasion kept that grin from twisting into a sneer.

Then came the newspaper accounts of Darly Lotz's death and the search for Lawrence Parker, a handbill offering five thousand dollars for information leading to Parker's arrest, newspaper ads soliciting information, generally illiterate letters insisting that Parker was everywhere from Pioche to Pocatello, and letters full of vague promises and demands for money from private investigators. There was no correspondence from Stuart Dahlman.

And two drawings initialed "L.P." In each the same nude figure stood in quarter-profile. Beneath the swirl of wind-stirred hair, the features were indistinct. The expression, conveyed by heavy pencil strokes around the mouth, was not.

"How do these tell you that Parker's alive?"

"From what Flora told the Sheriff, he drew those the day he killed Daryl. They're the only ones he did of her—"

The screen door slammed into the side of the house. Janet Harkness's eyes jerked wide. The back of my skull exploded, the world turned over, porch splinters dug into my shoulder. I got my head turned just quickly enough to see the blur of boot. I jerked back, the heel clipped my chin, I rolled off the edge of the porch into the daffodil bed.

"Thievin' son of a bitch!" The voice was a loud hollow rumble, like a vivid but meaningless memory. I scrambled back from it, got to my feet.

He towered above me on the porch, a big man who'd been big long before age and inactivity had covered his frame with fat. His old longjohns were soiled a lumpy yellow at the crotch; a month-long menu of meals dribbled over his huge stomach. His jowly face was dark and swollen with blood. "Gimme my money, you thievin' son of a bitch!"

Jess Harkness watched him quietly. His wife seemed frozen. Then she moved. "Dad, stop it!" Her hand twisted into the rank cloth of his sleeve. "He isn't the one!"

The old man threw back his arm, and his daughter went with it, stumbled into the rocking chair. He stepped heavily off the porch. "You govamint issue son of a bitch!"

I backed away from him. His huge fists were scarred and lumped and dappled with liver spots. "Careful, Mr. Lotz."

"Goddam crook!" Tobacco-stained spittle flew from his mouth, beaded on gray stubble at the edge of his jaw.

I continued to back away. Jess Harkness remained silent and still in his chair, watching.

The old man lumbered ahead. I felt the fence against my heel and stopped. His big fist started back, then forward. When it reached the top of its arc, I stepped aside.

Confusion replaced the rage in his eyes. He couldn't stop the blow. The fist sailed past me, the arm, the shoulder; he toppled onto the fence, grabbed at it, wheeled slowly, fell heavily, lay sprawled on the grass. His eyes were open, staring into the blue sky, seeing nothing. His big gut and chest rose and fell rapidly; his breath wheezed from his gaping mouth.

Then Jess Harkness was beside me. "You all right?"

My head and chin and shoulder hurt, but I was all right. "What about him?"

"He'll be okay. Want Jan to take a look at that chin?"

I rubbed at it. The pain was sharp, and my hand came away streaked with blood. My shirt was spattered with it.

"Ought to get a damp cloth on it, anyway." He turned toward the house.

"You going to leave him there?"

"Yep."

Janet Harkness still sat in the rocking chair, stunned. She turned blank eyes to her husband. "Is he dead?"

"No."

"Oh." She sounded, if anything, disappointed.

"Hon, could you get Jack a cold cloth for that chin?"

"Oh!" She started, as if awakening. Taking my jaw in her hand, she tilted it up. "That really should have some stitches. I'll be right back."

I sat in the rocker, leaned forward, dripped blood onto the worn wood. "What the hell was that all about?"

"I'd guess he thought you were Dahlman. You're his size, he was dark like you, your suit's about the color of his uniform. You had the pictures in your hand."

I shook my head, watched the pattern the small red drops created on the wood. "Crazy old bastard."

"Yeah," he said. "Thanks for not hurting him."

Pete Lotz had managed to sit up. His gaze passed over me as if I weren't there, found Harkness. "I fall?"

"Yep."

"Gonna help me up?"

"Nope."

The old man grunted, reached out to a fence slat, and slowly pulled and twisted himself to his knees, his feet.

Slowly, old, he moved to the porch. He gave me a long, puzzled look. "I seen you somewhere?"

"Nope."

The question faded from his eyes. Nothing replaced it. "Hungry," he said, and shuffled into the house.

"He been this way long?"

"A couple years."

"You thought of a rest home?"

"He's going to die pretty soon, Jan wants to see it."

Then she was back, fussing, wiping and cleaning my chin with a cold wet cloth, patching it with a crossed pair of Band-Aids. "Still ought to see about stitches."

I did a damage survey. My shirt was stained with blood. The elbow of my jacket was torn. My trousers were stained with grass. Three daffodils had been crushed under my fall.

"I can save that shirt if I can get it in cold water," she said. "Take it off. You can borrow one of Jess's."

"All right. But I've got another shirt in my car." I slipped out of my jacket, started to unknot my tie.

"I'll get a pan started," she said, and fled.

I stripped off my shirt and draped it on the porch rail, then stepped into the yard and headed toward the Wagoneer.

Harkness fell in beside me. "You need the scrapbook?"

"I don't think so, but thanks."

I opened the rear door and unlocked my trunk and pulled out an old Stanford sweatshirt. While Harkness studied the trunk's contents, I jerked off my boots, slid out of my trousers and into a pair of jeans, slid back into my boots.

"Rigged for the desert, huh?"

"For about everything." I had fishing gear, a broken down 30.30, several changes of clothes, sleeping bag, packets of dried food, a camera and tape recorder and some electronic hardware, a paperback copy of *Moby Dick*, two jugs of water, cups, and a fifth of Glenlivit.

I folded my clothes and put them in the trunk, then shut it and the door.

"You sure you're okay?"

"Fine. And thanks again for your help."

I offered my hand. He took it. "Where you headed?"

I hadn't really thought about it. But there wasn't much more I could do out here. "Back to Reno, I guess."

"You might want to take the Gerlach road back."

I'd like nothing more. But sometimes the west section of that road was a road and sometimes it wasn't. "No problem, this time of year, all the water?"

He looked over the Wagoneer, me. "You could make it."

"Why would I want to?"

"It runs pretty close to the old Dahlman place."

I gazed into his lumpy, ugly face, his calm brown eyes.

"Might not be anybody around, though. The fellow that owns it now comes and goes."

"You know him?"

"Of him. Dolores Dahlman's nephew. A photographer. Name's George, Gabriel George. He might be able to help you."

# 7

The he road out of Winnemucca was a gravelly strip through sageflats and low hills. The land loomed desolate, ominous, starkly lovely—the pale range haunches stained green by runoff, the ragged range crests pinion-dark and snow-white, the tan and sandy playa shimmering with still water.

After a while I passed the rotting foundations and big-puddled playa that had been Jungo, then the cattailed spring and hillside mines and abandoned shacks at Sulphur.

Then the Black Rock Desert.

From the road, dirty white sand tufted with sage spread out to the old lake bed that surrounded the sheen of silver that was the Quinn River sink. Far beyond it in the haze rose the pyramid of black rock that gave the desert its name.

The road deteriorated. Pockets of sand, slick and soft, shoved my front wheels, sucked at the back wheels, scraped oil pan and differential. The bottoms of washes were a quarter-inch of cracked, dried mud over a slick sandy goo; I had to blast down into the muck, jerk and slide through, spin and buck up the other side, and get ready for the next one.

For over an hour I fought the sand, ears tuned to the hum of the engine, eyes flickering from gauges to sand to the brown hump of range ahead of me that seemed to get no nearer. Until, finally, it was nearer, finally it was there, and I pulled up onto dirt, rock. At the top of a rise, I stopped.

The Wagoneer was splattered with mud and lumps of sand, the undercarriage was coated with thick gray gunk, the tail pipe was loose, but it seemed all right.

Then I made myself a drink and sat on the fender and looked at the desert. The late afternoon sun spread golden light on the land, the silence.

It was a big silence, soothing, serene, made bigger, more soothing, more serene by the sounds that whispered in it: shush of wind, clack of rock, scrape of brush, hiss of sand. Beat of heart.

It was what I had come for, the big silence.

I sipped scotch and thought of nothing, let the desert take me, let the gritty wind scour the faces from my mind, the blackness from my heart, the blood from my hands.

Silence and emptiness. And time. Silent, empty time—epochs, eras, eons of time compressed into the rock, carved into the hillsides—so much time that the past in which human life did not exist became the present, as did the future in which all trace of humanity has vanished from the universe. In the big silence under the empty sky, time itself became meaningless, and death, and life.

Silence, emptiness, time. Nothingness. Abounding. And nothing mattered. Not even me.

My drink was finished. I had another, reluctant to leave. It wasn't enough, this brief communion. I needed not merely to experience it, the grand nothing, but to become it.

But I didn't have time.

I fired up my rig and aimed it at the sun.

Soon the spoor of civilization began. Narrow dirt roads wandered off toward ranges in search of water and minerals and ranches. Fences appeared, a distant glint of windmill.

I turned on the radio and found, through one of the atmospheric quirks of the desert, a strong clear signal from KUNR, and Mozart. Then I saw ahead the jagged pile of red rock and the road Jess Harkness had told me to watch for.

For a quarter-mile the road edged a narrow wash in which a brown trickle nourished willow shoots and cattails. Then it bent over a low roll in the earth, and the Dahlman—the George—place came into view.

The ranch hadn't been worked in years, and the desert was reclaiming the land. The dusty-yellow house was in good shape, but the few outbuildings were weathered and spine-busted, the corral gapped and falling in on itself. Sage invaded abandoned hay fields.

The road showed fresh tracks of a heavy-treaded vehicle, but I couldn't see one. I parked at the house, turned off the motor and Mozart, and climbed out. I could still hear Mozart, drifting from behind the house.

Long-vanished feet had trampled the sandy earth into a hard path. I followed it around the house. The music grew louder, clearer. I rounded the corner and stopped.

The radio dangled on the limb of a cottonwood. Beneath it a smallish young woman in stylish bright colors swayed mirage-like to the music before a large canvas spread with muted desert colors. The shapes on the painting were blocky, abstract. The shapes on the painter were not.

To avoid startling her, I moved slowly into her line of sight. My caution didn't help. Suddenly aware of me, she jerked back from the easel, her eyes huge and full of fear. The brush in her hand dropped to the dust.

My grin didn't help. But even startled, fearful, she was pretty—smooth pretty features, small pink pretty mouth. And with her eyes, more than pretty. Big and brown, they made the pretty face around them richly human.

I kept grinning, put a hand slowly near my ear and made a twisting movement.

My pantomime reassured her a bit. She turned down the radio, then bent and retrieved her brush. I felt soft scrotal shiftings.

I took a slow step forward, and a guess. "Miss George?"

That smoothed the stiffness from her face. "I'm Dolly George, yes."

I moved closer, still smiling. I took out a business card. "I'm inquiring into a matter concerning the previous owners of your ranch." That, stretched enough, was true.

She examined the card, then my sweatshirt, my face. "I don't know anything about that. My father might. He'll be back any time now."

"I'd like to wait for him then, if you don't mind. I could do it in my car. I don't want to impose."

She tucked the card into the pocket of her blouse. She took a small step back, slowly sucking the length of me into her eyes. "You don't look especially imposing."

The soft slap of sexual glove was as unexpected and as day-brightening as her presence. "Ah," I said, "my disguise is working then."

A smile threatened her mouth. "It's the sweatshirt. Stanford men are notoriously effete."

"Notoriously."

To hide her smile, she turned and dropped her brush into a mason jar of muddied turpentine that stood with assorted paints and brushes on a small folding table.

I moved closer. To avoid too obviously studying the girl, I studied the canvas. She studied me.

"Well?"

"It's very good."

"No it isn't."

She was right. "The composition is sound."

"But?" Her eyes fixed on mine. Fun danced in their darkness. "I have little ego invested in this, Mr. Ross. Take your best shot."

"It's all there, but it doesn't quite add up to the desert. I've seen a lot of attempts to do it abstractly. I've never seen one that succeeded."

"Why is that, do you suppose?"

"I'm not sure. It's the sort of thing you can't explain—at least I can't. The forms and colors are there, but when they're fused, the desert gets lost in the activity. It's like the sound of silence—what's the shape of nothing?"

"You are an artist yourself, Mr. Ross?"

"Jack," I smiled. "No. I took an art course once."

"Sophomore level, no doubt."

Mozart ended, the delicacies of Chopin began. "No doubt. But think of your father's photographs. They're remarkable, but they're in black-and-white. Have you ever seen a color photograph of the desert that really worked?"

"You know my father's work?"

"I'm a fan."

"An art critic, perhaps?"

"Student, maybe."

She nodded at the radio. "As well as a fan of Horowitz, a connoisseur of fine music."

"I took a course in Music Appreciation, too. Student."

"At Stanford?"

"I studied law at Stanford. The finer things in life I learned of at UNR."

"I was under the impression that at the University of Nevada the finer things consisted of swilling beer and shooting at highway signs from a moving pickup."

"I'm Nevada born and bred. I already knew that stuff."

"So, Mr. Jack Ross," she said, her small mouth pursed smaller, her eyes full, "you know everything."

"More like a little bit about a lot of things."

"I see." The corners of her mouth twitched. "A sort of Jack Offal Trades."

That could have been nasty. She knew it. Her sudden smile told me that it wasn't.

"I have a response to that, but it's obscene, and I don't know you that well. So," I bowed, "I surrender."

"How well would you have to know me—" She stopped. Her face changed; a charge I hadn't known it held diminished. "You put up a good fight. That must be Nevada." She laughed. "But Stanford made you a good loser." She waved a small hand toward the table. "I have to clean up. Why don't you wait inside. There's beer in the refrigerator."

She didn't strike me as the beer type. A Manhattan, maybe, strong dark bourbon, a hint of dry vermouth, a bit of red fruit. But I didn't say so. I went inside.

The house was cool, dim in the waning light, filled with smells like memories—long-spent sweat, dead smoky fires— and, mixing caustically with it all, a new, sharp scent of chemicals. The furniture was worn but serviceable, the linoleum on the kitchen floor faded by the passage of boots and time. The stove was black and old, the refrigerator white and new. It held basic foods and two cases of Coors.

I popped one at the small table, numbed by my pleasure in the discovery of Dolly George, confused by the numbness.

She came in, got a beer, and sat across from me. "So, Mr. Detective From Stanford, who are you looking for?"

"Berkeley."

"Berkeley who?"

"You went to Berkeley. Only a Bear could knock Stanford and misuse pronouns doing it."

She laughed. "I went to Yale. But I teach at Cal."

"You certainly don't teach art."

The laugh deepened. Swathes of red colored her cheeks, her big eyes glittered, her teeth flashed white. She was very pretty. I had to fight the impulse to tell her so.

"Now, really, who—whom are you looking for?"

"I'm helping a girl whose grandmother, Dolores Dahlman, owned this place. I—"

"Dolores Dahlman was my father's aunt. I was named after her. But I never—this girl, she'd be my . . . cousin?"

"Sort of, at some removes." Glory Dahlman was as far removed from Dolly George as I was from the Supreme Court.

"Wait till Dad hears about this." She shivered with excitement. "I—are there others, relatives, family?"

"Not that I know of."

"The girl—is she a girl? I mean, how old is she? What's she like? What's her name?"

"Glory. She's twenty or so." But I wasn't ready to tackle the rest. "Dolly, could we wait for your father? It's a bit involved."

"All right." She drank more beer, her big eyes watching me over the can. "What happened to your chin?"

"I got mugged by a senile eighty-year-old."

I told her of my set-to with Pete Lotz and soon had her pressing her hands to her face against the laughter. I laughed too, and watched her.

This time the impulse would not be resisted. I told her she was very pretty.

She stopped laughing. She didn't stop smiling. Her eyes focused on me, seemed to deepen.

# 8

The door at the front of the house slammed. Dolly rose and went to the refrigerator. Footsteps thunked toward us.

Gabriel George hesitated in the doorway. He wore tan workpants and shirt, heavy lace boots, and a sweat-stained old cowboy hat. His arms and thick shoulders were draped with camera cases and equipment bags. He gave me a quick look, his daughter a longer one. "Be right with you." After a moment, he was.

A closely-trimmed white beard crept up his face nearly to his eyes, which behind square-cut rimless glasses shifted from blue to gray. His beard seemed to continue up over his ears and around his head, and above it his pale pate showed several old scars.

He took the beer his daughter gave him in one hand, my hand in the other as she introduced us. "Jack is a private investigator, Dad. He's working for Dolores's granddaughter."

His eyes shifted colors. "Dolores had a granddaughter?"

"The girl's father was named Stuart. That's the name of your aunt's son, isn't it?"

He sank slowly to the table. Still, his body seemed older than it had in motion. He was, I guessed, sixty-five.

"Yes. There can't be too many Stuart Dahlmans around." He drank long from his beer. "But you said, was?"

"I gathered from his daughter that her parents had been dead for some time."

**43**

"Dead." He took another swallow from his beer, and the can was empty. His daughter moved to get him another. "The last time I saw him he was only four, but even then he was spoiled so bad by his mother, and the Indian she had helping around the place. . . ."

"The Indian would have been Haskell Dan?"

"You know Haskell?"

"I play cards with him."

"He used to trail that kid around. . . ." His eyes changed, as if he had withdrawn behind them. "Trailed him like a noon-day shadow, Dolores used to say." He smiled at the memory. "The last I heard Stuart was in the army."

"That's where he was when she died."

His gaze fixed on his beer can. "I should have kept in touch. I tried to, with Dolores. She was my mother's sister. After my parents died, she and Barney brought me out to help on the place." He looked up. "Dolores Dahlman is responsible for whatever it is of value that I've ever done. I cut some hay for her, and she gave me room and board and a way of seeing and something to see it with. I. . . ."

His daughter watched him with big eyes full of feeling. Looked at that way, I thought, a man must feel blessed, the undeserving recipient of unearned Grace.

"I should have kept in touch. But when I left, I just drifted around the West, learning to use what she'd given me. I'd write, when I could, but I was rarely in one place long enough to get letters. I got enough to gather Stuart was a disappoint-ment to her. Then she was gone and. . . ."

Something in him shook, settled. "Sorry. You don't need this. I don't either. What we need is another beer."

He got up, pulled three Coors out of the refrigerator with one hand, and set them on the table. "The girl, the granddaugh-ter—is it me, my family she wants to find?"

"I don't think she knows you exist." I finished my beer, popped another. "She wants me to find her grandfather."

He seemed confused. "Barney Dahlman died years ago. His grave's on a hill out back."

I shook my head. "Her maternal grandfather."

I told them the story of Lawrence Parker and Flora Magnusson and Daryl Lotz. Dolly's big eyes fixed on my mouth as I spoke, as if capturing the words and transforming them into inner images. Her father's eyes, behind his glasses, shifted from gray gravity to blue sorrow. Sometimes, listening, he slipped behind them and didn't come out.

Dolly spoke first. "Glory's other grandfather—he's a murderer."

"He's wanted for murder, but I think the charge has more to do with Pete Lotz's juice in Humboldt County than with the facts. I wouldn't want to try to get a conviction on it."

"There's no question that Rose was this Parker's child?"

"There's no way to prove it now, of course, but Glory's grandmother said so, and no one has seriously questioned it."

"Rose and Stuart Dahlman, how did they die?"

"I don't know." Doomed by love, Glory had said.

He suddenly looked tired. "Some legacy for her, huh?"

Glory had used the same word, but with pride.

We each popped another Coors. Dolly watched us. Some of the affection she directed at her father seemed to spill over onto me. I felt warm.

"But how did you get here? We're the other side of the family."

"As a matter of fact, Mr. George, I think maybe the whole thing started with you." I told him about the photograph at Cal Blass's. Gabriel George was to the high desert what Ansel Adams was to Yosemite. Any poster-sized print of the Nevada desert was likely to be his work.

"Which shot was it, do you know?"

I described it as Glory had.

He grew thoughtful. "Stuart got the sketches here. Dolores had them. A young guy had given them to her for a couple nights sleep in the barn and a few meals."

"That sounds like Parker, all right."

"So," Dolly said, "he really is alive."

"Not necessarily," I said. "It was forty years ago. It does

argue that he got through the desert. Stuart Dahlman thought so. So did Pete Lotz. On the other hand, Haskell Dan told me he was dead."

Gabriel George leaned slowly back in his chair. "Did he tell you how Parker died?"

"No."

He seemed to disappear for a moment.

Dolly leaned forward, breasts brushing the table. "But how did Stuart Dahlman end up with Parker's daughter?"

"Stuart told Lotz he'd try to find Parker," I said. "He must have gotten as far as Flora, met Rose that way."

Gabriel George came out from behind his eyes. "I'm still not sure I understand how that brought you here."

"There wasn't much logic to it," I admitted. "But since I was in this part of the country, I thought I'd see if there might be something left here that could help."

"After forty years?"

I laughed. "I know. But when I learned that you owned the place now, I took a chance you might be here. I—well, I've enjoyed your work for a long time."

"High praise, Dad," Dolly smiled. "Jack's a critic of the arts." Her smile deepened. "And a master of self defense. Tell him, Jack. About the mugging."

We were all laughing when I finished. But Gabriel George's laughter didn't last. He seemed troubled.

"That sounds like Pete," he said. "The old bastard."

"You know him?"

"Everybody in Northern Nevada knows Pete." He turned to his daughter. "What would your mother say if she knew you were letting me suck suds on an empty stomach?"

Dolly rose. "She'd say it served your stomach right. What about some eggs? Jack, you'll have some with us?"

Her father waved his big hand over the beer cans. "You better get something in your stomach too. And we could use the company. We're driving each other nuts out here alone."

I accepted.

As Dolly went to the stove, I told Gabriel George again how

much I enjoyed his photographs. With a sudden energy he led me to his darkroom, a small rectangle stuffed with chemicals, solution pans and enlargers and expensive-looking pieces of equipment whose functions eluded me. In the next bedroom, prints of desert scenes lay over the bed and desk and chest like a profusion of square, colorless flowers. I admired them, and he talked about them.

As the desert darkened outside the window, I listened to him, learned more about photography than I thought there could be to know. But what I learned didn't explain the disturbing and at the same time satisfying quality of the finished prints. I said so.

"Thanks. But I don't know if I can explain them. I—what do you see in them?"

"I don't know, I—" But I did know. "Nothing."

He laughed.

"No," I said. "It's a positive nothing, an absence, I. . . ." I smiled. "I guess I can't explain them either."

He rubbed the back of his big hand against his beard. "I don't understand myself how it happens. I'm thinking only about composition and light, and then when I develop, it comes rising up, that—I guess nothing is as good a word for it as any." Within his white beard his mouth twisted in a faint smile. "I'm not very articulate about this, I—"

His daughter's bellow rolled into the room: "Men eat!"

"See what I mean?" he laughed. "We get wacky out here."

We washed up and went into the kitchen. We ate silently, concentrating on the food. No one spoke until Gabriel George had filled three cups with coffee.

"That was very good, Dolly," I said. "Thank you."

Her face, flushed from the heat of the cooking and the food, seemed to have sucked up some of the color from her bright blouse. "Do you suppose it's worth a ride into Reno?"

Her father looked at her quickly. "You're going back?"

"I'd better."

He pointed at the blackness behind the window. "But not tonight. Jack, you're not planning to drive back now, are you?

From the looks of that jeep out there, you had a little fun in the mud today. You'd better give it a blow. And we've got more talking to do, about my . . . our new family."

If Dolly seriously had wanted to leave, the mention of new family changed her mind. "The couch is comfortable enough for a critic."

"Thanks. I've got a sleeping bag, I'll make do."

She laughed. "Good. Gentlemen, you may do the dishes."

# 9

As I washed the dishes and thought about his daughter, Gabriel George dried them and stayed behind his eyes. When we finished, he grabbed a handful of beers. "Let's go out."

I followed him to the small front porch. Dolly sat at its edge. Her father sat beside her. I sat beside him.

An old Land Rover with big, sand-grabbing tires rested beside my rig. Above them the night sky was deep and starry, around them the night silence was big and deep and still. In the starlight the desert smoothed into shadowy shapes.

"Tell us about our . . . cousin," Dolly said.

I described Glory Dahlman physically.

"What's she like?"

I realized I wasn't sure exactly what Glory was like. "She's a little different. Haskell Dan said that she had visions. You'd probably say she was a little spacey."

"What does she do—go to school or work, what?"

There was no way around it. "She's a prostitute."

The silence got bigger. I was at my beer.

"She works in a house?" Dolly said. "Like Mustang?"

"Mustang's another world. She free-lances. A couple of the casinos let them in, but it's very discreet."

"So she's like a call girl. But isn't that illegal?"

"Brothels are licensed on a county-by-county basis in Nevada. What Glory does is illegal everywhere in the state."

"Is she. . . ." Something choked off the words. Before she

**49**

could find others, her father spoke: "Let it go, Doll. It doesn't matter. She's still Dolores's granddaughter."

Dolly let it go.

We sat and watched the desert and the night, felt the heat rise from the earth and disappear into the emptiness above it, listened to the stirrings of the night breeze.

"Maybe you need to understand about Dolores," Gabriel George said finally. "She was an original, even back then, when half the people in Nevada were eccentrics."

He told us about Dolores Dahlman. She spent her childhood in a wagon her parents drove from fence-mending to hay-cutting jobs around the Great Basin. At thirteen she left her family at Battle Mountain and made her way to Reno, picked up a year or two of formal education, and at sixteen she was in the desert teaching the children of ranchers.

She had a lot of teaching jobs, because she taught the kids not what their parents wanted them to know but what Dolores wanted them to understand. That the ranch land really belonged, by treaties never rescinded, to the Indians. That women in Nevada were just more stock. That miners and their machines were destroying the land. That life meant whatever you thought it meant. That there was more evidence against the existence of God than for it, but that if God did exist He was one strange-humored sonofabitch.

So she would teach for a few months and then move on. Until, barely twenty-one, she ended up owning the ranch we sat on, through circumstances which neither Dolores nor the president of a Lovelock bank ever chose to discuss.

Not that the rest of Northern Nevada didn't masticate it into a salacious goo, for Dolores was as quirky a woman as she was a teacher. She said and did as she chose, dressed in overalls and a flannel shirt and lace-up boots, shot two men—one fatally—and was prosecuted for neither, had thirty-seven proposals of marriage and countless proposals of relations less formal, some of which she accepted as the mood struck her. At forty she married Barney Dahlman, a hand on a neighbor's place and twenty years her junior, because she wanted a child and he looked to be the best of the bulls.

I enjoyed Gabriel George's story. I'd heard similar tales from my grandfather of the people who in the vast barrenness of the desert allowed each other to work out their lives pretty much as they pleased. I'd even met a few of them. Each year there were fewer to meet.

"Saved me, the crazy old woman," he said. "She got me interested in things, the desert, history, art. She did anthropology out here before anybody at the university knew how to pronounce it. She read everything, and made me read it too. She had an old box camera," he said, his voice getting slower. "She'd picked it up in Reno at a pawn shop, taught herself how to use it. She taught me to use it too, to see with it. How to see without it, too. If it wasn't for Dolores, I'd still be heaving hay for a living."

He shifted again, drank from his beer. "I guess the point of all this, Jack, is that Dolores would be the last person to care what her granddaughter was doing, as long as she was doing what she wanted to."

After a moment he pushed himself to his feet. "Desert got me today. It's bedtime for these old bones."

"You aren't going to work in the darkroom?" Dolly asked.

He bent over to kiss the top of her head. "I'm beat."

I got up. "Good night, Mr. George. Thanks for your hospitality."

He offered his hand. "My friends call me Gabe, Jack."

I returned the steady pressure of his grip. "Thanks."

After he went inside, Dolly and I sat in the quiet of the night. Then the silence was invaded by the distant drone of a light aircraft circling over the Black Rock Desert.

"What's a plane doing out here?" Dolly asked.

"Could be a rancher. Or smugglers."

"In Nevada?"

"Nevada's full of isolated old lake beds, like the Black Rock, that make perfect landing strips. A couple of years ago a man asked me to find his daughter. I learned that she had a pilot boyfriend, and that they were out of the country. In her apartment I found her phone bill. She, or somebody, had made several calls to a Gerlach number. That didn't figure. I checked a few things, then called the Sheriff. We watched the plane land out on the Black Rock a few nights later, and made sure it didn't take off. There's a guy in Reno who says I owe him a hundred thousand dollars because of it."

"What happened to the girl?"

"Then, nothing. The pilot got time, and one of Cal Blass's goons did too. They didn't prosecute her—until they caught her six months later coming over Carson Pass on a motorcycle with its bags stuffed full of cocaine."

"Is that what you do, in your work? Get involved with dope smugglers and . . . ?"

"And prostitutes? Not often. I get caught up in street business some times, but mostly I find people."

"I wasn't disapproving, Jack. About Glory. But I've heard the stories about pimps and violence and drugs. I'm concerned. Curious too, to be honest."

"Don't worry about Glory. She knows what she's doing."

"I—what's she like, really?"

"I don't know. I just met her last night. As I said, she's spacey, seems to think life is some kind of impromptu theater. But she's young. You'd probably get along fine."

She smiled. "Are you suggesting that I'm spacey too?"

"No. You're very bright, very pretty, and very nice."

"Is that all?"

We were at sexual play again. "You tell me."

"What about affectionate, considerate, and passionate?"

"Tell me about it."

We sat and talked as the night chilled and darkened, the air stilled, the stars neared. The dark smelled faintly of dust and sage. Dolly smelled faintly of a subtle musk.

Dolores Anne, I learned, was thirty-three, the middle child of Gabriel and Alice George, and an Associate Professor of Music at Cal-Berkeley. She was ten months out of a ten-year marriage to a cellist. The wounds hadn't completely scarred over. She was here to see if the desert air might hasten the healing process.

She had two brothers. The elder, Hayes, managed the family business dealings in Nevada. The younger, Bobby, was a pro golfer of little success whom I'd seen play on TV a couple of times.

"I haven't heard much about him lately."

"He lost his card. He's trying to get it back."

"Problems?"

"He's just so—it's all fun to him. He was partying instead of practicing. And he lost a lot of money in Las Vegas, and Mom won't pay it this time." She smiled. "But he's getting his life together. He's practicing, working. And he's getting married. He'll be all right."

After a while, I told her about myself. Dolly learned that I was the long-divorced father of a teenaged daughter, that I had chosen not to practice law because it seemed so unrelated to justice, and that I was considering giving up the investigation business.

"Why?"

I didn't want to talk about the whys. "I've been doing it a long time," I said instead. "It's time for a change."

We sat together in the night.

"I like your father," I said.

"He likes you."

"Good. I like you, too."

I might have seen star-shine in her big dark eyes. "Are you hitting on me, Jack? With my dad not twenty feet away?"

"Call it an overture. Announcing my interest."

After a while, she said: "What are you contemplating so deeply?"

The same question Glory had asked. "Pheromones."

"What?"

"Pheromones. Lewis Thomas has a wonderful essay on them. He describes a male moth who awakes one morning feeling unaccountably great, so great that he swoops off for a frisky fly, just for the joy of it. So he's having this great fly, and he notices there's a bunch of other guys out having a great fly too, and that's great, because it's such a wonderful day for a fly, a glorious day for a fly. And then he comes around a corner and—O ho! Look what we have here!"

"The source of the pheromones? A female moth?"

"Amazing how it works out, isn't it."

She smiled. "Has it a point, that particular story?"

"Just that that was pretty much my reaction when I came around the corner of the house today."

"I see," she said. "And in this story, what does the female moth say upon being discovered?"

"Thomas doesn't tell us—probably feeling unqualified to speak from the female point of view."

She stood up, smiling. "From this female's point of view, it's late. I can make up the couch for you."

"My sleeping bag's less fuss."

"I'll get you a pillow."

I got up and got my bag from the jeep. In the living room, Dolly was plumping up a blue-cased pillow. I spread my bag over the couch, and she placed the pillow at its head.

"Thank you," I said.

"You're welcome." She looked at me, a smile playing at her mouth, her big eyes strangely somber. "Good night, Jack."

"Good night."

She stepped past me, stopped at the door, turned. "What the hell took you so long?"

"What?"

"That's what the female moth says. 'What the hell took you so long.'" Then she was gone.

I dragged myself out of my boots, jeans, and sweatshirt, switched off the lamp, and crawled into my bag. For a minute I lay listening to Dolly move in the room across the hall.

I closed my eyes. I saw nothing. Then I heard nothing.

# 10

Thunder rumbled, steadily, like an aboriginal drum. Then it was a drum, and an insistent, hard-pounded piano, a swell of voices, and the rich rasp of Bonnie Tyler complaining of the death of good men, gods, and heroes.

My eyes opened. Sunlight flooded the room. Holding her radio, Dolly sat in an old chair across the room. Her hair was pinned behind her head. She wore a yellow sundress.

She smiled. "The street-wise Hercules lives."

I struggled to sit up. "I—good morning."

"Try afternoon," she laughed. "It's three o'clock." She rose. "The coffee's fresh." In a yellow swirl and flutter she was gone.

After a trip to the jeep, I stepped from the bathroom—clean, shaved, dressed in grey slacks, a blue shirt, and a soft, worn, old gray Harris tweed jacket. In the kitchen, Dolly examined the result as she poured me a cup of coffee.

"Do you always dress this way in the desert?"

"When I'm trying to impress someone," I said, sitting.

She smiled. "You don't miss a beat. Fifteen hours in never-never land and you pick right up where you left off."

"Sorry. You should have rousted me."

"I was afraid to touch you. I thought you were dead. Are you hungry? I can—"

"Too soon. My heart hasn't started beating yet." She laughed. "Besides, you want to go."

"We might as well wait and say goodbye to Dad."

So we waited. We drank coffee and talked. She was right: I was still at it. Had I been a desert bird, I'd have been all tail-fan and feather-puff.

I told her stories. I went through my repertoire of past stupidities and adopted, in a moment of inspiration, the persona of the "street-wise Hercules" who flooded the Augean stables only to be swept away with the manure. I recounted crafty tracking that had led me to the wrong destination, fearless wronging of rights, brilliant cerebrations that put me in the right pew in the wrong church. Hercules Bumbling.

And Dolly laughed, her big eyes glowing, teeth flashing, pretty features coloring. She liked to laugh: her face seemed to slip naturally into expressions of incredulous amusement and outraged delight; her mind was quick and anticipating, eager for ironies, alert to the nuances of nonsense.

So I told stories and she laughed.

I didn't care if I never went back to Reno.

Out the window the sunlight was softening when Dolly broke off a laugh, held up a hand: "I think that's Dad."

In a few moments, as he had the evening before, Gabriel George stood in the doorway. "Thanks for waiting for me," he said quietly. "Give me a minute."

Quickly he was back, accepting the can of Coors his daughter offered. He didn't sit. "Are you packed, Dolly?"

"Mostly," she said. "I'll only need a minute."

"I want to show Jack something." He turned to me. "Let's take a walk."

I followed him out the back door, then up a nearby hump of low brown hill, through the sage whose silvery new growth was graying with dust.

At the top, a sageflat spread back to the base of another, higher, hill. In its center a white picket fence enclosed a small square of sand and two fairly new gray-black granite headstones.

"I put these up when I bought the place," he said. "His was wood, hers a piece of marble the wind had blasted."

Barney Dahlman, Dolores Dahlman. Husband and wife. He

had died at twenty-four, she at sixty. They had shared only a few years. Now they shared the big silence of the sand.

Gabriel George took a small swallow from his beer. "I just thought if she—Glory—ever wanted to see the graves, and I wasn't here, she'd know where to find them."

"I'll tell her," I said, puzzled.

"Does she know about Barney, her other grandfather?"

"I don't know. She didn't mention him."

"The forgotten man," he said, his voice strange. "But he always was, even when he was still here. A woman like Dolores is always going to be the center of things."

He leaned against a corner post. "Barney could have been her son, he was that much younger, pretty much still a kid. He was a hand on a neighbor's ranch, he'd drifted in from Oregon, I think. He . . . well, nobody saw much special in him, but Dolores did. She started hauling him around on her exploring, showing him things, got him interested in what she was interested in. When she was pregnant, they got married. Independent as she was, she didn't want a child of hers to have to deal with illegitimacy. You know how that could be, out here, back then."

I knew better than he ever could.

"And then Stuart was born. And a couple years later, Barney died. Horse threw him, broke his neck."

That was the end of his story. The point of his story hadn't been made yet. "You want me to tell Glory all this?"

"I guess."

The light had begun to shift, tilt, soften, to spread shadows over the land. Distant ranges cut like dark serrated knives into the pale evening sky. Gazing out at the desert, he said: "You come out here a lot, don't you?"

"Not enough," I said. "Not lately, anyhow."

"Do you know why you come?"

The question didn't strike me as strange. Still, I wasn't sure I could answer it. "I started coming when I was a boy, with my grandfather. Hunting, sometimes, or proving up a couple of old claims he had. I like it out here."

That wasn't an answer, and he knew it. But I wasn't quite ready to tell him about the big silence.

"I have a hard time talking about it, too," he said. "My wife has never understood, Dolly and her brothers think I'm nuts. But they're Californians. They don't understand Nevada. They think Nevada's Las Vegas and Reno. They come out here and look at all this and they don't see anything."

"Nothing?"

"Not anything. You know they're not the same, Jack."

He looked at me, both offering and inquiring. He was offering himself, and inviting me into his desert world. I didn't know what he was inquiring after.

When I didn't speak, he drained his beer. "Guess we better get back."

We turned and trudged down the hill. At the cottonwood behind the house, he stopped. "You can tell Glory that Lawrence Parker is dead, Jack."

I waited.

"What I told you about the sketches last night, that was the story Dolores told. But Barney. . . ." He looked down at the beer can in his hand; slowly he crushed it.

"Parker made it through the desert, but he wasn't . . . a man anymore, a human being. Haskell found his briefcase in the desert and trailed him to a pile of rocks. He was alive, but he was like some kind of dying, rabid animal. Haskell thought his mind must have gone pretty fast out there."

"What happened?"

"There was nothing they could do for him. He was in pain, insane, dying. Dolores had Haskell shoot him. Barney and Haskell took his body into the desert and buried it."

"Just like that?"

"I know what it sounds like. But if you knew Dolores—they were simply putting a suffering creature out of its misery. They did things like that out here back then."

Not quite like that. "They didn't notify the Sheriff?"

"He had a bullet in his heart. There'd have been questions, maybe even charges."

"And they passed on the reward, the five thousand Pete Lotz put up, for the same reason?"

"Yes."

"Why did Barney tell you about it?"

"It bothered him. We were out looking for strays and passed the place where they buried Parker. He just told me."

"Guilt?"

"Not exactly. It just . . . bothered him."

"Does anyone else know this?"

"Just Haskell Dan."

In Nevada, anything is possible. Even this. But something was haywire.

"I—do you want me to tell all this to Glory?"

"Yes."

"Can you show me where he's buried?"

"It's been so long, I don't think I could find it."

And I didn't think he was telling me the truth.

Haskell had told me that Lawrence Parker was dead. I could believe that.

Glory had told me that Haskell had killed Parker. I could believe that he had told her that, could even believe that it was true.

I couldn't believe what Gabriel George was telling me.

He saw that. He turned away from me. "We better not keep Dolly waiting," he said. He walked across the dust and into the house.

I walked around to the front of the house. Three pieces of expensive leather luggage sat on the porch. I put them in the back of the Wagoneer, then leaned against the fender and watched the sunset.

# 11

Shafts of sunlight tilted skyward from behind a lumpy distant range before they came out. Dolly gave her father a hug. He showed her into the jeep.

"Thanks again for the hospitality." I offered my hand.

"Whenever you're out this way, stop in, Jack," he said, taking my hand but withdrawing behind his eyes.

I eased the rig around the yard, started down the dirt road. Gabriel George shrank in the rearview mirror until we dipped over a wrinkle in the land and he was gone.

I headed west, into the dregs of the day. Darkness descended in layers as if the desert were undergoing a succession of washes in Gabriel George's solution pan.

The scattering of lights that was Gerlach appeared like a constellation. I slowed, hit the highway, turned south, pressed the accelerator. We sped past the lights of the gypsum plant at Empire and into a darkness lit only by stars and the infrequent flash of eyes in the brush. We drove through the star-lit, star-shadowed desert in silence.

I enjoyed the silence. I felt Dolly's eyes on me.

Skirting the dry bed of Lake Winnemucca, we eased around a low range and caught a glimpse of moonlit Pyramid Lake.

"God," Dolly said, "it's so beautiful."

Bare black ranges rose up against the softer blackness of the sky. The black of the water glistened within the pale confines of narrow sandy beaches. Anahu, the tufa island that gave the lake its name, spired into the still silence.

"Dad's been trying to get this for years."

I didn't reply, drove along the Truckee River through the thick sageland to Wadsworth and the interstate.

Dolly shifted in the seat. "You and Dad were up on the hill a long time."

"He was telling me about Dolores and Barney."

"And about me?"

"No. What should he have told me?"

"Oh, maybe that I'm an over-protected, thoroughly-spoiled, thirty-three-year-old brat."

"He didn't mention it."

"I—" She stopped, choking something back. "How about the fact that since my husband divorced me for another woman I've been sleeping with damn near anybody who asked?"

"No."

"Does that bother you?"

"No. Does it bother you?"

"It did, for a while. Maybe it still does. But I think I understand it now. Do . . . you?"

"Yes."

"I hope so. I . . . it's become important to me."

The darkness of the canyon enclosed us.

"Jack, is what seems to be happening, with us I mean, is it really happening?"

"Yes."

"So fast?"

"That's why Nevada wedding chapels are open twenty-four hours a day."

She laughed. "I know. My mother told me once that she was in my dad's bed less than seven hours after they met."

"We can't beat that."

She laughed again.

The interstate slipped out of the Truckee River Canyon, and Reno and Sparks appeared before us, clusters of neon lights from the two downtowns surrounded by squares and rectangles of yellow lights that spread to the foothills, thinning as they climbed into expensive developments, finally vanishing as if within the mountains themselves.

The city neared. My spirits lowered. Because it was still there, all that I had fled. Hanging heads.

No more, I told myself. No more.

"Pardon me?"

"No more." A snatch of wonderful old poetry rose into my mind. *"And brood on hopes and fears no more,"* I quoted; the next lines came unbidden: *"And no more turn aside and brood/ Upon love's bitter mystery. . . ."*

"You're the mystery, Jack," Dolly said warmly. "A lawyer who won't practice law, a detective who quotes Yeats, a Stanford man and a street-wise Hercules, a moth. . . ."

"In Nevada, anything is possible."

"We're possible?"

"In Nevada," I repeated, "anything is possible."

"It all seems so . . . strange, unreal."

"In Nevada, nothing is as it seems."

"You've got it all worked out, I see."

"All but where we're going."

"An art critic such as yourself? I assumed you were going to invite me to see your etchings."

Dolly said nothing about my apartment and the vodka gimlet I made her. She sat where Glory Dahlman had the night before. I sat beside her.

In a sudden nervousness that I found somehow touching, she picked up the book on Will James. "Is this any good?"

"I don't know. I haven't read it yet."

"Are you a student of cowboy art too?"

"Mostly I'm interested in James. Do you know about him?"

"He wrote horse stories? And illustrated them?"

"That's what he did. He drew, and he wrote fiction. But more than that, he *was* fiction. He wasn't Will James, he was Joseph-Ernest Default, a French Canadian from Quebec. He'd apparently picked up a dream or vision of the West from pulp magazines. And he came to Nevada, concocted a fanciful tale about his parentage and history, and then proceeded to live as if it were true. He just made himself up."

"Like Gatsby?"

"There were differences. He married, but apparently he never told his wife who he was. He wrote his autobiography, told the world his story. Then he had to live it. It killed him; he died of alcoholism at fifty, in Hollywood."

"Like Fitzgerald." She reached for her gimlet. "If you already know about him, why are you reading the book?"

"To see if I can find out why."

I let her finish her drink before I kissed her. I rose, pulled her gently to her feet, and led her to the bedroom. We undressed one another slowly. Then we made love.

Her body, small under my hands, smooth under my lips, trembled in urgency. Soon, urgently, she led me into her. Soon, her hands clenching my shoulders, her thighs clenching my hips, with a strain and buck of pelvis and a series of soft hoarse cries, as if giving birth, she came.

I didn't. I didn't need, or want, release. I needed and wanted the opposite: a yoking, binding, cleaving, joining.

So I stayed within her, moving slowly as her fingers traced my bones and muscles and scars, read the story of my life, a life that seemed to be undergoing radical and ineradicable transformation, until her breathing changed, her body took on another, deeper, urgency, began to thrust itself at mine, grew taut, tense, hard, and she—we—came.

I lay with her, holding her, stroking her, thinking of nothing. I continued to hold and stroke even as her breathing deepened. I held her and stroked her until she was asleep.

I wouldn't sleep, not after my fifteen hours the night before, but I didn't care. I lay with Dolly and thought of the past two days with her, imaged her smile, her big bright eyes, her small strong hands, brought into my mind a tilt of head, movement of mouth, stretch of limb, bend of back, I listened to her laughter. . . .

I awoke with a start. Alone.

I'd known she was gone before I awoke. Absence woke me.

The sky out my window was a pale but deepening blue.

Dolly hadn't been gone long. The sheets still bore the imprint of her body, its warm scent. But she was gone.

I sat on the edge of the bed. Then I got up, went to the kitchen, looked for a note. There was no note in the living room, no note anywhere.

I slipped into a jock and shorts, a tee shirt and sweat socks and running shoes.

Outside, I checked the Wagoneer. Her luggage was gone.

I shuffled east to the Truckee River trail. I began to sweat. Gradually I increased my speed.

I ran with the river for over an hour, past the *Gazette-Journal* building, around the sewage plant, past the Grand, into Sparks, in and out of the small parks that line the river's edge, under highways and streets, past warehouses, past weedy fields, as far as the trail went.

Then I ran back. I listened to the river and thought of nothing, felt my body losing strength and pushed it harder, till it burned, and then pushed it some more.

At Wells and the heavy morning traffic, I stopped running. Chest heaving, face caked with salty sweat, legs rubbery, I walked back home, still thinking of nothing.

I put on Mr. Coffee, showered, shaved, dressed in a suit the brown of a Hershey's bar and sporty enough to require no tie at the neck of my pale rose shirt.

I went in to my office and watched my message recorder blink and finally allowed myself to think about Dolly George.

I didn't know why she felt she had to sneak away, but I did know it didn't bode well for me. I didn't know where she had gone or how she had gone there. I knew I could find out. I also knew I wasn't going to. Not for a while, at least.

I didn't want to find her. I wanted her to come back.

I recognized that as a piece of prideful masculine silliness. I also recognized that as the way it was.

I also, dimly, recognized something excessive, nearly hysterical, in my reaction. I didn't know what that meant.

Still ignoring the blink of my recorder, I picked up the phone, took out the number Glory Dahlman had given me, and dialed. I wanted to tell her about the family she didn't know she had, get out of her life. And get her out of mine.

No answer.

I punched the recorder, listened to the voice of my former brother-in-law and constant friend. "We need to discuss a little business."

I didn't want to discuss business with Frank Calvetti. He was a homicide detective with RPD. But I knew that when I went to the desert I'd left some loose ends behind. I had to tie them up. I called him.

"Ah, back already," Frank said. "I thought you'd gone to the desert. Knowing you and your illusions, I also thought you'd be out there for forty days and forty nights."

"And remove myself from the source of such scintillating wit? What do you want?"

"I want to know how the hell you do it."

It was an old game he'd enjoyed playing since we'd been kids. "Do what?" I asked wearily.

"Get yourself tangled up in everything that comes down the pike. Or in this case, the river."

"And what came down the river besides California's garbage?"

"A body."

And so it started again. No escape. "What body?"

"The body of an old Shoshone named Haskell Dan."

# 12

Haskell Dan's body had been found trailing from a snag downstream from his trailer park eight hours after I'd left him in the Hilton. The coroner indicated that his lungs held enough water to fix the cause of death as drowning.

In the desert, death by water.

The pattern of bruises around his head and body, Frank said, was consistent with the damage the river might do.

"What are you in it for?" I asked. "Hardly sounds like enough for homicide."

"True," Frank said, "except for one little thing."

He was going to make me ask. "What little thing?"

"A little bullet hole in the belly."

I closed my eyes.

After a moment, Frank spoke: "Still there?"

"Unfortunately." But Frank was right. Whatever it was that had led to Haskell's death, I was already enmeshed in it. That's how it had been going. "Just tell me, will you?"

Haskell had been shot in the abdomen, an inch or so above the appendix, by a .22. The slug had bumped a rib, but still had a nice set of grooves for ballistics. The lab troops hadn't come up with a match, but they were still looking.

RPD had found blood in the dust before Haskell's trailer, along with his footprints and the prints of spike-heeled shoes.

None of the inhabitants of the trailer court admitted to seeing or hearing anything.

"So what do you want from me?"

"You were in the Hilton that morning frying your brains, I understand, and talking to Haskell Dan."

"He talked to me."

"And?"

"He asked me to help a friend of his find her grandfather. That's what I've been doing in the desert."

"The friend would be the Wicked Witch of the West who flew into the Hilton, I presume. What's her name?"

"Why?"

"They left together."

"She didn't kill him, Frank."

"Thanks. I'll write that down. Jack Ross says the hooker didn't kill the Indian. That ought to wrap up the whole case for us. My superiors will be ecstatic. They may, however, want a detail or two—like the *name* of the hooker who didn't kill the Indian."

It didn't matter. She didn't kill him. "Glory Dahlman. I don't know where she lives." I gave him her phone number.

"Anything else?" I didn't answer. "You all right, Jack?"

"Peachy."

He slipped from cop to friend. "I know what this is for you, Jack, what's been going on lately. If you need—"

"Just find out who killed Haskell Dan. And without me."

"Jack. . . ."

"I'll be in touch," I said, and hung up.

I called the number Glory had given me. Still no answer.

So Glory had left me that morning, gone to the Hilton, left with Haskell, and not long after that he'd been found gut-shot in the Truckee. The police wanted to talk to Glory.

I checked the phone book for the address I wanted. Then I sat at my desk, thinking about, seeing, nothing.

After a while I realized that I was seeing something. The envelope on the top of my pile of mail. It bore a sticker with the return address of Juanita and Malcom Springmeyer. I opened it and found a check signed by Malcom Springmeyer. The signature was ragged, barely controlled. Like the note: "For services rendered."

I looked at the check until, as if in a dream, a faint scattering of spots seemed to rise from the ink of the signature, to clump into vague shapes that became human heads hanging by knotted strands of hair. . . .

To dispel the vision, I tore the check in half.

I tore the halves in half, let the scraps flutter down.

I tore the envelope.

Then I tore another envelope, this one unopened.

Then I had the stack of mail in my hands and was ripping it apart, hurling paper.

Suddenly I was up. A sweep of my arm sent lamp and phone and recorder crashing to the floor, a grunting heave overturned the desk and I was out from behind it, ripping law books from shelves and smashing plants and tearing down plaques and pictures and certificates and flinging them blindly, blindly, blindly. . . .

I became aware of myself.

I was aware that I was in the corner by the door, on the floor, my back wedged tightly between the walls.

I was aware that it was entirely possible that I might sit there in the corner on the floor forever.

I was aware, in a way I hadn't been, of the seriousness of the trouble I was in.

Through a large hole in the window the sounds of the street drifted over me.

Slowly I climbed to my feet.

My office was destroyed.

I left it that way.

I went back into the bathroom, washed away sweat, adjusted cloth, put in acceptable order my disguise as a human being.

Then I left.

Outside, in the middle of Second Street, in twisted frame and shattered glass, lay my law diploma.

I left it there.

# 13

Sun Valley hunkered in a hollow formed by bunched-up brown hills at the north edge of the city. On the valley floor a few trees tried to shade ragged blocks of mobile homes. Some were bright with paint, surrounded by little lawns or rock gardens, picket or pole fences—neat little retirement places or starter homes for young couples. Others—most—slumped battered and wind-scoured within squares of bare earth littered with sagging sheds and rusting tools and cracking tack and oxidizing vehicle carcasses.

Pickups sported gun racks and mud-flaps; big bikes wore heavy chrome. The scattering of horses I saw were shaggy, empty-eyed, prematurely aged by hard, even violent, use. The scattering of people I saw were the same.

At Artemesia Street, at the narrow end of the valley, the tarmac dissolved into desert dust. A tumbleweed-choked barbed wire fence demarcated a lot filled with disemboweled and lobotomized automobiles rusting in the sun like the work of a crazed sculptor. In the center sat an old double-wide trailer, paint peeling from its sides. A bright red tricycle stood in the dust before the door.

A tricycle-sized girl answered my knock. She was four or five, raven-haired, neatly dressed. Her eyes were brown and serious. She stared up at me with a child's big silence.

"I'd like to see Mrs. Flora Baker, please."

"Gramma!" she shouted. "It's a man!"

The door opened onto a drape-dimmed living room. I could make out a couch beneath a velvet painting of a matador. I could hear Big Bird singing on the TV. Then I heard a low, slow-cadenced voice. The child stepped aside.

The room was lighted only by the lavender nimbus around the television. My eyes, adjusting from the midday glare, everywhere met eyes. Youthful faces swam before me—framed portraits on the walls, small frames and plastic cubes of snapshots on every flat surface large enough to hold them.

I fought off the eyes, searched for the body that went with the voice I'd heard.

She sat in an overstuffed chair. Under a house coat, her body was bloated and shapeless. The object of old desires, inflamer of long-stilled blood, Flora Magnusson Baker. Although the drawings had stylized her features, something in the set of the wide mouth identified her.

There was no fat in her face. In the dimness it seemed curiously youthful. Deep shadows ringed her eyes.

I told her who I was. "I wonder if we could talk."

She appraised me, probably from long habit, as if I were a suitor. Finally she turned to the child. "Emmy, hon, Sesame will be on again later. Why don't you go ride your trike."

The child rose, turned off the television, and went outside. An air conditioner hummed softly.

"She's a cutie," I said.

"You want to talk about Emily? You don't look Welfare. Can't be the Sheriff, in that getup."

"I'm a private investigator, Mrs. Baker. I've been doing a job for your granddaughter, Glory. I've got some information for her, but she's not answering her phone. She told me to check with you if I couldn't reach her."

"'Fraid I can't help you," she said. "Haven't seen her for a week. What you been doing for her?"

I settled into a chair. Only an unlit pole lamp separated us. She obviously didn't want to turn it on.

"Glory asked me to look for her grandfather."

"That stuff again. Did you find him?"

"No."

"Figgers. If he ain't dead, he sure ain't gonna want to be found." She hesitated. "Is he dead?"

"I don't know. There's some evidence that suggests he might have made it out of the desert."

"Wouldn't surprise me. He was a funny sort, Larry, with his drawings and his talk, but he was tough."

"Tough enough to snap Daryl Lotz's neck."

"Daryl's own fault. Even at that, it wasn't like Larry wanted to kill him. When he saw Daryl was dead he was like a little kid, crying, carrying on, scared."

"What happened out there in the dunes?"

She told me, in succinct phrases, as if time had reduced the memories to small bits of tile to fit into the mosaic of her life. It was the same story I'd heard from Spoon White.

As she spoke I grew aware of an odor, faint but distinctive, that seemed at once to emanate from and to enclose her.

"Sounds like a pretty clear case of self-defense to me."

"That's what it was."

"Is that what you told the Sheriff?"

"He just heard what Pete Lotz told him to hear."

So Glory Dahlman's grandfather was not a murderer.

"Is there any question that Lawrence Parker was the father of your first daughter?"

"Rose? Nope."

"But your father and Pete Lotz weren't so sure?"

"Old fools." She shook her head as if the gesture pained her. Her blonde hair was thin, lusterless. "I told 'em, but they still made their deal. For my baby. Between the two of them I learned everything I needed to know about men."

The scent seemed more pervasive, a quirky combination of odors I couldn't identify. One might have been rosewater.

"You don't think much of us?"

"You're good for two things, and they both happen at the same time, in bed. After that, who needs you?"

I smiled, then nodded at the wall beside her hung with young faces like fleshy fruit. "These are all yours?"

"Seven girls, four boys," she said with quiet pride. "And grandkids."

"And no husband. How did you support them?"

"A little of this, a little of that. A lot of Welfare." Her gaze drifted over the photos. "I liked getting pregnant and being pregnant, and I like having the little ones around. What I didn't like was having some yahoo laying around and expectin' me to wash his dirty underwear just 'cause he could get himself to stand up and be counted once in a while."

It was roses I smelled, masking a medicinal odor. And something else, something rank, rotting. Brilliant detective that I am, I finally induced that the woman was ill.

"Emily is the only child with you now?"

"I've had her a couple years. Glory sees her all the time, though."

"She's Glory's daughter? Parker's great-granddaughter?"

"I guess. Not that it matters. These are my kids, my family. Larry has no claim to them. No man does."

Her voice had sharpened, but she wasn't angry. She was wary, an old she-beast protecting her cubs.

"Do you have any idea where I might find Glory?"

"Why?"

"As I said, I've been trying to find her grandfather for her. I need to talk to her."

"You said, Mr. Detective," she said. "There's nothin' to say what you're saying is true."

"I can't prove it, but I am working for Glory. Haskell Dan asked me to. I've found some things she'd want to know."

She took that as a ploy, rejected it. "You come slicking in here talkin' about Lawrence Parker, but you keep askin' questions about Glory. You tell me you're just a private detective, but you got cop eyes."

Suddenly it was clear. "You know about Haskell Dan."

"I can read. It was in the paper."

"No, you know Glory was with him when it happened."

"Was she?" The she-beast, backing into her lair.

I eased off. "As far as that goes, Flora, I don't need to see Glory. I can tell you, and you can tell her."

"Go ahead." She didn't trust me, but I didn't care.

"I was told that Lawrence Parker survived the desert. There's some evidence—some sketches of you, in fact—to verify this, but it's not concrete. I was also told that Parker's dead, buried out in the Black Rock. There is no evidence to support this. But I did find other relatives of your granddaughter's. The old Dahlman place out near Gerlach is owned by a man named Gabriel George, Dolores Dahlman's nephew, Glory's cousin. He wants to meet her."

Interest flickered around her eyes, and doubt. "Stuart never said nothing about any cousin. What sketches of me?"

"The ones Parker did of you in the dunes. Stuart found them when his mother died. He sold them to Pete Lotz. He also got Lotz to give him money to find Parker."

"So that's what it was all about."

I sat, waited.

"Stuart come sniffin' around, with Haskell hanging over him like a guardian angel. He—well, he was a good-lookin' man, big like you, almost as slick a talker. My youngest was two, and I had the urge. Once I was pregnant with Lily, I gave him the gate, or tried to. Then come to find out he'd been at Rose too, she was pregnant with Glory. She was willing—he was so full of flimflammery about how he was going to make it big and get rich and get her out of the Valley—so he married her when I told him no. Tell the truth, I never really understood him wantin' to marry either one of us. Stuart Dahlman was a lot of things, but not the marryin' kind. Poor Rose found that out soon enough."

Talking of her dead daughter seemed to weary her. Her eyes filmed over. Then suddenly they cleared.

"But that's what was back of it all. Pete Lotz and the reward and Larry Parker. That son of a bitch."

"He never mentioned any of it to you?"

"Told me Haskell'd found the briefcase. Didn't say nothing about the dunes, pictures, or money. Asked about Larry, had I seen him, did I know anything about his family."

"Gabriel George has another relative he didn't know about. Lily—your daughter by Stuart Dahlman."

"Guess so."

"Is she in Reno?"

"Sings around town, her an' this little band she's got." Her eyes shone. "God, you oughta hear that girl sing."

I asked her for, and after a moment's hesitation she gave me, Lily's address. "I'll tell Mr. George. Will you tell Glory about him?"

She didn't answer. I listened to the air conditioner and the shallow, rapid wheeze of her breathing. The odor in the room was growing richer, ranker.

"I don't know if I'll be able to."

"Why not?"

The skin around her eyes tightened. She was trying to trust me. "The cops are looking for her, aren't they?"

"They want to talk to her. She was seen with Haskell just before he was shot. They don't think she did it."

She seemed unconvinced.

"How did you know Glory was with Haskell, Flora?"

"She told me she was going to talk to him, said that Haskell knew this guy . . . that was you, I guess."

"You haven't talked to her since?"

Her head moved slowly sideways.

"She may still get in touch with you."

"It might be too late," she said slowly. "Turn on the light a minute, will you?"

I flicked on the pole lamp. As my eyes adjusted to the light, her face came into focus: the face of death.

The skin that in the dimness had seemed youthful was slack over bones. What had seemed shadow was a sunken gauntness. Her blonde hair was so thin I could see her scalp, and beneath it, her skull.

"What is it, Flora?"

"The Big C."

"There's nothing—"

"They tried drugs and x rays. But it's too far gone."

"How long?"

"A month. Tomorrow." She saw something in my face. "It's all right. No real pain. And I—well, I'm ready. It's all right. But I've got to find Glory."

I thought I knew why. "To take Emily?"

She nodded. "I—would you turn out the light?"

I did. "You were a friend of Haskell's?" she asked.

"Yes."

Her hands tightened again in her lap, twisted. "Can you find Glory for me?"

"I can try. Where does she live?"

"She's got a little apartment over by the university."

"Friends?"

"She never . . . Glory lived pretty much inside herself. Lily was the only one she was ever close to."

"What about Emily's father?"

"Only Glory knows. She said it wasn't one of the Valley boys, had this story about some rich old guy, but I never really . . . Glory always had stories. More like dreams. Her mom had them too."

"There's nowhere you can think of that she might have gone? Nobody she'd go to?"

"Just Lily, an' she hasn't seen her."

I let my eyes leave hers and drift over the dim room. Cheap furniture, ridiculous painting, young faces, eyes.

"Is there anyone who can help you, anyone you can call?"

"Lily. Neighbors. I'll be okay."

I rose. "Is there anything I can get you?"

"I'm fine." She smiled. "It's too bad, though, you didn't come around sooner, before I got the change. It could of been interesting, to see what we could of come up with."

Then her face, her eyes, did something, and her weary, bloated, cancer-riddled body; something in me stirred, the same something she had been stirring in men since she was a barefoot girl on a little hay patch outside Winnemucca. Now she was old, bred-out, dying. Yet there it was.

"My loss, Flora."

Her dying eyes followed me out the door.

Her great-granddaughter's eyes followed me to my jeep, followed it around and out the dusty yard.

A white pickup followed me back to town.

# 14

I spotted him less than a half-mile from Flora Baker's trailer. He gave me enough room to stay just out of license plate-reading range, but he made little effort to conceal his presence or purpose.

I led him out of the valley, took North McCarren to Virginia, played games with two stop-lights and pulled in at the Little Wal so suddenly that he had no choice but to drift on past. I couldn't get a good look at his hat-shaded face, couldn't quite identify the small logo on the door of the truck. I did get the license-plate number.

The Little Wal was crowded, a late lunch and early drinking bunch, has-been and never-was jocks, ag students, university administrators, middle-aged businessmen, and women. The women were not young enough to be students, traveled in packs of three or four, had bright smiles and hunter's eyes. The women watched the men. The men watched the women. From the walls, athletes immortalized in blown-up prints watched it all with blank, white-centered eyes.

I got a beer and called Frank Calvetti. He wasn't in, so I left my name and Glory's address. I called a contact at DMV, gave her the white pickup's license, and told her I'd call back.

I finished my beer and went outside. The nose of the white pickup peeked from behind the corner of a Standard station. I pulled out, letting him follow me. We weren't going far.

In five minutes I was on The Strand, winding through a

quiet, shady neighborhood of substantial old brick and stucco and frame houses slowly being fragmented into apartments for university students. The house I wanted was an old Queen Anne webbed with wooden staircases; the apartment I wanted had the look of a converted basement garage.

I parked in the shade of a gnarly old apple tree. A half a block away, the roof of the white pickup slid along a low hedge and stopped.

A crumbling concrete drive lined with flowering strawberry plants led to the door. I knocked, expecting and receiving no answer. I picked the lock and stepped inside.

It was a large square room notched in one corner by a small bathroom, outfitted in another with kitchen equipment and a breakfast bar. The former garage was carpeted in blue and contained a king-sized water bed with a headboard stuffed with books, a lovely old cedar wardrobe, a pair of dressers antiqued in blue, a brick-and-board bookcase filled with paperbacks, a walnut veneer and aluminum tubing desk. Pillows and stuffed animals filled corners and created cutesy tableaux; bright colored posters announcing movies of the forties and plays put on by UNR and Reno Little Theatre interrupted the institution white of the concrete walls. Everything was neat. Bare surfaces were dulled by dust.

I tried to understand what the apartment told me about Glory Dahlman. It certainly didn't tell me she was a hooker.

I went into the tiny bathroom and tossed it. Everything you'd expect. Which is to say, nothing.

I checked the wardrobe. Wherever Glory had gone, she'd traveled light.

The dresses hanging in a neat, almost formal row ranged in style from skimpily to formally to bizarrely seductive. They were all black. They seemed, hanging bodiless, more ghoulish costume than attire, the accoutrements of Halloween theatrics. On the cedar floor lay at least a dozen pairs of black spiked-heel pumps and an old, one-eyed, stuffed doll.

One of the dressers was filled with little girl clothes, the other with underwear both for wear and for show, with jeans and blouses and sweatshirts.

I tried the desk. On its top perched a small framed snapshot of Glory in a subdued and sensible summer dress, with Emily, about three then, in her arms.

The single drawer contained a book of good paper bound in good red leather. In neat fat oval letters the first page was titled "heart bleeds."

Each sheet contained a brief, cryptic poem. The most recent was dated four days before:

> A dream demon lover
> Is better than none
> When that demon's one
> Lover of babies all
> Drowning in tears
> And mothers of night
> Wearing nightmares of years
> And dead lovely ladies
> Who rot in the grave . . .
> Can grandpa save?

I couldn't make much of it, or of any of the others: incoherent images, jingle of rhyme.

I made more of the rest of the drawer's contents.

The bank book showed me that Glory Dahlman had deposited and withdrawn money in an account at Nevada National Bank for nearly three years. Most of the deposits were weekly, for a couple hundred dollars; most of the withdrawals were in August and January, for about a thousand dollars. Her last deposit brought the total to twenty-seven hundred and change.

The neat collection of grade slips showed me that for three years Gloria Dahlman had been attending the University of Nevada-Reno, taking mostly courses in the English and the Speech and Theater departments, earning mostly As and Bs.

The neat collection of handbills from college and Little

Theatre plays showed me that Gloria Dahl had acted in a number of local productions, most recently playing Lady MacBeth and Lucy Van Pelt. The neat collection of reviews clipped from the *Gazette-Journal* told me that she'd played them well.

The neat entries in the small notebook showed me that Glory had "engagements" roughly twice a week with what appeared to be, by the initials beside each, a fairly constant group of about two dozen men. On the inside cover of the notebook were three telephone numbers.

As Haskell Dan had said, she was not what she seemed. Not quite.

On the wall beside the breakfast bar hung a telephone and a small corkboard bearing a blue flyer. Poor Lil, it announced, would open a two-week run at the Silver Saddle Casino the next night.

The first number in Glory's notebook I recognized as her grandmother's. I called the second. No answer. I called the third. A female voice, not Glory's, answered with a distant, sleep- or drugged-slurred "Yeah."

"May I speak with Glory, please."

"Go fuck yourself." The line went dead.

I called a contact at the phone company and asked her to check out the numbers.

I looked around the apartment of Glory Dahlman, Gloria Dahlman, Gloria Dahl. Mother, student, thespian, hooker. Missing. I found nothing to indicate where she might be.

Back in my rig, I sat for a moment. The white pickup was still with me. I decided to let him hang around a while. I cranked up and headed toward town.

I was on my way to Lily Baker's. But she lived less than six blocks from my building, so I stopped to make a couple of calls.

My diploma was no longer in the middle of the street.

My office was still a shambles. But my recorder was working. It blinked at me.

I righted the desk and chair, picked up the phone and the message machine. I turned it on and listened.

"Mr. Ross, this is Frederick Ripley. I may have a job for you. I'm at the Hollister Ranch."

I had no idea who Frederick Ripley was. I did know where, and what, the Hollister Ranch was.

I played the message again. Frederick Ripley was not so much terse as imperious, his tone that of one used to giving commands that he was used to having immediately obeyed.

I erased the message.

I called Frank Calvetti. He still wasn't in.

I called my friend at the phone company. One of the numbers belonged to Lily Baker, the other to Leon Whipple.

I knew Leon Whipple. I didn't want to think about what it meant that Glory knew Leon Whipple.

From my window I could see the white pickup parked a block and a half down the street. I called my friend at DMV. I listened, decided that maybe I would just trot out to talk to Mr. Frederick Ripley.

The pickup was registered to the Hollister Corporation.

# 15

From the low top of Windy Hill, I could see below the Hollister Ranch, the house gleaming white even in the dark shade of tall poplars. At a significant distance from it, a grid of white fence spread across the old pasture land in squares of ten acres planted with expensive homes that flashed, from glass and pools and paint, the sun-signals of success. Around most, like living lawn decorations, sleek pampered horses nibbled at the grass.

I twisted down the hill to Del Monte Lane, found the unpaved road I wanted and stirred dust up to the house. The white Ford pickup continued on down Del Monte Lane.

Larger, older than others in the neighborhood, the Hollister Ranch house sat regally in the shade, two wide, green-shuttered stories to which a screened porch added substance and a pillared portico lent aristocratic authority. It spoke not of recent success but of long-held dominion, not simply of money but of money in the service of power.

At the top of the parking loop, vehicles nosed toward the door like patient saddle horses: a black Lincoln, a brown Bentley, a beautiful '54 T-bird the deep waxy green of about-to-ripen cherries, a pickup the twin of my recently departed shadow. The logo on the door was the discreet encircled H of the Hollister Corporation. It was Pete Lotz's Circle Lazy L stood up and branched with money.

There were no real horses here, no pasture. The house sat in the center of sixty acres of thick, smooth lawn. Just left of the stairs leading to the door, chunks of turf were being torn from the earth.

I parked and got out. Then I recognized him. I stood in the afternoon sun, chilled, numb. I vowed silently that I would believe nothing of what I was told in that house.

He was of medium height, square of shoulder and jaw like his father. His swing seemed effortless, generated enough power to keep downtown Reno gaudily aglow for a week. Divots lay scattered ten yards in front of him. A dozen white balls lay at his feet. Others gathered in tidy concentration at the foot of a catalpa tree a hundred and eighty yards away.

He gave me a large-toothed grin. I grinned back, feeling icily gleeful. He came over.

Open, sun-stained, surrounding eyes as dark as his sister's but not so large, his face showed no sign of the high, hard living that, word had it, had kept him a no-name after years on the pro tour.

"Afternoon. Bobby George. You looking for me?" He tried hard to let me see that he hoped I wasn't.

"Jack Ross," I said. "I'm here to see Frederick Ripley." I nodded at the circle of balls beneath the catalpa tree. "You've got that shot down?"

"I've got them all down. When I can keep my mind on what I'm doing. That's why I'm here. It's easier to behave here."

"In Reno?"

He grinned. "I know. There's more action in this town than— but the family's been here most of the summer. They make me be a good boy."

It was a curious admission to a stranger, reflected the innocent arrogance of one who had always had more of everything than he could possible want. His sister had it too.

"You here for the war council?"

"I don't know what I'm here for." I nodded at the collection of automobiles. "What's the occasion?"

He shrugged his square shoulders. "Freddie whipped in from San Francisco a few days ago. He's been huddled up with my mother ever since, so it must be business." As if that weren't enough, he added: "Ripley's president of Hollister, Mom's board chair and chief stockholder."

"Any idea what the confab is about?"

"I don't muck around in the business, except to cash my dividend checks. Mom and my brother are the only business types in the family." A question settled into his dark eyes. "You don't look much like a business type yourself."

I didn't know why Bobby George was chattering, or what he wanted from me, and I didn't much care. If he wanted to chat, I'd chat. And believe nothing.

"What type do I look like?"

He gave me a read. "All I can tell is you're probably an ex-jock with a nine handicap who plays a hook and has trouble inside fifty yards."

"I'm carrying a twelve, and I can't get a half-wedge within thirty feet of the hole. I'm a private investigator."

"What . . . what does Ripley want a detective for?"

"I don't know yet," I said. "I haven't talked to him."

He was silent for a moment. Then the grin returned. "How about that. You're the first private dick I've ever met. At least officially. I might have had one on my tail from time to time. Hey, you . . . ?" His gaze frisked me.

"I'm licensed to carry a gun. I don't."

He relaxed, grinned. "I suppose you don't wear a trenchcoat either."

"In Nevada?"

"No gorgeous women always panting with lust for you?"

I thought, nastily: Just your sister. But I said, grinning: "Alas."

"Yeah," he grinned. "Come on, let's go find Freddie."

He led me up the stairs and under the portico. As he reached for the door, from the dimness of the screened porch drifted a throaty female voice full of maternal resignation: "Shoes, Bobby."

He turned. "Hey, Annie. didn't see you there."

Shadows stirred. She stepped into the light. She was as maternal as a bejewelled G-string.

Her short hair was a shade blonder than blonde, her eyes subtly made up to accentuate their sea-grey shimmer, her oval face smoothed with something besides skin. Her high-breasted body swelled against the lines of her blue sheath dress. Her wide mouth, a glossy-lipped implement of pleasure, in repose settled somewhere between pucker and pout. It moved.

"Please don't wear your spikes inside again, Bobby. You're destroying the floor."

She addressed Bobby George, but she looked at me. A faint fault line appeared on her forehead; she was older than I'd first thought, at least thirty-five.

"Sorry," Bobby George said. He popped off one spiked shoe, then another. "Annie, this is Jack Ross, a private eye. He's looking for your old man. What's up—you been working out at the Bounce Awhile Motel?"

She was not amused. She was, although she tried to hide it, apprehensive.

I offered my hand. "How do you do, Mrs. Ripley."

She examined my hand as if it might contain a weapon. Slowly she lifted her own, soft, adorned with nails like fat blood-colored hearts. "You are working for my husband? On what?" Her face tightened. "I'm sorry. I just. . . ."

"I don't know, Mrs. Ripley. I—"

"He's upstairs in the office. Bobby will show you." She turned, stepped from sunlight into shadow, and was gone.

Grinning, Bobby George opened the door. "I guess you're right, Jack. I didn't notice any lustful panting there."

"You were looking at the wrong person."

He laughed.

She had been right about the floor. The small foyer we stood in led to a long hallway, the fresh coat of hard wax on which could not disguise the pits left by Bobby George's golf shoes. Now without them, he shoved himself forward, skating down the hall. I followed in more conventional fashion.

In the middle of the hall two large doors faced each other. Through the one on the right I saw a dining room, with archways into a den and into a kitchen, a warren of pantries.

As they dispensed sustenance, those on the left provided comfort: a living room dominated by a baby grand piano, several smaller sitting rooms. All had dark wainscotting, delicately patterned wallpaper, paintings hanging from shadow molding. Furniture gleamed with layers of wax.

Two dark-haired young women occupied the living room. The taller paced before a window with the insouciance of the well-trained fashion model. The smaller sat at the piano. She was not playing. I let Dolly George sit there.

Her brother led me down the hall. I addressed his beveled back. "Your family doesn't live here?"

"Just Hayes, my brother. He handles the Nevada operations. We grew up in San Francisco. My grandfather used to summer here, and my dad stays here sometimes on his way in and out of the desert, but mostly it's a tax dodge."

That figured—literally. Nevada's tax laws encouraged companies to incorporate in the state. The Hollister Corporation had ever since R. Hayes Hollister tore his fortune out of the Nevada mountains and the men who mined them and hauled it to California well over a half-century before. Nevada metals had financed real estate, banking, and manufacturing ventures. Nevada laws protected them.

The hall ended in a staircase which we climbed to another hallway extending back to the front of the house. Four closed doors interrupted its length. Bobby George stopped at the first one, gave it a thump, and pushed it open.

The room was small, with more dark wainscotting below pale plaster, more heavy old furniture. One wall was lined with books, mostly statutes of various states. Another, broken by a closed door, was hung with a black-and-white photograph of a desert landscape. In the third, the mass of Mount Rose, dark green pine capped with snow, loomed beyond the window behind an old oak desk. The desk looked well used. The man standing beside it did not.

Not fifty, he wore his thick sandy hair short to control its wiry tangle, wore an exquisite blue pin-stripe three-piece suit to control the thirty excess pounds he carried on a tall, slope-shouldered frame. His long, well-fed face was nearly as smooth as his wife's. His eyes were blue, blank.

"Here your detective, Freddie." Bobby slumped into one of the leather armchairs angled toward the desk. "What's up? You decide I need a babysitter?"

Frederick Ripley ignored him. "Thank you for coming, Mr. Ross. I'm sorry for such short notice."

His deliberate phrasing articulated that he wasn't sorry at all. He had called and I had come. For the president of the Hollister Corporation, it would always be thus.

I let him think that, and said nothing.

"Ca'mon, Freddie. What's going on?"

"Run along and play," Ripley said evenly.

Bobby flushed. "With all the corporate security we've got, if you're hiring a private detective, there must be a private problem. Private means family. Problem means me. This's got something to do with Vegas, doesn't it?"

Again Ripley ignored him. He motioned me to the other chair. He sat at the desk, turned his blank gaze on Bobby.

"Yeah, okay," Bobby said finally, rising. His grin flashed. "See you, Jack. Maybe you can give me a detective lesson, so I can find out what's going on around here."

Frederick Ripley's eyes followed him out. Then they turned to me. "Would you care for something, Mr. Ross?"

A row of bottles stood on a low table against the back wall. "The Napoleon Brandy looks mighty tasty."

He didn't know whether to approve of my choice or disapprove of my levity. He glanced to the side as if searching for a minion. Finding none, he rose and went himself to the table. While he poured, I gave the photograph a longer look.

A twisted cottonwood and a castellated rock formation stood sharply etched against a plateau stippled with sage and rising to blend with a sparsely-starred sky. Shadows without sources deepened the emptiness. The effect was eerie, as if tree and rocks, in their crisp presence, were at once created and consumed by the surrounding nothingness.

"Filters," Ripley said, placing a snifter half-filled with brandy on the small table beside me. "Gabe did that with a special kind of filter. But perhaps he told you that?"

That game we weren't playing. "He told me many things."

Ripley sat at the desk. It held a phone, a pair of pens in an onyx holder, and a boxy old intercom with its switch in the ON position.

I love it when people think I'm stupid. It makes my job so much easier. And so much more fun.

"Now then, Mr. Ross. Curiously, Bobby was correct. The matter we need to discuss does not involve the Hollister Corporation. It's a family matter."

"The Ripley family or the George family?"

He sat up in his chair, blocking out Mount Rose. "The Georges are my family, Mr. Ross. I went to work for Hayes Hollister thirty years ago. He put me through law school. Moreover, he took me into his confidence, into his home as well as his business. When he died, he charged me with the care of both. I take neither charge lightly."

I took a sip of the brandy. "I'd guess you don't take much of anything lightly, Mr. Ripley—especially yourself."

His blue eyes pulsed. He sat back in his chair, hands folded over his paunch as if to help his suit contain the bountiful fruits of good living.

"I've had you checked out, Ross, since Dolly came to her mother this morning with her curious story. I was surprised to learn that you come recommended both for your expertise and your discretion. You are also said to be honest."

I'd been demoted. No more Mister. Just another lackey. But honest. "The last of a dying breed."

His eyes remained blank. "I have a few questions."

"It's your brandy."

"You have a law degree and retain membership in the Nevada Bar, yet you've never practiced. Why?"

"I got it right the first time."

He gave me the same silent look he'd used on Bobby George. It didn't take with me. On the other hand, if we were playing games, I'd play this one for a while.

"I got the degree to please my grandfather, who was a small bail bondsman and private investigator whom I'd helped since I was a teenager, and to satisfy an ambitious wife. In law school, I realized that I preferred investigation to litigation, but my options seemed limited to law enforcement. Vietnam delayed the decision, and ended my marriage, so I went to work with my grandfather. Then he died. I expanded the bonding business until I could hire someone to run it, and I now concentrate on investigations. I pay my bar dues because as an officer of the court I can get information more easily and offer my clients more confidentiality."

That part was smooth, an oft-fingered old coin. What followed was freshly-minted and crisply-edged.

"I am expert, discreet, and honest, by reputation. By character I am little inclined to indulge the whims and condescensions of the monied, whether they be thoroughly spoiled brats or corporate executives."

It was wasted on him. "How seriously do you take your ethical responsibilities as an attorney?"

"I didn't take a course in legal ethics. They couldn't find anyone in the profession qualified to teach it."

He didn't laugh. He didn't smile. Then, as if his synapses had received a sudden charge, his blank blue eyes flared. "And how do you feel about extortion, Mr. Ross?"

Although I was Mister again, I'd had it. I'd tried my best to insult Frederick Ripley. Now I insulted his brandy, draining the snifter in a gulp.

"The way I feel about this conversation. The way I feel about the fact that someone else is listening to it over the intercom. The way I feel about being tailed most of the day by a pickup with a Hollister Corporation logo on its side. The way I feel about playing silly fucking games."

I rose. "If you've got something to say to me, say it. Otherwise, I'm gone."

"Not if you know what's good for you. I'll have you—"

# 16

A small sixtyish woman in a beige suit and pumpkin blouse came briskly through the connecting door. Her eyes were as intelligent as her daughter's. I rose.

"I'm Alice George, Mr. Ross. Please forgive our ruse, and our rudeness. But we didn't know if you were involved."

"Alice," Ripley said, "we still don't know—"

"Yes, we do. Between what Dolly told us and what you learned, it was already clear. But why don't we simply ask." Her eyes hadn't left mine. "Mr. Ross, are you involved in an attempt to extort five hundred thousand dollars from us?"

I couldn't help it. That one surprised me. "No."

"Thank you." We sat, and she turned to Ripley. "Now, let's get down to business. Show him." Frederick Ripley might be the president of the Hollister Corporation, but there was no question who was the boss.

From a drawer he took a manila envelope and placed it on the edge of the desk. It was addressed to Mrs. Alice George at the Hollister Ranch, Reno, in square block letters in ballpoint pen, with a Reno post mark.

I reached inside and withdrew three sheets of paper. The top sheet bore a block-lettered message:

WE CAN IDENTIFY HIM. THE EVIDENCE WILL
COST $500,000. SMALL BILLS. YOU HAVE A WEEK.
INSTRUCTIONS TO FOLLOW.

The second sheet was a copy of a photograph of a desert scene, the photograph Glory Dahlman had described. The third sheet copied a drawing of the same scene.

I held the two landscapes up before me. In the drawing, the lines were stylized, the hills consciously mammarian, the canyon gynecological, as if trying—unsuccessfully—to make a sexual something of the photograph's philosophical nothing.

"Well, Mr. Ross?" Ripley again sat back in his chair.

"Gabriel George is Lawrence Parker."

"How long have you known that?"

I should have said, "Since I met him." If I hadn't been whacked senseless by his daughter, I could have. "Just now."

"He didn't tell you?" Alice George asked.

"He told me that Parker was dead, shot by an Indian named Haskell Dan."

She frowned, started to speak, didn't. Ripley did. "You have drawings like these?"

"I do. About twenty of them."

"How did they come into your possession?"

"A hooker gave them to me."

"The Dahlman girl," Alice George said. "She's the only person who has these drawings?"

"Your husband used to trade them for meals and lodging. They're probably scattered all over Nevada. The Humboldt County Sheriff has some. And some were stolen from Glory. This is probably a copy of one of them."

Alice George frowned. "Mr. Ross, is there a possibility that the girl, Glory Dahlman, could have a part in this?"

"Anything is possible. But if Glory knew Parker was alive, knew his identity—and this envelope was mailed before she talked to me—she wouldn't have needed me."

"It might not be that simple." Ripley leveled his blue eyes at me. "This drawing and photograph suggest that Parker and Gabe George are the same man, but as evidence they are worthless. The blackmailers would want more than this. And you now have it. Or are in a position to get it."

I got it. The reason I'd been summoned. "You think Glory knew who Gabriel George was and hired me to prove it?"

"We don't know that, Mr. Ross," Alice George said. "We do wonder if that might be the case."

"My initial response to that, Mrs. George, is no. I believe that Glory doesn't know who Lawrence Parker is."

"I see." She sat straight and small in the chair. "But you can see, Mr. Ross, that we will want to talk to her."

"That's all she wants. She's Parker's granddaughter."

"Are you certain?"

"Her grandmother has always said so."

"What does she want, Ross? What's she after? She's a prostitute, are you sure she doesn't—"

"Let it go, Frederick." Alice George turned to me. "We will be happy to welcome Glory into our family."

I had difficulty not believing that. Alice George's eyes were frank, warm. Ripley's eyes were blue and blank. "Which brings us back to the matter at hand. Extortion."

"Forget it," I said. "Mrs. George, your husband is wanted for murder in Humboldt County. But he'll never be convicted, never even come to trial. Even if the D.A. was an idiot or susceptible to some sort of pressure and decided to prosecute, your husband would never be convicted, not with the legal help you could get, certainly not in this state."

She frowned, uncertain.

"Mrs. George, if the citizens of Nevada discovered that your husband had managed to parade around under the nose of the law for forty years, they'd probably elect him governor."

She turned to Ripley. "You didn't tell me this."

"No, I didn't." He shifted in his chair. "Ross is correct, but only generally. It remains possible that Gabe might be arrested, tried, and convicted, if not for murder then on some other charge. We might also be charged—aiding, and abetting, that sort of thing. We are not prepared to take the risk."

His "we" was almost monarchical. I didn't know whom it included. "Is that also Mr. George's position?"

"He doesn't know about this."

"You haven't told . . . ?"

"He's in the desert, working," Alice George said. "Telling him about this would only upset him, and interrupt that work. Perhaps for no good reason." She leaned forward. "As for turning himself in, which you seem to be suggesting, we've discussed it over the years, but it always comes to the same thing: Why? What is to be gained? The boy Gabe killed is long dead. Why bring it back up, upset everyone, involve the children—to say nothing of the publicity that would attach to Hollister Corporation because of it—if, as you say, nothing significant is likely to result?"

I still didn't know what was really going on. "Mrs. George, your husband has lived with this, carried it around on his back like a burlap bag full of fool's gold, for forty years. Wouldn't he like to get rid of it?"

"My husband would tell you that the weight of that useless ore, and the bruises it formed on his back, make the difference between Gabriel George and Lawrence Parker."

"Are we talking about guilt?"

"It's deeper than that. That sketch was drawn by Lawrence Parker. The photograph was taken by Gabe George. They are not the same man. By turning himself in, he would become Lawrence Parker again. At least he thinks so. Since he doesn't want to do it, I don't want him to either."

When I didn't respond, she smiled. "I know this isn't easy to understand."

It wasn't that difficult. She had lived her adult life loving a man wanted for murder, protecting that man. She was still protecting him.

"What do you want from me, Mrs. George?"

"We would like you to tell Glory Dahlman that we'd be happy to talk to her. We will welcome her into our family."

Ripley slid his chair back from the desk. Taking that as a sign the discussion was over, I started to rise. Alice George, with a quick flash of brown hand, stopped us both. "There is one other thing, Mr. Ross. We still have a couple of days before we're to hear from the blackmailers. I'd like you to see if you can find out who they are before then."

"Alice," Ripley said quickly, "I don't think—"

"Mr. Ross can be trusted. That seems clear enough."

He looked at her, his smooth-fleshed face stiff. "It's—the fact is, the more I think about it, the more I come to agree with Ross. We should just ignore the whole thing. It doesn't balance," he said. "As Ross says, the risk to Gabe is minuscule. If we take it, one of two things will result. These people will try to use what they have. Almost certainly it will cause Gabe no harm. Or they will try to get to us again, and probably expose themselves in the process." He turned to me. "Do you agree, Mr. Ross?"

I was Mister again. "Essentially. Especially given the fact that the threat to Gabriel George does not really exist. Lawrence Parker did not murder Daryl Lotz."

They both stared at me.

"Parker killed Daryl Lotz, but he didn't murder him. The only witness to the event, Flora Magnusson Baker, is certain of that. She told me so less than two hours ago."

"She would testify to that?"

"She's dying, she'd never get to a trial. But I'm sure she would be happy to give the authorities a statement. She would be glad to get the truth out, about everything."

Alice George seemed stunned. "Thank you, Mr. Ross. You seem to have . . . eliminated our problem. But there's something else. The fact is that my home, my family have been invaded. I want to know who is responsible."

Here was another she-beast protecting her cubs. And her mate. "This perhaps strikes you as vengeful on my part, Mr. Ross. It may be. But I will not have my family threatened. I had no family for most of my youth, just a father who sent me to the best schools so that he was free to . . . do his business. In a very real way, I didn't become a human being until I met Gabe. He became my family, and then the children completed it. I will not have *anyone* endanger them."

I said nothing.

"Can you find these people, Mr. Ross? I want to know who they are. We will double your regular fee, to ensure your exclusive efforts until the matter is resolved. We will also award you a substantial bonus if you are successful."

"I have a client at the moment. Glory Dahlman."

"She hired you to find her grandfather. You have."

"But she doesn't know it. I found her grandfather, but now I can't find her. Neither can the police. Haskell Dan, the Indian your husband told me killed Parker, was murdered two days ago. Glory was the last person seen with him."

Her eyes filled with distress.

"She didn't kill him, Mrs. George."

"But . . . she's disappeared?"

"That isn't certain. She just isn't around."

"I see." Alice George used that expression a lot. I guessed that she saw a lot. I also guessed that she didn't see everything. "But in order to find the blackmailers, I'd think you would try to learn who stole the drawings from Glory. So there's no problem. Find Glory, then find the extortionists."

There were more problems than I could shake a stick at. I mentioned one. "Neither you nor Mr. Ripley has bothered to explain why you've had me followed all day, Mrs. George. I feel about that the way you do about the extortion attempt."

Her face lost all expression. Ripley frowned. "Hayes?"

She slumped back into the chair. "My son, Mr. Ross. He was here when Dolly arrived and told us about you and Glory Dahlman. He—well, I apologize for him. I'm sure he thought he was helping. The fact is, my son is convinced that everyone but himself is a fool or idiot or both—he has much of his grandfather in him."

Any of R. Hayes Hollister would be too much to have in another person. I accepted her apology. "All right, Mrs. George. I'll see what I can dig up. I—how many people know that Gabriel George is Lawrence Parker?"

"We know," she said. "My father knew. When Gabe and I married, my father got Gabe all the official documents he needed—birth certificate, social security number, that sort of thing. And Dolores Dahlman knew. No one else."

"Stuart Dahlman?"

"I—he's Dolores's son? Glory's father?"

"Stuart Dahlman has been dead for twenty years," Ripley said. "Your father knew about him, Alice. When I was here, he had me keep track of the boy and Flora Baker. There was never any indication that Dahlman had any knowledge of either Gabriel George or Lawrence Parker, but your father took no chances. Then Dahlman and his wife killed themselves."

"Do your children know, Mrs. George?"

Her face took on a darker tint. "There was never any reason to tell them. But even if they did, they certainly wouldn't set out to blackmail their own father."

I turned to Ripley. "Your family?"

"What family I had is long dead."

"Your wife?"

"My wife knows nothing." The statement was so forceful as to be nearly absolute. "I won't presume to tell you your business, Mr. Ross, but as Alice suggested, the extortionists must be in league with whoever stole the drawings from the Dahlman girl. So these questions seem totally irrelevant."

He had no notion of how relevant they were. Or perhaps he did. But I just said, "They do, don't they."

Alice George sat up on the edge of her chair. "What are your chances of identifying these people?"

"Good. People who do this sort of thing are stupid."

As she nodded assent, Ripley took out a checkbook. "Of course, Mr. Ross, this does not go beyond this room."

"No one else in the family is to know about it.?"

"No," Alice George said. "For now, at least."

Ripley shoved a check across the desk to me. It was written on a Hollister Corporation account. "That is a sufficient retainer?"

"Ridiculously sufficient." I rose.

"You will begin immediately?"

"I already have." Had I ever.

Alice George rose. "When will we hear from you?"

"Shortly."

She offered me her hand. I accepted, as I had accepted the brandy, the check. "Thank you, Mr. Ross." She went through the connecting door.

"What happens to the extortionists, once I've identified them?"

Ripley's blank blue eyes seemed to take another sudden charge, brightening. "I'm not certain that I understand your question."

He understood my question perfectly.

I understood something too. The little trick he did with his eyes was effective, but that's all it was, a trick. There wasn't a whole lot more to Frederick Ripley.

"Forget it," I said. "I'll find my way out."

# 17

Chopin, strangely played, drifted up the staircase. I tracked down to the ground floor, along the hall chewed by Bobby George's cleats, to the doorway of the drawing room.

She played the piece Horowitz had rendered so lovingly as we stood under the cottonwood tree engaged in our first wit-and-word sexual grapple. But she played with a furious energy, distending the melody into grotesque shapes.

I left her to it.

Ann Ripley was no longer on the screened porch.

Bobby George, still in his stocking feet, stood close to the house, as if in its shelter, hanging onto the elbow of the dark-haired girl who had been pacing inside. She stood rigidly in his grasp, her profile suggesting the patrician lines stamped on old gold coins, her gaze the emptiness in those gold eyes. Bobby at once seemed to comfort and plead. His eyes briefly met mine, exposing a deep bleakness.

I left him to her. Or tried to. As I was opening the door to my rig, I heard gravel crunch. "Hey, Jack!"

The girl was striding into the house. Bobby was picking his way painfully toward me. His expression was working itself into a grin. It was working hard. "So, what's up?"

"I can't tell you."

"Sure you can," he grinned. "It's about me, isn't it? Me and Vegas."

"What about you and Vegas?"

"You know. The two hundred grand I dropped at the Starlight."

"It didn't come up in the conversation." He didn't know whether to believe that. "You getting pressure to pay up?"

"Naw, they—" He shuffled, wincing as the gravel dug into the soles of his feet. He fought to retain his grin. "They sent a couple letters, but there's nothing they can do. And they're not about to mess with the Hollister Corporation. They get nasty, Mom'll just have to buy the place."

"So why would you think that's what I'm here about?"

He shrugged, winced. "Hey, you know, just checking. I thought at first, when you got here, that maybe you. . . ."

"I don't do that kind of work."

He forced his grin wider. "What kind of work do you do?"

"The kind that tells me you're a fella with a problem."

"No way," he grinned, lying. "I mean it's not me. I . . .- could I hire you?"

"To do what?"

"I—it's Tracy. She's got this . . . problem. I'm going on the tour, and I can't leave her. I need. . . ."

"A babysitter?"

"I can pay you," he said quickly. "I'll have a trust check in a week or so, I can—"

"What's her problem?"

The pain in his eyes didn't come from sharp gravel. "It's my fault, I never thought—I mean, a couple lines, that's all we did. And all of a sudden that's all she—"

"If your girlfriend has a coke problem, she doesn't need a babysitter, she needs a substance abuse program."

He looked down again. "I know, but—if I could just figure out where she's getting it. I mean, while I was in L.A. requalifying, even Hayes couldn't keep her. . . ." He sucked up air as if he were trying to reinflate his grin.

"Don't you have anyone here who might keep an eye on her? This is a big place, you must have a staff to run it."

"Just Hernando and his wife. He keeps up the grounds, she cleans the house. They're so old they can hardly move."

"Hollister security?"

"It's all in San Francisco."

"Who helps Hayes?"

"Nobody. Like I said, this is all pretty much a tax dodge. Tracy was going to help him while I was in L.A., but there wasn't anything for her to do."

I'd gotten what I wanted from him. I slid into the Wagoneer. "If she needs help, you better get it for her."

He forced his grin. He seemed to feel that as long as he grinned, he could hold back the world. "She doesn't want help. All she wants is cocaine."

I didn't know what Bobby George wanted. I didn't feel like waiting out his grin to find out. He saw it, turned, and picked his painful way back to the house.

I drove toward Del Monte Lane, glad I'd escaped that big white house without having to listen to any more lies. I'd already been fed so many I had heartburn.

Fifty yards from Del Monte Lane, a white Ford pickup sat on the shoulder. As I approached, its back wheels suddenly spat a shower of rocks at me; the pickup spun, swung, slid, and came to a stop. The driver leaped from the cab and planted himself a yard from my bumper.

Hayes George was a bit shorter than his brother, but as wide- and thick-shouldered, with a bull neck supporting a head so heavy that its weight seemed to give him a permanent and pugnacious forward lean. His features were larger, rougher-cut than Bobby's. Now hatless, in jeans and a cowboy shirt, he glared at me, his mouth twisted and mean.

I climbed out. "Master Hayes, I presume."

His hands were fists, lump-knuckled as if from old breaks. "You're finished, asshole."

The voice was amazing, deep, resonating as if it caromed through canyons in his chest. Had he been any bigger, it would have been as intimidating as he thought it was.

"You got it. I'm finished. And as soon as you move your spymobile there, I'll be on my way."

"You'll go when I fucking well say so. First you're going to tell me what you're trying to do to my family."

"Go ask your mother."

His mouth twisted into a grin. "I'm asking—no, I'm telling you, you piece of shit. You think we're all idiots?"

"You make a pretty good case for one of you, anyhow."

The grin spread. His front teeth were capped, or false. Scar tissue cornered his mouth. I wondered how mean he was.

He told me. "You tell me what's going on or I'm going to bust your bones."

Well, it had been a long day already, and it was only mid-afternoon. It had not been a good day. I was tired. Tired of being lied to. Tired of being used, set up.

"I don't know what's going on, and I don't much care," I said. "I do know that if you don't keep a civil tongue in your head, I'm going to take you over my knee."

He wasn't afraid of me, I had to give him that. Half my size, he leaned his head at me as if it were a battering ram. Like some misbegotten mutt—half pit bull, half rat terrier, and all fight—he quivered. Then he came.

He charged low, doing the bar-brawler's shuffle. I ignored the feints, stepped outside the right he aimed at my head and hit him with a hard left behind the ear that sent him tumbling into the side of my jeep.

He wasn't hurt. He was surprised, grinning, pleased. He came again, slower, looking to take me down where I lost my edge in speed and size. I feinted right, stepped left and hit him with a right above the eyebrow, a chopping left at the temple that put him on his hands and knees in the gravel.

I stepped back, astonished at how much better I suddenly felt, at how much I enjoyed hitting a George.

I was breathing deep, and sweating. I could feel the dust gluing to my face and neck. I was ready for a drink.

But there was no quit in him. Quickly he was up, gravel clinging to the knees of his jeans, his forehead empurpled and lumping up. He grinned, crouched.

"Don't do it, Hayes," I said, taking a step back. "I'll beat on you till my hands break, and then I'll use my boots. I'll hurt you bad, if I have to."

That stopped him. He still wasn't afraid of me, but he knew enough about what we'd been doing to know I was right.

Suddenly he whirled back toward the pickup, reached in and came out with a double-barreled shotgun in his hands.

He stomped back toward me, the twin black holes pointed at my belly. My insides churned.

The knot forming on his forehead was as ugly as his eyes. The thick finger on the shotgun's trigger was outlined in white. "You're going to tell me what I want to know or you're going to have a load of double-ought up your ass."

Hayes George wasn't going to fire that shotgun. Not at me. Not in broad daylight. He'd have to be crazy.

I thought that he might very well be crazy.

"Look, Hayes, if you'd just talk to your mother—"

"Talk my ass. That's all any of them can do, talk. They'll talk themselves into the poor house. I don't talk. But you'd better."

He was right. As long as the words were coming, the double-ought shot wouldn't. "What do you want to know?"

"I want to know what you're up to. Now."

"I'm helping a girl find her grandfather."

"Don't give me that shit—maybe Dolly Dimwit will fall for it, but don't try it on me. What are you and that Sun Valley slut trying to pull?"

"Glory Dahlman? You know her?"

"I know everything. Except about you."

I didn't think he knew everything. But I was beginning to get the lay of Hayes George's land. It was wild country, craggy promontories, deep crevasses choked with rank growth.

"You must be pretty sharp at that." I forced my body to relax, shoved my hands in my pockets, stood exposed and vulnerable. "How'd you know to pick me up at Flora Baker's?"

A cold superciliousness displaced the heat in his eyes. "You dumb shit. I followed you there from your office."

It was possible, given the shape I'd been in. "Hey, look, I

may have made a mistake. Maybe instead of beating on each other we ought to be exchanging information."

It was pretty bald, but he seemed to buy it. He was filled with what had to be a colossal sense of himself. "The mistake you made was a lulu. And you'll pay for it."

"No—you really do know what's happening, don't you?"

"I know enough. What's that bitch up to?"

I took that to mean Glory. "I can't say. Your mother made me promise not to. I—how do you know her, anyway?"

"Forget her. You're the one who's under the gun here."

I no longer had any idea what to make of Hayes George. I took a deep breath, slipped my hands from my pockets, straightened up. "Hayes, you're either going to have to trust me or shoot me. I'm working for your mother."

"This morning she didn't know you existed."

"This morning I wasn't working for her. Now I am. So either pull the trigger on that thing or get out of my way."

"You want it one barrel at a time or both at once?"

"Shit or get off the pot, Hayes."

Slowly the shotgun lowered. Slowly Hayes George smiled. "Had you going there for a minute, didn't I?"

I was confused. He saw it. "You handled your fists all right, Ross, but you don't dissemble worth a damn. But what can you expect from Stanford. No sophistication, elan. You wouldn't have lasted a week at Harvard."

"Harvard?"

"Dissembling is an art. You're strictly an amateur."

I stared at his grin. Without changing that grin, he added: "What you need to know is this: the old lady lets that fat wimp Ripley run our business into the ground, the old man's a hermit, Dolly gets her little feelings hurt and starts spreading her legs all over town, and Bobby loses his PGA card 'cause he plays so crummy, he loses a quarter of a million in Vegas and this time his mommy won't bail him out, and he hooks up with a nose-nellie—they're a bunch of babies. They need a keeper. That's me. And if you ain't real careful, I'm gonna see that you do get both barrels where the sun don't shine."

"No you're not."

He grinned, dropped the shotgun even lower. "You're right."

He was, had been, laughing at me. I was either an idiot or he was genuinely crazy.

Now he laughed out loud. "Oh shit, she's cute."

"Who?"

His laugh deepened, became a strange guttural bellow. "You're the detective, asshole. You figure it out."

He wheeled and leaned his way back to the pickup, climbed in, fired it up, slammed the accelerator, jerked the wheel, and showered me with gravel.

# 18

I found a stool and a glass in the nearest bar, a square of concrete block bedecked with beer signs on South Virginia.

I tried to sort things out. I no longer knew who was lying to me and who wasn't—if there was anyone who wasn't.

Haskell Dan was dead.

Glory Dahlman seemed to be missing.

Forty years before, Lawrence Parker and Flora Magnusson had tangled limb and loin in the dunes north of Winnemucca. Now their families entangled like untended rose bushes. I was trying to untangle them and bleeding all over the place.

I sipped vodka and went back over the past three days. It got me nowhere. I went back to work.

I drove up into a neighborhood of small frame houses and large old cottonwoods, quiet streets and neat little lawns. Lily Baker's house was a tiny old box that seemed supported against the sag of wood-weariness by layers of paint so thick they might have been troweled on. I parked at the curb and got out and started up the brief walk, watching the girl on the small shaded porch watch me.

She sat in a battered platform rocker covered in faded purple velour. She had Glory Dahlman's wide mouth, her high cheekbones, but had them in an open face with more flesh on it. Her hair was lighter, longer, her eyes a lighter blue.

I stopped at the two-step stairway. "Afternoon."

"You're right so far." She had a big friendly smile.

"Lily Baker?"

"Two for two."

"My name's Jack Ross. I'd like to talk to you."

"You're off to a good start."

"I talked to your mother today. She sent me to you. I'm trying to find Glory Dahlman."

Her eyes sparkled. "You don't look her type."

"What type is that?"

Her grin widened, her mouth opened, and suddenly, wonderfully, she was singing:

> *Tell her your love dreams*
> *She'll make them come true*
> *Dream a dream lover*
> *She'll be it for you*
> *She's the queen of hotel rooms*
> *She's an artist in bed*
> *She's all that you long for*
> *She's all in your head. . . .*

It was a big voice, rich and perfectly pitched, wide-ranging, full of country twangs and rasps and gritty growls, funny and poignant. Her voice pleased her. It pleased me.

"Hey, don't stop."

"Got to. She never finished it." Her big, scrubbed-looking face took on a pinkish hue of delight. "Sort of hard to tell where you'd go with it from there."

"Glory wrote that? About herself?"

She laughed. "It was gonna make us rich and famous." Her eyes sparkled again. "I take it you're not looking to . . . avail yourself of her services?"

"She availed herself of my services. I need to tell her I've done it."

She was a good-sized girl, as tall as Glory and carrying fifteen more pounds, with heavy breasts forcing the face of Willie Nelson on her tee shirt into a wide-eyed grin. Her thighs stretched smooth her faded jeans. Her feet were bare.

"She's not at her apartment?"

"Hasn't been, apparently. She left the Hilton the other morning with Haskell Dan. She hasn't been seen since."

The sparkle dimmed in her eyes. "I read about Haskell. I—it didn't say Glory was with him. Is she in trouble?"

"The police want to talk to her, but not for the same thing I do."

She looked away from me, stared out into the quiet afternoon. "I liked Haskell. He was always real nice to Glory and me. I'll miss him." She looked back at me. "Does Glory know who . . . ?"

"If she was with him, which seems likely, she may have seen who did it. She's probably hiding from him. Or them." That, at least, was what I chose to believe.

Lily Baker calmly took it where I had chosen not to. "Or they've got her. Or she's dead too."

"I hope not," I said.

"Me too."

She was, I knew, within a month or two of Glory's age. Her big open pink-tinted face made her seem years younger. Her calm made her seem centuries older.

"What sort of thing were you doing for her?"

I told her.

"That again." She shook her head slowly, smiling. "Crazy girl. She can't leave that stuff alone, can she? So did you find the world-famous Lawrence Parker?"

"Yes."

Her smile widened, crept across her wide mouth as if she were savoring it. "You're kidding. Really?"

At my nod, her smile became a grin. "Well good for her. Good for Glory. She finally won one."

"Now all I have to do is find her so I can tell her."

"Yeah." Her grin lost some of its energy. "Well, I don't know what I can tell you, but why don't you grab a piece of porch and we'll see."

I sat on the edge of the painted planking and leaned back

against a post. "Your mother said you and Glory were close, that if she contacted anyone it would be you."

"I guess," she said. "But I haven't heard from her for a week or so. Not that that's so unusual. We're close enough, I guess, but you couldn't say Glory is really close to anybody. It's just that I'm somebody to talk to, we grew up together, we're half-sisters. . . ."

"And aunt and niece."

"You really are a detective, aren't you." But if her relation to Glory and to the twisted coupling that created it had ever bothered her, she was long over it. "But that's the valley. It gets a little out of tune out there sometimes."

"Lily, if Glory were in trouble, is there anywhere she'd go, anybody she'd go to for help? Somebody at UNR, a teacher or director, somebody in Reno Little Theatre?"

"No. At least, she's never mentioned anybody."

"I—is there a man she, I mean . . ."

"You mean does she have a pimp?" She laughed. "It isn't like that, Jack. Glory just goes to parties, see, and she meets these guys, and if she likes them she gives them her number. She doesn't just go out and pick guys up. And there's only a few of them."

"Do you know any—"

"No."

"There's no one she'd call on for help?"

"Just me and Mom, I guess. I don't—except maybe Whip."

"Leon Whipple?"

"You know him?"

"Unfortunately."

"He—he thinks he's Emmy's father. If Glory was in real trouble, she might ask him for help."

"Who is Emmy's father?"

She shrugged her wide shoulders, making her breasts tremble prettily. She smiled fondly.

"Who knows. I don't think Glory even knows. She might have once, but the way she makes up these fairy tales about herself, most of the time she doesn't know what's real and what isn't. As soon as she found out the valley'd trapped her, she came up with this yarn about some rich old guy who'd been picking her up and driving her into the hills in this big car and how she's just waiting for him to come back and haul her off into the sunset." She shook her head. "Might still be waiting for him, for all I know."

"There was no rich old guy?"

"They don't usually congregate in Sun Valley," she said dryly. Then she grinned again. "But who knows. If one of them critters wandered into the valley by accident, Glory'd be the one to corral him."

I laughed.

"Boy, the stories that girl could tell. Whenever something happened that she didn't like, why, she'd just change it! Even when we were little. I mean, some kid would give her a hard time in school, and by the time we got home she had a tale to tell Mom that was so far from what really happened it was crazy. I loved it. I couldn't wait to see what she'd come up with—her stories were always so much more interesting than the truth. And she made them up about everybody. She was the granddaughter of a famous artist, her mom and dad had died in this wonderfully romantic love pact, my mom was this fantastic creature who drove men wild, drove her grandfather to murder. And she was going to be famous too, a great poet and actress, and I was going to be the greatest singer in the world, and she'd write all my songs for me. She believed it all, too. Still does." She smiled. "But at least it kept her out of the trap."

"What trap?"

"Kids. For girls in the valley, a kid is the spike that nails your foot to the floor. If you get a kid while you're there, you're there forever. Or someplace just like it. All my sisters got caught, except one. But Glory managed to have Emmy and still get out. Just dreamed her way out."

"I'm not certain she got very far, Lily."

She tried to frown. It was not an expression that came naturally to her. "You mean because she . . . goes with men?

Hey, different drummers, you know? At least she isn't stuck in some tin box out there with a bunch of rug rats squalling all day and some smelly dude belching and farting and smacking her around. At least she's still got a chance to end up with something decent for her and Emmy. Hey, with Glory anything can happen."

I believed that. "How did you get out?"

She grinned. "I figured it out early, watching my sisters. So about the time these guys started after me, I just laughed. Or started singing. I'd sit on the hood of the car and pick and sing my little old heart out all night long, but there wasn't a way in the world they were going to get me into the back seat." She laughed. "Sometimes it took some doing, too. I mean, there were a couple I wouldn't have minded snuggling down with. I'd just have to sing louder and think real hard about Anemone."

"Your sister?"

"One of my sisters." She laughed again. "The second flower in Mom's garden. Rose, Anemone, Daisy, Aster, Crocus, Iris, Lily. Quite a bouquet, huh? But she's the only one who kept her britches on and got out. So I knew it was possible."

I smiled.

"So, how are you going to find Glory?"

"Have a little talk with Whip, I guess."

Again she tried to frown. "You really know him? I mean, he can be. . . ."

"We get along all right." I stood up, stretched. "Well, thanks for the help, Lily."

"No problem." She smiled again. "You really did find Glory's grandpa—Parker?"

"I really did."

"I don't suppose he's a famous artist."

"Close enough," I said. "He's a photographer."

She laughed. "It's like she just dreams this stuff up and it comes true for her. When you find her, tell her to start dreaming real hard that I'm a tremendous hit tomorrow night and get a recording contract and meet a rich guy who wants to carry me off on his white horse, will you?"

"Be glad to. But from the sample you gave me, I'd guess you don't need to worry about being a hit."

She flushed with pleasure.

At the bottom of the steps I had a thought.

I turned to find Lily standing, arm draped around the porch post. She seemed even larger from that perspective, deep-breasted, wide-shouldered and -hipped. Built for making and nurturing babies. The trap.

"Lily, what's the story with Glory's parents?"

The smile froze on her face. "They're dead. They've been dead for a long time."

"Glory's mother was Lawrence Parker's daughter. He'll want to know what happened to her, how she died."

"What did Glory tell you?"

"She was a little vague."

"Yeah. Doomed by love." Her wide mouth twisted as if she had bitten into bitterness. "That's all he's ever been to Glory, something else to make up a fairy tale about."

"Stuart Dahlman?"

"My father," she said quietly. "Everybody forgets that. He was *my* father too."

"And Rose was your sister. What happened, Lily?"

"I don't know. But if he killed himself, I'm a monkey's uncle."

I watched her.

"You talked to Glory, you know that she takes whatever there is and changes what she doesn't like to suit her. I try to see things the way they are. And my dad was this big, good-looking guy who never did a day's work that he could avoid, who first lived off his mother and then by selling dope, who spent his time trying to nail every woman in the valley, who wasn't good for much of anything except trying to figure out how he could get rich off somebody else."

It couldn't have been much fun, talking that way about the

man who had been her father. But she didn't flinch from it, nor did she seem especially upset.

"That's pretty much what your mother said."

"She never made a mistake about a man in her life. And the Stuart Dahlman she describes wasn't a guy who'd kill himself, especially over a woman."

"You never know, Lily."

"You're right. But there's one person who does. Glory. She was there, in the same room, in her crib. Too bad she doesn't remember it."

I still didn't know what to tell Gabriel George about his daughter's death.

"Yeah. Well, thanks again."

I was in the sunlight, halfway to my car, when she called my name. "I was just thinking. If Glory's around, she'll be at my opening tomorrow night, at the Silver Saddle. The only way she'd miss it is if she was . . ."

She couldn't say it this time. She didn't have to.

# 19

I drove back to South Virginia, remembered I hadn't eaten all day, pulled in at Marie Callander's, and filled up with a bowl of beef stew and a basketful of cornbread.

After I ate, I sipped a beer and watched the local news. The murder of Haskell Dan was not mentioned—old news. The new news was that a community college student had been found on Mount Rose with his hands tied behind his back and a bullet in his brain. A thirty-year-old woman who had been hitch-hiking with her four-year-old son on the interstate had tossed the boy from the pickup they were riding in; he was in critical condition in Washoe Medical Center, she was wigged out in the Washoe County Jail. Ranchers were complaining again about wild horses destroying the range in Northern Nevada. A California assemblyman had revived the notion that the solution to San Francisco's waste problem was to haul the garbage to Nevada and dump it in the Black Rock Desert, since there was nothing out there anyway. A low pressure trough was moving in, bringing unstable air and the likelihood of showers. The news reader told us to have a nice evening.

The air was already unstable. The sinking sun sent spears of light up from behind the Sierra and into a thick band of cirrus, pinking the sky. Gray loomed over peaks.

I got some gas and a case of beer, then headed south out of town. Soon I was past the junk, driving through the few fields in the Truckee Meadows that the developers hadn't planted with ticky-tacky. Past the Mount Rose and Virginia City turnoffs, the sulphur smell and wisps of steam of the hot springs at Steamboat, into Washoe Valley; under the loom of the Sierra, lots of three and four acres that supported a tract house, three or four vehicles, one or two horses.

At the top of the low hill overlooking Washoe Lake, I turned off and followed East Shore Boulevard past more tract houses. No pasture here, no lawns. Just sage sticking up from pleistocene sand worked fine by waves centuries still. What was left of the lake shimmered from gray to blue, like Gabriel George's eyes, in the twilight.

I found the road I wanted, climbed the sandy hillside, found the house I wanted. Wind-driven sand had stripped most of its paint, chewed shake shingles, scoured windows. In the small yard, sand settled around a junked pickup, tireless trailers, a collection of empty beer kegs. The wind had driven garbage and tumbleweeds into the lower strands of the barbed wire fence, piled on more garbage, and formed a barricade against which sand duned in smoothly-rippled waves. Under a scrawny poplar beside the house two motorcycles sat in neat, snug canvas covers.

I drove through the fence and parked and pulled the case of beer from the back seat. Slowly I trudged through the sand to the front door. It opened before I reached it.

Like the house, the woman standing in the doorway was worn and unkempt. She wasn't pretty, although she had been. The prettiness had been drugged and drunk and beaten from her face. A mane of stiff, tawny hair hung around it like some dead desert growth. Below a pink band covering her pancaked breasts, the unicorn tattooed on her stomach bowed its head so that its helixical horn pointed at the crotch-snap of her jeans. She wore glittery silver high heels.

A fly rested at the corner of her mouth, another creation of ink and needle and pain. Her eyes were glazed, perhaps permanently. "What do you want?"

"Hello, Veronica," I said. "Whip around?"

She looked at my face, at the beer in my hands, and she shrugged her bony shoulders. "He's asleep."

"You want to get him up?"

She did not want to get him up. Her mouth tightened, the fly danced. "Get lost."

"It's your choice. Either he's pissed because you got him up, or he's pissed because you didn't."

It wasn't much of a choice. But Veronica Hardesty had chosen to place herself in the position that forced her to make that kind of choice all the time.

"I don't suppose you'd just leave the beer and get out of here?"

I smiled.

She scratched her shoulder nervously. Then she turned and moved slowly, like a bit of fur that would creep past a sleeping snake, into the house.

I followed. Tools and junk food containers and empty cans lined the short hall, sand stiffened the shag of the carpet, piles of dog dump clung to it in various stages of solidity. In the living room a broken-down bike and its oily guts stood beside a new color television; before it on a swaybacked couch, a boy about four and a diapered and pacified one-year-old of indeterminate sex sat transfixed before a rerun of *Charlie's Angels*.

I went into the kitchen as Veronica Hardesty continued down the hall. I dropped the beer on the small table, sat, took out a beer and popped it, swallowed, and stared out the window. The view was lovely—Mount Rose, Slide Mountain, pine and rock and small snow-patches darkening in the shadows created by the setting sun.

A sharp growl sounded from the back of the house. Then Veronica Hardesty scurried in, her heels clicking on the linoleum. She grabbed and opened a beer, brushed newspapers and Big Mac cartons and food scraps from a patch of table across from me, and set the beer can in the formica clearing. She backed away to the wall beside the window, her eyes fixed on a spot over my head.

Then I felt him behind me. My stomach tightened, but I didn't turn around. I listened to him breathe, thought perhaps I could smell him. But the whole house smelled of grease and garbage and shit, a sweet rankness that clotted my nostrils. Then he stepped past me.

"Ross." He took the beer, tilted it, and poured at least half its contents down his corded throat.

"Whip."

Leon Whipple was as tall as I, not as heavy, but rangy, all bone and tendon and thick slithering veins, his arms dark with tattoos, face dark from the desert sun, long hair dark with dirt. His black jeans were stained blacker at the thighs, his black Harley-Davidson tee shirt at the armpits.

In his angular face his eyes, still full of sleep, still were hard. "Been a while."

"Some," I said.

The last time I'd seen Leon Whipple he'd been deep in conversation with the Governor of Nevada, out on the Mansion lawn, at the annual Multiple Sclerosis picnic. The Governor had seemed extremely interested in Leon Whipple's views.

He finished his beer in a swallow, set the can on the edge of the table, sat, and grabbed another. His elbow thumped the table and the empty can clattered to the floor. Veronica Hardesty remained against the wall, her back pressed to the peeling flowered wallpaper as if nailed to it.

"So," Leon yawned, "what's goin' down?"

"I need some help, Whip."

He grunted, drank. "Always happy to help out a friend, Ross. You know that."

I did. I also knew that he was always happy to come at a friend with a tire iron, should the spirit move him.

"I'm trying to find a friend of yours—Glory Dahlman."

Veronica Hardesty writhed against the wall as if struggling to free herself from it. Leon Whipple's body stilled. "What for?"

"She hired me to find somebody for her. I did. Now I can't find her to tell her."

That wasn't going to do it.

'Besides, she may be in trouble. I know the cops want her. I'd like to find her before they do."

"What kind of trouble?"

I told him what I knew.

"Sounds like trouble, all right."

Veronica Hardesty struggled away from the wall. "Serves the bitch right."

"Shut up, Ronnie," Leon said almost pleasantly. "So you got any idea where she might be holed up?"

"That's why I'm here, Whip. I sort of figured that if she was in real trouble, she might come to you."

"That whore doesn't know what real trouble is," Veronica spit, advancing a step toward us. "The filthy little—"

"Shut up," Leon said.

"Like hell I will," she hissed, advancing. "Goddam whore calls up in the middle of the—"

The glaze of her eyes became nearly opaque as he pushed up from the table. He gave me a small smile, turned to her.

She stood frozen. "Whip, don't. I didn't—"

His arm rose, flashed, his open hand swatting the top of her head with a dull swack. Her arms, hands, jerked up; she hunched her face into them. "Baby no. I'm—"

Calmly, methodically, he slapped her, knocking her hands away from her face, backing her against the wall. The older child glanced briefly at his parents and went back to the television; the younger sucked the pacifier deeper into its mouth and stared at the screen.

Shortly, Veronica Hardesty was a sniveling heap on the floor. Leon Whipple looked down at her, then turned and came back to the table, giving me a little shrug of shoulder as if inquiring if I had an objection to lodge.

I didn't. Veronica Hardesty had made her bed.

Five years before I had been hired by Harold Hardesty, a Sacramento stockbroker, to find his daughter, a senior at UNR who had disappeared a semester before she was to graduate. I found her with Leon Whipple, pregnant, unicorned, with a recently-broken nose. I made the mistake of telling her that her father had sent me. She came at me with a knife. Leon pulled her off. We had a beer and talked. I left, came back the next day, sat with Leon and drank a case of beer and watched. That night I called Harold Hardesty, told him that I couldn't find his daughter, and tore up his retainer check.

I finished my beer, popped another. "Glory did get in touch with you, didn't she?"

He sat, nodded. "She called me, yeah."

"What did she say?"

"Said she needed a ride."

I saw in his lean hard dirty face, his hard eyes, that he knew where Glory Dahlman was. I also saw that he wasn't going to tell me.

"I'm trying to help her, Whip."

"I already helped her."

I drank beer, thinking, trying to find another angle. Veronica Hardesty had quieted. Slowly she sat up, leaned against the wall. Without looking at her, Leon said: "Get the stash."

She struggled up, stumbled forward, slid carefully past him and out of the room.

"There's this other problem, Whip. Emily."

His face tightened. "What about her?"

I shrugged. "It's just that her grandmother is dying. Cancer. She could go anytime now. Emily's with her. If Flora dies before Glory comes out of hiding, well . . . you know what'll happen."

He knew. The county would take the little girl, and Glory would play hell getting her back from the bureaucracy.

Leon knew that, but it didn't disturb him. "I took care of Glory. I'll take care of Emmy."

I thought of the little girl I had seen, and tried to imagine what would happen to her in this house. I stopped trying to imagine it.

Veronica returned with a small mirror, a razor blade, a tightly-rolled twenty-dollar bill, and a bindle of white powder. She placed them before him, placed her hand on his arm, slid it up and around his neck as she moved behind him.

He opened the packet and emptied half its contents onto the surface of the mirror. "Want a toot, Ross?"

"Thanks," I said. "I think I'll pass."

"Good shit," he said, going to work with the razor. "This is Cal Blass's personal snort—not that stuff he stomps all over before it goes on the street."

"Enjoy," I said.

He chopped the cocaine into four neat lines and through the twenty-dollar bill took one up each nostril. He held the mirror and bill out to me and, when I shook my head, shrugged and brought them back over each shoulder. Veronica Hardesty took the bill and greedily sucked the powder from the glass.

When she finished, I said: "You're sure she's safe?"

"They'll never find her." He grinned, exposing a darkness of departed molars. "I took her to the last place you'd ever think of looking for a chick like Glory."

"Who are they? The ones she's hiding from?"

He shrugged.

I tried once more. "Did she tell you what happened? Who shot Haskell Dan?"

"When I talked to her, she didn't know he got it. The guy was shooting at her."

That shook me. "I—who was it?"

"If I knew, Ross, you'd know. There'd be a nice write-up in the obituary column."

"And she doesn't know why?"

"Not a clue. But she ain't hanging around to find out." He popped another beer. "You looking for this guy?"

"No, not really."

He grinned again. "You happen to stumble onto him, you'll let me know, won't you?"

"I just might do that, Whip." I pushed away from the table. "Will you be seeing her?"

He looked at me.

"If you do, tell her I found her grandfather. He wants to meet her."

"You're shitting me. That old story of hers is true?"

"More or less."

Veronica watched me. Her thin arm draped over Leon's shoulder. Her hand massaged the hard muscle of his chest.

I nodded to her. "Nice to see you again, Veronica."

She gave me a strange, evil, triumphant smile. "Go fuck yourself."

I didn't do that. I did leave.

# 20

I drove slowly down toward the lake, feeling a little better. I had not allowed myself to think about Glory Dahlman's fate. Now I could. She was alive, hidden. One body I wouldn't be finding.

Across the small basin, yellow lights marked in a ragged line the base of the Sierra and Franktown Road. Old and new money lived in private comfort amid the big trees and the boulders that lay like mountain scat on the brief foothills. Some of that money was cocaine money. It was time to visit Cal Blass.

I drove around the lake in the thickening darkness, through the big pines, past the old cabin marked with a small plaque where Will James wrote *Smoky*, and turned off Franktown Road onto a narrow strip of asphalt that slithered through trees and rock to a square of parking lot before Cal Blass's wood and brick sprawl of a house, and discovered that Gabriel George was being blackmailed by a member of his own family.

Amid two dozen automobiles in the parking lot sat a fifty-four T-bird the deep waxy green of about-to-ripen cherries.

Everything fell into place. I knew who had stolen Glory Dahlman's sketches. I knew who had known enough to send the extortion letter not to Gabriel George but to his wife, and who had known she'd be in Reno.

What I didn't know was why. But I was about to find out.

I parked beside the T-bird, got out, and headed up the

flagstone walk. The house spread in squares and rectangles through pines that filled the night air with the heady scent of gin. Light splashed through windows onto gray rock and brush and a tiny creek that tumbled toward the distant lake. The breeze carried a garble of voices beneath the masochistic taunts of Pat Benetar.

Cal Blass was having a party. Cal Blass was always having a party. And always doing business.

The front door stood open. I walked into a large, woody room—parquet floor, redwood beams, paneling, big mahogany fireplace in the stylized shape of a smoothly-tapered spruce.

The girl at the open French door was like a sapling, long thin bare limbs, hands ribbed and fluttering at her sides as if in a swirling breeze. She turned, showing me the stunted fruit within the top of her bikini. Her face was young, her eyes dull, her patrician nose red and wet.

"Hello, Tracy," I said.

She peered at me. "Do I know you?"

"No. Where's Bobby?"

"Who knows?"

"Is he here?"

The pale leaf of her hand fluttered vaguely toward the French door. "They're down there. Everybody."

I could see them. A redwood staircase Z-ed down through the pines and rocks to a brick patio from which a pool spread around huge spruce and pines that cast phallic shadows over the softly illuminated water, the huge hot tub, the portable bar, the lounge chairs, the people who collected and cavorted in groups of twos and threes and fours.

They wore everything from business to birthday suits. Most of the men were in their forties or more, most in casual dress. The women were in their twenties or less, most in some stage of undress. Under the blare of Pat Benetar, their voices chirped with the irritated rush of the coke-stoned.

I knew several of the men: a state senator, a partner in a small Reno casino, the head of a local ad agency, two of the best criminal lawyers in town, the aging scion of a Basque ranching family. All held glasses in, and female flesh under, their hands.

I focused on the woman in a lounge chair beside Cal Blass. She'd changed from the blue sheath to a pale green silk blouse and dark green skirt, but the hair was still a shade blonder than blond, the oval face still smoother than skin. Cal Blass was leaning close to her, his head bent over her breasts as if he would suckle. He was talking to her, but she was not listening. The eyes that I knew were sea-gray found mine. Fear settled into Ann Ripley's face.

I made my way down the stairs to the patio. Stoned, sybaritic eyes noted, dismissed, my presence. Cal Blass was so engrossed in Ann Ripley's breasts and the sound of his own voice that, before he knew I was there, I flopped into the chaise across from him.

"Good evening, Mrs. Ripley."

She sat as if frozen.

Cal Blass spoke. "You got in, Ross. Unless you've got a hundred grand on you, you won't get out."

He didn't look especially menacing. Under hair like dirty straw his face was square, eyes light, nose and mouth small and faintly cherubic. Above the conspicuous bulge in his white bikini bathing suit, his body was a sagging layer of pleasure fat over once-hard muscle. He was an ex-skier, a downhill daredevil who'd found the good life and the fast lane with a different kind of snow. He was also, in his way, more menacing than Leon Whipple. Cal Blass's way was final. He did not break people's legs. He had the legs and everything attached to them disappear.

"Lighten up, Cal." I smiled, out of the corner of my eye watching two big shadows moving across poolside toward us. "And you can call off your dogs. I'm not here for trouble."

"You *are* trouble, Ross," he said. "But not for long."

"I don't think so. Not with the collection of guests you've got here." The big shadows neared, became big men. They slipped behind me. A shadow lay like a pall over Ann Ripley's bright blond head.

"Can you take the chance, Cal? I mean, you've got all these folks gathered for some conviviality and a toot or two, among whom are several prominent members of the legal and business community who would not like it known that they indulge in this sort of fun. But goodness gracious, what must they be thinking? They know I know them. They know I'm the very soul of discretion, but that I can be one vindictive son of a bitch if somebody jacks me around. They must be desperately hoping that you don't jack me around."

He leaned back, for Ann Ripley's benefit tugging his swim suit to better show the contours of his genitals. She didn't notice. She was still staring at me.

"Not quite, Ross," he said with a small smile. "The problem disappears when you do."

"Ah," I said, enjoying myself, "then another appears. When my carcass is found, these good citizens will realize that I was last seen alive being escorted from your home by your employees. And you know how good citizens are. Someone will feel compelled to mention this to the authorities."

His smile grew. He too was enjoying this. "But what if your carcass is never found."

"There's that," I acknowledged. "But there's also the question of whether your employees can get the job done." The shadow covering Ann Ripley's head grew larger.

"I could do it myself." But he was still smiling.

"But not here, Cal. Goodness, what would Mrs. Ripley think? To say nothing of your other guests?" I grinned. "Face it. What we have here is a classic Mexican standoff."

"No," he said. "What I have here is a minor interruption in an otherwise delightful encounter with a lovely lady." He gave Ann Ripley an admiring leer. "But what you've got—well, you run a terrible bluff, Ross, but you've got a certain ballsy . . . panache." He grinned, as if delighted to have the opportunity to use the word. Then his gaze drifted from my face, swooped down to Ann Ripley's breasts, lingered, lifted. "Is this slug a friend of yours?"

"I—yes," she said in a small strained voice.

"In that case," he said, a fat tongue sliding over his cherub-lips, "I consider it a favor to you." He tugged at his swim suit, shifting the genital lump, promising another favor to Ann Ripley. "All right, Ross. Get on your horse."

"Golly," I said, "before I've done my business?"

"What business?"

"Where's Bobby George?"

"How should I know?"

"He's here somewhere."

"No."

Something in his smile told me he was telling the truth. I looked around. Tracy was in the pool, bare breasts bobbing.

"That's his fiancée. He's got to be close."

"No," Ann Ripley said. "He's not here. We came alone. I mean, together. I drove Tracy out here."

Blessedly, Pat Benetar stopped howling. In the sudden big silence, voices hitched, lowered. I lowered mine as well. "Where is he?"

"Home. At least he was. They . . . had a fight."

Suddenly her eyes were pleading with me. I didn't know what they wanted.

"Satisfied, Ross?" With a guitar blast, Olivia Newton-John began demanding that everyone get physical.

"Where's Glory Dahlman?"

Again, Ann Ripley's face froze.

"Look around. You see her?"

"That's why I asked."

"Glory comes, she goes. Right now she's gone."

"I know that. I want to know where she's gone."

"Glory's a hooker, Ross. I don't run hookers." His eyes flicked past me. The shadow over Ann Ripley spread. I could hear raspy breathing behind me, feel body heat in the heavy air. "Now, in deference to this lovely lady, I've tried to be hospitable. It runs counter to my instincts, but I'm going to give you one more chance to leave. In one piece."

I didn't know if he knew where Glory Dahlman was. I did know that he wasn't going to indulge me much longer.

I got up. "You're a true gentleman, Cal."

As if awakening from a dream, Ann Ripley shook herself, rose. "I have to go. Would you give me a ride, Mr. Ross?"

"Hey, not yet, lovely lady." Cal Blass struggled up. "The party's just starting."

"No," she said, edging away from him. "I mean, I'm sorry, I've . . . enjoyed it. But I have to go." She turned to me, eyes pleading again. "Mr. Ross?"

"Sure," I said. I looked at the pool. Bobby George's fiancée bent her classical head over a spoon in the hand of a paunchy man in a large-flowered shirt. His other hand cupped one of her bare breasts. "What about Tracy?"

"I . . . she won't want to come. I'll leave her the Thunderbird." She stepped around the hand that Cal Blass had put out to stop her. "Can we go? I really am very late."

What she was was very nervous. Or afraid. I looked back at the girl by the pool. Her head was tilted back, eyes closed. Ann Ripley was right. She wouldn't want to go.

"Come on," I said.

Cal Blass wasn't finished. He placed a hand on Ann Ripley's arm, brushed her hip with his bulge. "Stay. I've got everything we need to make you feel really good."

She backed away. "No. I—I have to go." Her voice was tighter, higher pitched. Panic, fear, smeared her eyes. She was, I realized, a woman out on the edge of herself.

She was also, her emotional state notwithstanding, a remarkable sexual presence. Both Cal Blass and I had felt it; it had prompted, in part, our little performance. Now, in the line of her limbs, the slant of her carriage and the thrust of her breasts, a sensual energy surged and pulsed. Standing still, she seemed to sway, seductively.

She backed away from Cal Blass. "Please, Mr. Ross."

Cal Blass sagged in disappointment. He sagged all over. He took out his disappointment on me. "This goes on the list, Ross. I won't forget it."

Quips lined up in my mind like shooting gallery ducks, but I looked at him and spared the creatures. Blass was in no mood for my jokes. I shrugged, took Ann Ripley's arm, and led her toward the house.

At the stairs she stumbled, leaned against me. Her hip was warm against mine. She shuddered. "That awful man."

"Let's get out of here."

We climbed the redwood stairs. At the top she shuddered again. "Poor Bobby."

I led her into the house, looking for the photograph that had brought Glory Dahlman and Bobby George together and started the mess I was tangled up in. I didn't see it.

We walked through the house, out and into the night.

# 21

We drove through the darkness in silence. Ann Ripley remained tense. I remained inordinately aware of her.

We passed the chaos of rock and mud and broken trees that was the slide that swept down the Sierra on a park full of picnickers a few years before. In the starlight, half-buried cars leaned like old tombstones.

"Why are you looking for Bobby?"

"I wasn't, until I saw the T-bird. He usually drives it, doesn't he?"

"Everybody drives it."

That didn't concern me. "How did you end up out there?"

"Bobby and Tracy had a fight. He stormed out. She asked me to give her a ride. I thought she wanted to go for a drive, to get away for a while. But she wanted to come out here. Then he invited me in and . . . I was curious, I suppose. I wondered what Tracy wanted there. Then I . . . found out. I wish I hadn't."

The lights of Reno paled the night sky ahead.

"I thought that stuff—cocaine—wasn't addictive."

"Anything can hook the addictive personality. Booze, food, sleep, sex." Death.

"She was such a lovely girl just a few months ago. So refined." Her voice was nearly wistful, as if refinement were a quality she had long yearned after for herself.

"Have they been engaged long?"

"A few months. Bobby met her when he was playing in a tournament in Vegas. She's been here most of the spring, helping Hayes while Bobby got his golf card back. Bobby said he didn't dare leave her where other guys could get a look at her, and if he took her with him he'd never make a putt. He . . . if he'd just stayed with her, it they'd been married, maybe she wouldn't have. . . ."

"Marriage usually doesn't solve that kind of problem."

She laughed, briefly, bitterly. "Marriage doesn't solve any kind of problem. Most of the time it is the problem. I—you wouldn't have a cigarette?"

"Sorry," I said. "I gave them up."

"Me too. Or tried to. Do you suppose I'm an addictive personality too?"

I didn't know what kind of personality she was.

We left Washoe Valley and Reno glowed before us, a few patches of cloud sucking up a soft gray light above it.

"I—why were you looking for the Dahlman girl?"

"You know about her?"

"No," she said. "I mean, just what Dolly said. That she was a relative? The granddaughter of Gabe's aunt?"

"Yes," I said, troubled by her voice. It was flutey and artificial. "Alice George wants to meet her. So does Gabe. But I haven't been able to find her."

"She's disappeared?"

I told her about Haskell Dan, and what I knew about Glory's part in it.

"Somebody's trying to kill her? Who? Why?"

"I don't know. I don't even know if, for sure."

We approached the Del Monte Lane turnoff. "She's a . . . prostitute?"

"Sort of. She's also a student at UNR, and she acts in local theater. The reviews say she's pretty good. The hooking is . . . I think it's a kind of acting to her too. And it pays her tuition."

I drove through the fenced darkness. Then, as I slowed to

turn onto the Hollister Ranch road, she said: "I'd rather not go in yet. Could we go up to Windy Hill for a minute?"

"Why not?" I wasn't especially looking forward to what I would have to do in that big house. I drove past, and we climbed up the low hill to the top.

A newish Pontiac was parked before the boulder barrier near the edge of a steep, rocky incline. In the faint amber light from a distant street lamp, a shadow-head appeared over the back seat cushion. Another shadow-head rose, attached to the first, and dragged it down.

Ann Ripley shifted uncomfortably. "Let's sit on a bench, shall we?"

I followed her between boulders, around a stunted pine and wind-torn spruce, to the dirt path that traced the edge of the promontory. Three benches commanded a view of the Truckee Meadows. She took the one in the center. I sat beside her.

In the middle of the wide valley the Grand rose like a flood-lit feudal castle. Beyond it, Sparks spread toward the desert hills, the lights of serfs' hovels fading into the darkness. Downtown Reno was a chaos of bright color within a tree-darkened moat of old residential neighborhoods.

Ann Ripley sighed, shivered. "I used to love to come here when I was a girl, to look at the lights."

"You're from Reno?" Somehow that surprised me.

My question seemed to surprise her. "I—lived here for a while. I'm sort of from nowhere."

We sat in silence and watched the lights. Below us, the Hollister Ranch seemed distant, inconsequential.

She shuddered again, as if she were cold. But the night was almost balmy, the air as comfortable as a cloak. I stood up. "I can't offer you a cigarette, but I have some scotch."

"That would be lovely," she said.

I went to the Wagoneer and took out the scotch and two plastic glasses. No shadow-heads appeared in the back window of the Pontiac. The car trembled.

Back beside Ann Ripley, I poured two fingers of scotch into the glasses and handed her one. She sipped. "Thank you."

I sat as far away from her as I could get without sliding off the bench. It wasn't far enough. Her breasts rose and fell softly with her breathing, the pale light doing a shine and shadow dance on her silk blouse. Suffering the first sharp symptoms of sexual distress, I drank the scotch as if it were medicine.

She didn't drink. She gazed out at the lights, lost in them and in herself.

Her reverie was shattered by the flatulent blast of a motorcycle. It roared up the hill and pulled into the turnout. As the yellow headlight caught and held us, we turned. The light vanished, the throb of engine ceased. The shadows of the two riders seemed one, another two-headed beast.

Ann Ripley turned back to the lights. Then the new silence exploded with music. A boy in a jean jacket came around the trees, a ghetto-blaster the size of a suitcase on his shoulder. The girl behind him tried to move with the music, tottered at the edge of the rocks.

The music was a cacophonous yowl. Ann Ripley looked at me as if in pain. I got up and went over to the boy. His lean face was not yet fully formed, his body bone awaiting flesh. He looked at me as if I were a blur, a mist.

I shouted to make myself heard over the screech and wail of guitar. "Would you turn that down, please."

He tried to focus on me. Then he slowly twisted one of the dozen silver knobs on the huge machine. The sound faded.

"Thank you," I said. "We're trying to enjoy the quiet and the lights. We'll be gone soon."

"Yeah, man, the lights," he said with a sibilant drug-slur. "Maybe you want some Barry Manilow or something, huh?"

"What we want is silence."

"Hey, yeah. Silence. Lotsa fucking silence up here."

The girl wandered to the bench, sat heavily, sagged against his shoulder. Her face was also thin and unformed, her hair a wind-blown tangle. Her eyes closed, her head slid lower into the hollow of his shoulder. The muted crash of sound ended, and The Waitresses began a sing-song taunt.

"How's that, man?"

I looked at them, these children. They weren't much older than my child. Already they were burnt out by drugs, by life. I reached over and turned the radio off. The boy didn't object. The girl didn't notice.

I went back to Ann Ripley and the scotch.

She watched me refill my glass, held out her own. "I've never heard that song before. I—is that what they call punk or new wave or whatever?"

"More or less."

"Maybe they've got the right idea, the kids. At least they see sex for what it is—don't confuse it with . . ." She tilted the glass high. "Is that what she does—Glory?"

"I suppose so."

"Good for her." The declaration was forceful, tinged with bitterness. "I wish I'd had that much sense."

I drank my scotch. I didn't want to hear about her problems. She was going to tell me anyway. "You may have gathered from that last remark, and one or two others, that my marriage is . . . not so hot." She laughed that short bitter laugh that seemed to come so easily to her. "We have a modern marriage. My husband sleeps with whoever he wants, and so do I. Only I don't want. So I sleep with nobody."

"I'm sorry," I said, wishing she'd shut up.

"Don't be. It's a mutual agreement. My husband likes them young. And I haven't been young in years. Maybe I never really was." She laughed again. "Must be a lot of young things in Reno these days. He hasn't been home at night since we've been here."

"You do nothing when he's gone?" I couldn't help it.

"I've lost my taste for it—sex, love, whatever you want to call it."

"Seems like an awful waste." I couldn't help it.

She drank, held out her glass. "It's all wasted. I mean, it's there and then its gone. You feel something and then you don't. It isn't like you can collect it, save it." As I refilled her glass, she smiled. "Besides, I've got what I want, live the way I want to. I have a house. I decorate it. I shop for it. I travel when I want."

"Thrill a minute," I said.

She turned her face toward me, and I saw that the scotch, or something, had hit her hard. Her eyes shone, a cruel smile twisted her wide mouth.

"What do *you* want, Ross? You want to be in the back seat of that car over there? You think that's what it's all about? Believe me, I'm an expert in back seats, they're the emptiest, loneliest places in the world."

"Maybe." I was depressed.

Suddenly she rose, swayed, caught herself. "Come on. I'll show you."

"I'll take your word for it," I said. "We'd better go."

I got up and she stepped into me and thrust her wide, widely-parted mouth at mine and pressed her body against mine and slipped her arms under my shoulders and pulled me down.

I put my hands on her shoulders and carefully pushed away from her mouth, from the soft crush of her breasts, the press and heat of her belly and thighs.

She stepped back, laughing. "You don't like me, Ross? Come on, I know what boys like too."

Her laugh was bitter, and something more. Something close to hysteria. She seemed even more a woman on the edge.

"I'll take you home," I said, ignoring her eyes.

I retrieved the scotch bottle, discovered it nearly empty. The two children slept on the bench; in each other's arms, still, they seemed even younger, vulnerable, huddled together against the lotsa fucking silence of the night.

A man and a woman sat on the fenders of the Pontiac. The lights of downtown Reno glittered in the wide space between them.

Ann Ripley was on the edge, literally. She stood above the yawning darkness, staring out at the lights and the darkness. Before the spread of lights she was a stunning sensual silhouette. I nearly staggered under a sudden sense of *déjà vu*. I

shook myself, but I couldn't shake the sense that I had seen
Ann Ripley standing there before.

Then she turned and slowly made her way to the car. "I'm
sorry," she said softly.

"It's been a strange evening," I said.

"Yes," she said. "Strange." I started the engine and we drove
back down the hill.

Softly flood-lit, shadow-shrouded, the big white house
hunkered in the trees. Only the two white Ford pickups sat
before the empty garage. I parked beside them and got out.

Ann Ripley did not get out. I walked around to her door and
opened it. For a moment she sat staring at me. Then, with a
flash of nylon-sheen, she slid her legs from the car and stood
beside me.

"I—I'm sorry."

"You've already apologized, Ann. It wasn't necessary the
first time." She no longer seemed drunk, or hysterical. She
seemed deeply unhappy. I put a hand on her silk shoulder. "I'd
help if I could."

Her blond head bowed. "Nobody can help."

Her head lifted and she tried to smile. Then she moved from
under my hand, slowly, toward the stairs. As she reached
them, a shadow stepped from the screened porch and became
Hayes George.

# 22

He wore the same mean-mouthed grin. It, and he, seemed larger as he leaned over us like something out of a child's nightmare. "Cute. Lady Chatterley and the gamekeeper."

"Shut up, Hayes," Ann Ripley said without energy. She climbed the stairs. "Get out of my way, please."

He didn't move. I climbed a stair and stood behind her.

"I know Ross can use his fists. How is he with the rest of his equipment? That magnificent machine of yours get a decent grease job?"

She looked into his face. I couldn't see her expression. Hayes George could. It pushed him slowly aside. Ann Ripley moved past him, opened the door, stepped through it, shut it.

"My sister wasn't enough for you, Ross?"

I wasn't going to start with him. As calmly as I could, I asked: "Is your mother here?"

"She next on your list?"

"Is she here?"

"She's out in the desert."

"Why?"

"To see if the old man's still fucking goats. How the hell do I know?"

"Ripley?"

His smile twisted. "What is this, Ross—bullshit? Do you try to bullshit everybody you can't fuck?"

I'd tried. I sighed. "Hayes, am I going to have to beat on your head every time we meet? I will, if that's what it takes to get a straight answer out of you."

He smiled. Suddenly I had the feeling that I was being had again. Then he began to laugh, a deep rumbling.

"I guess you're right. It hardly becomes a Harvard man to pursue such a bellicose course, particularly when the opposition is such an ineffectual creature."

"Where's Ripley?"

"Out. Chippying, I'd guess. And Bobby's out either begging some crap table to relieve him of what little money he's got or looking for the object of his now unrequited love. Nobody here but me and my darling little sister. You want another crack at her, or was once enough?"

I had to either ignore that or hit him. I ignored it. "You know Cal Blass?"

Something in his eyes changed. "Yeah, I know him."

"You know the layout of his place?"

"I've been there. Who hasn't?" He wasn't exactly defensive. Guarded.

"Tracy's there. It's not a good place for her to be. You think we could get her out of there?"

He grinned. "It might be fun to try. The two of us—" Then he stopped grinning. "She feeding her nose?"

I nodded.

"Leave her there. It's where she belongs, she'd just go back. She's a coke-whore, Ross. She'd sell her ass for a snort and her soul for a gram. My knot-head brother's got enough problems. He sure as hell doesn't need her."

"He doesn't seem to think that."

"He doesn't know his putz from his putter. Stupid little bastard even thinks you can win in a casino. Thinks if you just tell a coke-whore you love her, she'll plug her nose. What nose she's got left. He's a fool."

"I'd still like to get her out of there. The two of us, what sort of chance do you think we'd have?"

It interested him. The nastiness I'd thought perhaps permanent slid from his face. "I don't know. We could get in. His muscle might be fun. You carry a piece?"

"No."

He smiled. "I didn't think so. You probably don't want to borrow one of mine, either."

"No."

"Yeah," he said with a small sneer. "But that ain't the problem, anyway. The thing is, Cal Blass's is where the coke is, and Tracy-chickie is right where she wants to be. She won't want to leave, and if we have to drag her out . . . well, even at Stanford they must have mentioned little things like kidnaping, forcible abduction, that stuff."

That stuff, in this situation, was nonsense. But it told me that Hayes George wanted his brother's fiancée to stay in Cal Blass's chemically-created seraglio. It didn't tell me why.

"What do you want with her, anyway? I thought you were supposed to be looking for Glory Dahlman?"

"I am," I said, wondering how he knew that. Wondering what else he knew. "And I better get to it."

His face changed again. "You don't want to see Dolly? What's the matter, Annie wear you out? Or is Dolly just a bum lay? Figured she must be, if that fiddle player'd walk away from that nice fat trust fund of hers. You play your cards right, you could get it. All you have to do is put up with her dumb-shit notions. You could *teach* her how to fuck. Pretty easy money, Ross."

"Hayes," I said, "was your mind this twisted at birth, or did you have to work to make it so ugly?"

He smiled. "I should think, Ross, that it would behoove one in your so-called profession to refrain from jumping to conclusions—particularly in those cases where you haven't the slightest conception of what you're dealing with."

So far as he was concerned, I had no idea what I was dealing with. I did know I was tired of dealing with it. And afraid. He might be contagious.

"Right," I said with disgust. "See you around."

I turned, stepped off the porch onto the short stairway, angry, half-sickened by the disease Hayes George carried.

I was on the second step when the jolt of fear stiffened my spine. I wheeled, leaping to the side.

Hayes George grinned down at me. "I couldn't decide whether you were brave or stupid, giving me your back like that." His big head leaned at me, his deep voice softened. "Stupid, Ross. Very stupid."

Very.

I backed down the remaining step, backed across the gravel, backed halfway to my jeep. He stood before the door of the big white house and grinned at me.

I headed home.

For a while I tried to fit things together. Then I stopped. I just drove, slowly, toward and then into the casino glare. The downtown streets were crowded with tourists, many with plastic drink glasses in their hands, drifting among the casinos in inebriated search of the lucky table, the cold dealer, the due machine.

Somewhere in that hyped and hustling mess Bobby George might have been throwing his money away. It couldn't be a whole lot. If he had welched on big markers in Vegas, he wouldn't get a line of credit anywhere in the state.

I thought, briefly, about looking for him, then said the hell with it. Bobby George and his silly scheme didn't matter.

I left downtown and drove the few blocks to my building.

In the mess that was my office, my message machine blinked insistently at me. I sat at my desk and pushed a button and looked out through the broken window at the street and the lights and the dark swell of Peavine Mountain against the slick blackness of the sky, and I listened.

Frank Calvetti wanted to know if I'd found Glory.

Flora Magnusson Baker wanted to know if I'd found Glory.

A white Ford pickup drove slowly down the street past my building.

I didn't call Calvetti or Flora Baker. I had nothing to tell them.

The white Ford pickup came down the street again, slowed,

and stopped across from my building. I couldn't see Hayes George. If he looked, he could see me framed in the window.

Then the door of the pickup swung open. It wasn't Hayes George that got out. It was his sister.

She slammed the door so hard dust puffed. She crossed the street with quick stiff strides. I heard her heels stomp on my stairway.

I swiveled in my chair, got up, moved around to the front of the desk as the office door crashed open.

She stood in the doorway, trembling, her face flushed, her eyes burning. Under her thin white blouse her braless breasts rose and fell rapidly.

"You son of a bitch." She came at me, her arms raised. I prepared to get hit.

I got kissed.

# 23

**D**amp with sweat and the slick of sex, we lay on the littered floor of my office. On my back, my chest heaving, I stared at the ceiling. On her side, Dolly lay within the loose curve of my arm, her head resting as it had the night before in the hollow of my shoulder, her breasts a softness against my skin, her hand slowly stroking my belly.

Slowly the maelstrom in my mind began to flatten, fill, still. Gone, it left me cold, achingly empty. I felt Dolly shudder beside me, sigh, fit her body into the curve of mine.

Then abruptly she pushed away from me. She sat up, laughing. "You're hell on a girl's wardrobe, Ross."

I turned my head to see her grinning at the torn silk panties dangling from a fingertip. Her blouse was ripped at the neck, her skirt crumpled and stained.

"Sorry," I said numbly.

"You'd better not `be," she said, grinning. With sudden energy she jumped to her feet. "Up and at 'em, Hercules. Why don't you make us a drink?"

But she didn't move. "Did somebody break in?"

"No," I said. "I did it."

She was silent for a while. Then I heard her footsteps padding across the room and into the apartment.

I stayed on the floor. I tried to understand what had happened, and why. I knew that all day I had suffered a deep, scorching sense of betrayal, that from the moment I awakened to discover Dolly gone from my bed I had seethed with rage at somehow having been used. I knew that all day I had been lied to. I knew that all day I had been struggling through a bramble patch of sexuality, from Flora Magnusson Baker's sensual swan-song to Ann Ripley's hysterical, self-flagellating urgencies. I knew that I had spent the day with violence, the violence of old killings, the violence of fists and words and threats.

Now, after making something not very much like love to Dolly on my office floor, I didn't feel much of anything. I didn't feel justified, excused, or absolved. I felt cold, empty. I felt that I had deserted myself.

Finally, I climbed to my feet and put myself together and went inside the apartment.

Vodka couldn't burn away the sour, ashy taste from my mouth. I drank it anyway, poured more, and in an empty silent cold like that of night in the winter desert fixed Dolly a vodka gimlet.

She returned wearing a big pleased smile and one of my shirts, its tail tangling at her knees. "My clothes are hopeless. This was simpler."

She took the drink, then the couch, curling her sleek legs beneath her. I sat in my chair, across the low table from her, as I had across from Glory Dahlman.

She sipped at her drink, watched me with her big eyes. What she saw sobered her. "It's been an awful day, Jack."

"Yes," I said.

"I'm sorry about this morning. I had to leave. I was . . . so confused."

"So was I."

"I woke up, remembered where I was and who I was with and how I'd gone to sleep, remembered the last two days, and there you were, so big and warm beside me. I felt. . . . But then I got confused. I was afraid that I'd misunderstood what was going on with us, that I was rushing into something that wasn't the same thing to you. I . . . had to leave, to get away from you for a while, to think."

She took a healthy slug of her drink. "Then this afternoon I saw your car at the house. I thought you'd come after me, but you hadn't. You left. I was hurt. And angry. Then tonight I saw you with Ann. I saw the way you put your hand on her, the way you . . . looked at her. That hurt even more. I felt betrayed."

"I'm sorry," I said. I was less cold, less empty. Somehow her pain was warming, filling me.

She shook her head. "It wasn't your fault. It—when I came in just now, I wanted . . . I don't know what I wanted—to kill you, maybe. But not for anything you'd done. I didn't even want to kill *you*, really. I wanted to kill all the other men I've been with, for what they let me do to myself. You . . . were just the closest."

I thought I understood that. I felt myself testing a small smile. "Glad I could be of service."

She smiled too, faintly. "But I really did want to kill you too. I sat on the porch and listened to you and Hayes, and he practically . . . *offered* me to you, and you just left. And I sat there and tried to think about everything, and all I managed to do was get more and more frightened. I thought. . . . Why didn't you try to talk to me today?"

"I guess I felt betrayed too. You'd left. I thought I'd been just another one night stand for you."

Her head snapped sideways. "No."

"I didn't know that. And I didn't want to talk to you and find out that really was the case. Besides that, I didn't know if I could believe anything you might say to me."

Her eyes widened. "You thought I'd lie to you? Why?"

"You told me a lot about yourself and your family, Dolly. You didn't tell me about the Hollister Corporation."

She looked down at the glass in her hand. "I know. I didn't want to—does it make a difference?"

"That your family is powerful and wealthy? Not to me. But it must to you."

"I just didn't want to complicate things, Jack. I wanted what was happening to happen because I was the person I was and you were the person you were, not because. . . ."

I almost laughed. "You thought it would change the way I felt about you? That I'd suddenly become . . ." I wriggled my eyebrows evilly, ". . . a Fortune Hunter?"

She smiled softly. "No. But it was always there, with everyone I met. I just didn't want it to get between us."

I set my glass down on the table. "I've got all the money I can use, Dolly. What would I want with yours?"

"Nothing. I know that." Then she smiled, happily. "But Hayes was right. You can have it if you want it."

"All I want from you is you, Dolly."

"You've got that, Jack. I think you know it."

I didn't know if I knew it or not. I knew I wanted to know it, to believe it. I told her so.

"I wouldn't lie to you, Jack. Ever."

"I believe that. But you have to understand, Dolly. I am, for the moment at least, a private investigator. I spend most of my time trying to get information people don't want to give me. That means most people lie to me. I lie to them, too much. I'm tired of lies. I've been hearing them and telling them for too long. I don't want any lies slithering between us. This is too important."

"Yes," she said quietly. "It is too important. So I won't lie. I won't even be femininely coy. I think I'm in love with you. If you took all the unhappiness I've been through in the last year and rolled it into a ball, it would be like a grain of desert sand compared to the hunk of misery I've carried around in my throat all day. And right now, I feel so right just being here with you that you could ask me for the moon and I'd start building a ladder to it. I'm not going to do anything that would jeopardize that. From me you get nothing but the naked truth. What do you want to know?"

I thought of a dozen things I wanted to know. I wanted to know what, if anything, of all that I'd been told by her father and mother and brothers, by Frederick and Ann Ripley, was true. But I didn't want Dolly to tell me. I didn't even want to talk about it. I wanted to separate her from it all, to isolate the part of my life that contained her, to keep the thing growing between us free of contamination.

So I smiled. "I want to know if you're going to spend the night."

She chuckled, her face warming with pleasure. "Can we spend it making love?"

"We can try."

"Can we. . . ." Her chuckle deepened, became nearly ovarian. "Can we start soon?"

I laughed, hauled myself out of the chair. "Let me secure the place."

I checked the office door, the apartment door. I locked us in, and everything else out. I wished I could make it permanent.

Small, naked, smiling, Dolly lay on the bare sheet of the bed waiting for me. I undressed slowly, leaving on the small dresser light, taking in the substance and shadow of the body bathed in a soft yellow glow.

She watched me watch her, smiling, watched me slip out of my clothes and leave them in a pile and move to the bed.

"I feel like Medusa," she said as I eased onto the bed beside her. She fit her small hand around my erection. "You look at me and turn to stone. Are there snakes in my hair?"

We made love slowly, attending to one another, as if to negate the violence of our earlier coupling.

Until orgasm.

Dolly came for a long time, and in coming she went, disappeared, was no longer present with me.

And drifted back to me as I began to leave her. As if to prevent it, or to go with me, she clung to me, wrapped me in a net of limbs until at last I gave her all I had to give.

We stayed together for a long time, until the heat left our bodies, until she shifted beneath me and I slid from her.

We lay side by side, silently. Finally Dolly rolled away from me, gathered the bed clothes and spread them over me, crawled under them, pressed herself against me.

"I think we're onto something, Hercules."

"Could be. We'll have to try for a few centuries to make sure."

"But not tonight. I don't think I could . . . stand it."

"Not tonight."

We settled into each other, into the quiet calm pleasure of each other's presence, into the big silence of our togetherness. Into sleep.

# 24

I awoke to the warmth of Dolly's body in our chrysalis of bedclothes, of the sun pouring through the window, of my memories of the night. She stirred, sighed deeper into sleep.

I slipped from the bed, into my robe. In the kitchen I fixed the coffee and sat and listened to it cook. I looked into my living room, my home, at my books and pictures and small private treasures. They pleased me, but distantly, as if a nostalgia, like a cigar box of marbles and baseball cards and small shells discovered years away from childhood.

My home, the home of my seemingly endless childhood, had not changed. But I had. I didn't know quite who I was yet, but I knew I was going to start finding out.

I did know that I would not be a private investigator. I was through mucking about in other people's lives. It was time to get about the business of my own life.

I poured a cup of coffee and took it into the bedroom. Dolly slept. I went into the bathroom, shaved, set the shower steaming, and stepped in. The water washed away the last grains of sand and motes of dust of the desert I had lived in for too many years. I stayed under the water for a long time.

Then Dolly's dark head appeared over the edge of the shower door. Through the pebbled translucent glass her body seemed a lovely mosaic of flesh. My body swelled toward it.

"Save me some water, will you?"

"Why don't you join me?"

"Is there room enough for both of us in there?"

"No. Come on in."

I heard her laugh. The glass door swung open. Dolly's smile spread. "You're not Hercules, you're Priapus."

"With you, anyway."

"How nice for me," she said, and joined me in the sting and mist and heat.

After we got dry, Dolly sat at the kitchen table, again in my shirt, as I scrambled a pile of eggs. Then we ate, drank coffee, and talked. Eventually I told her what I'd decided.

"You're going to quit? Just like that?"

"I wish I could. But I have to finish a couple of things. Then I'm done."

"You know you don't have to do this for me, Jack. I don't care what you do."

"It's not for you, Dolly. I'm doing it for myself."

"What about downstairs? The business?"

"That too."

She lifted her cup in both hands. "What will you do?"

"I don't know," I said. "I'm a resourceful fellow, I can do a lot of things. For a while I may not do anything."

"Can you do that? Nothing?"

"I'll do something. But I'm not going to decide now. I've spent my life looking for things, Dolly, for people, for satisfaction, for fulfillment. I don't want to look for things anymore. I want to look *at* them, at what's around me, at what I've never seen because I was always so intent on finding what I was searching for. I'm . . . not being very precise about this. I hope you understand."

"As a matter of fact, I do understand. Precisely. I was looking for something too. Love, I thought. At least, that's what I called it. I was looking for someone to solve my problems, someone who would love me, love all my troubles away. All I found were more troubles. Until I despaired of finding that someone, and I started trying to take care of my problems myself. I stopped looking for someone to love me, and I went out to the desert with my father to try to learn to love myself. And around the corner came this Herculean moth in a Stanford sweatshirt."

I grinned. "I guess you do understand."

She put down her coffee mug, put away her smile. "I don't want to organize your life, Jack. Or shove you into mine. I certainly don't want to tell you what to do. But, since you're not going to do anything for a while . . . would you consider coming to Berkeley and doing it with me?"

We talked about it—carefully, not making plans but exploring possibilities. Dolly's teaching at Berkeley was important to her. She would never, she had realized, be more than competent as a pianist; but as a teacher she was, to her surprise, excellent. She had come more and more to find her identity in the classroom.

I envied her. I was abandoning my identity. Nothing in my life seemed very important anymore, except my daughter. And Dolly. I told her so.

She colored with pleasure. "You really should practice law. You'd be a killer in the court room—especially with a jury of women."

I laughed. "I want to get as far from the law as I can."

"Whatever you do, I hope it exorcises your demons."

"What demons?"

"The demons that look out of your eyes."

"It's that obvious?"

"Sometimes, Jack, you'll be right in the middle of one of your stories, and your eyes change, you look like you're having a nightmare, you get this . . . haunted look."

I twisted under the twin pressures of a dilemma. I wanted Dolly to understand. I didn't want to taint her with the gore of my life. But to make her understand, I had to.

"You need to know what's been happening to me, Dolly. For the last couple of years, everytime I took on a simple little case I ended up finding. . . . I found the manager of a Reno loan company in Sausalito, sucking on a rubber hose hooked to the exhaust of his boyfriend's car. I found a Harrah's keno runner raped and strangled and dumped in a grave in the sand. A nine-year-old boy buggered into catatonia in a kiddie-porn factory. . . ."

Dolly had paled. "My God, Jack!" She started to rise, to come to me. I stopped her.

"Two weeks ago, a man named Springmeyer, the branch manager of a bank, hired me to look for his wife. She'd gone to the grocery store three days before and hadn't been seen since. I . . . found her. In a salvage lot in Sparks. Behind the lot owner's trailer there's a wood shed. . . ."

I saw it again, the hard dirt floor, smeared with grease, spattered with dark coagulent blotches. The filthy mattress on the narrow iron bed. The rough plank walls papered with glossy magazine foldouts of beaver shots and splashed with blood.

I saw it again, and smelled it, the rank of gore.

And I heard it, heard myself, heard the animal cry that rose in me but could not escape into the silence.

"Oh Christ, Jack! What?"

"She'd been decapitated. Her hair was twisted around a spike, her head was hanging from it, from a rafter. Her blood had drained. . . ."

Dolly groaned. "Jack, please—"

"There were three other heads hanging there. Two still had some flesh on the bone. The other was just a little string of hair and a skull."

And then I saw the lot owner's son, his smooth young face, his empty innocent eyes. I heard his calm madness in my own voice. "He was just a kid. He envisioned himself a hunter. A descendant, somehow, of the mountain men. He had a theory that women had driven off all the game. So he hunted them."

Dolly was crying. So was I.

We struggled up, stumbled toward each other.

We were in the other room and I was pouring vodka before either of us spoke. "No wonder you look that way," she said quietly. "No wonder you want to walk away from it."

"Not want to. Will. As soon as I've finished this."

"Finding Glory. Can you find her?"

"Yes," I said. "But—" Finally there was no way around it. I had to bring the world back in to join us.

"There's another thing, Dolly. I'm doing a little job for your mother. It's practically done, in fact. But it's going to upset your family."

She stared at me, uncertain. "My family? What?"

"I promised your mother I wouldn't say anything to any of you. But she and your father will have to, and soon."

"When?"

"When is she coming back from the desert?"

"Tonight, I think."

I gave her her drink, looked into her big grave eyes. "It's nothing terrible, Dolly. It's stupid, silly, more than anything. But I just want to warn you. I've done what your mother wanted, but—I'm not responsible for it."

She worked up a small smile. "We don't kill the bearers of bad tidings, Jack. Although Hayes and Frederick sometimes want to." Her smile flickered, faded. "That's who it is, isn't it? Hayes?"

"Don't ask me, Dolly. I gave your mother my word."

She took my hand, entwined our fingers. "I know. But it has to be Hayes. I—sometimes I think he's crazy."

I'd felt that myself.

"It's not just the way he's so bossy and pushy, always trying to run everything in the family. He can be mean, ugly—like those things he said to you last night. And the way he plays these crazy games, so you never know who or what you're talking to. It's . . . sometimes I think that because he looks like my grandfather, he's trying to be him. I suppose you know what *he* was like."

Anyone with an interest in Nevada history knew what R. Hayes Hollister was like. But Dolly told me anyway. It was her own sort of horror story.

He was born in San Francisco in the mid-1890s, the only child of an alcoholic sailor and a tubercular waitress, who died bearing him. He grew up a wharf rat and by thirteen was making his way in the world with his hands—stealing, beating on folks, cheating at cards. By nineteen he had stolen and beaten and cheated his way to the Nevada mines, always a half-step ahead of the law and his victims.

In Goldfield, Hayes Hollister discovered high-grading—the practice of miners' hauling in lunch boxes and leather bags under their shirts as much high grade ore as they could carry away from the mine they were working. The ore he stole became chips, the chips a stake, the stake a crooked roulette wheel, the roulette wheel a partnership in a Tonapah saloon. During and shortly after the first world war the mines boomed, and Hayes Hollister ended up with silver and copper leases, a saloon, a hotel, and a couple of whorehouses.

And at the peak of the boom, he suddenly sold out. At twenty-five, R. Hayes Hollister was worth several million dollars. As had most of those who, one way or another, struck it rich in Nevada, he packed his fortune out of the state, back to California. He bought land, after the crash and during the depression bought more land, and went into banking.

He also became a patriot. The first world war had made him rich; the second, powerful. He built factories that built aircraft engines and trucks and munitions; he stole and beat and cheated his way into government contracts—all the while singing the praises of a country and a system in and through which a wharf rat could come to live in the most exclusive area of Nob Hill. He was militantly anti-communist, anti-union, anti-government, and pro-war. When Patton was stopped from entering Russia, he threatened an impeachment move against Roosevelt; when MacArthur was stopped from entering North Korea and China, he started an impeachment move against Truman. During the Free Speech Movement at Berkeley in the sixties, he armed a group of goons and offered them to the State of California to "keep the peace."

He died in his sleep in 1975, wealthy, influential, and still a thug.

"Once when we were small," Dolly said, "we all went to the Virgin Islands. My grandfather took us to the beach. When he went swimming, we saw his scars—on his chest, arms, back. Ugly things, from knives and . . . one of them was in his side, from a bullet. Then he told us how he got some of the scars. I started to cry. Hayes just laughed.

"He's my brother, Jack, and I love him. But he scares me sometimes. He's stuck here in Nevada, when he thinks he should have Ripley's job. So he gets in fights in bars, he gets wound tighter and tighter—sometimes you can see in his eyes, in his face, that he's going to have to do something violent or he'll explode. I—has he done it?"

"No. I—please wait. You'll find out soon. It's no big deal." Only an attempt to extort five hundred thousand from Alice Hollister George—small change, petty cash.

She was silent for a long time. "We're a strange bunch, Jack. Maybe it's because of the money, having all of it and having to protect ourselves from people who want it. But we're . . . fierce. We all think the others are crazy, but we love each other fiercely. We're all we have." She smiled. "Are you sure you want to get tangled up with us?"

I didn't tell her that I was already entangled with them. "I just want to get tangled up with you."

"Again?" She laughed. "You really do think you're Hercules, don't you?"

"The strength of love," I grinned.

"Is that what it is?"

"I've got all the symptoms."

"Strange disease, if it makes you stronger."

"Very. But this is Nevada, where anything is possible."

We went back to bed and made love. Finally, Dolly stirred. "I really do hate to come and go, but . . ."

I didn't want her to leave. Among other things, that meant I'd have to go back to work, and I didn't want to go back to work. But I would, one last time.

It took her a while to get presentable. I was dressed before she came out of the bathroom, her face smooth and shiny, her hair brushed and glossy. She wore another of my shirts, its tails covering much of her skirt.

"I had to throw mine away."

"I'll buy you another," I said. The thought of shopping for her pleased me.

We went through the apartment, into the office. The answering machine blinked at me. "Duty calls," I said.

"But not for long?" She looked up at me, her big eyes glowing at me the way they had at her father in the desert. "You're really going to quit?"

"I really am. As soon as I find Glory."

"Does that mean I won't see you till then?"

"No." I put my hands on her shoulders. "How would you like to see a show tonight? Nine o'clock, unless something comes up. If so I'll call."

"What could come up?"

I gave her a small kiss and a pat. "Nothing."

# 25

From my broken window I watched Dolly bounce light-footed across the street and hop into the pickup. As it pulled away from the curb, her hand rose above the cab and waggled a farewell. I watched the pickup until it was gone.

On my desk, my message machine blinked with electronic indefatigability. I punched a button and listened to words from the real world.

Jess Harkness identified himself in apology. "Pete snuck off this morning sometime around sunrise. He's in the Bronco, and he's got a shotgun. Hard to tell where he thinks he's going, and he probably can't get there anyhow, but I thought I'd better let you know."

I punched off the machine.

I flipped through the Northern Nevada phone book, got his number, and dialed. His wife answered on the first ring. Her hello was tight, raspy.

"This is Jack Ross, Mrs. Harkness. I just got your husband's message."

"Is he there? Have you seen him?"

"No."

"Oh." In that single syllable lay a poem structured by the antinomies that made up her feeling for her father.

"I'd like to talk to Jess for a minute, if he's there."

"I—we need to keep the line open, in case. . . ."

I let her not finish, then said: "I might be able to help. But I need to talk to Jess. I'll make it quick."

Static crackled, made me think of furtive footsteps in dry brush. Then I was listening to Jess Harkness. "Thanks for calling, Jack."

"No sign of him?"

"Not yet," he said. "The sheriff's looking, and the highway patrol. One of the neighbor's boys saw the Bronco out on the highway just after dawn. Nothing since then."

"You think he's headed this way?"

"I don't know. I know he's got his scrapbook with him. And your business card."

"And a shotgun."

"One's missing."

"How do you see it?"

"Hard to see much," he said calmly. "Since you left the other day, he's been restless, muttering, digging through his scrapbook. He might be trying to get to you. Shape he's in, he's probably asleep in a bar pit, or driving in circles in the desert, but I thought I'd better let you know."

"I appreciate it." For a moment the silence crackled. "How long have you known where Lawrence Parker was?"

"You found him?"

"Right where you sent me."

"It was only a guess. He still there, at his place?"

"As far as I know."

"Then there's no problem there. Pete doesn't know—" In the background Janet Harkness's voice was an importunate muffle of sound. "Excuse me a minute, Jack."

I listened to two hundred miles of current clatter. Then he was back. "Got to go. You'll keep an eye out?"

"Sure. You really think he can get here?"

"Hard to tell. He's capable of some amazing things."

Amazing was a good enough word to describe the kinds of things Pete Lotz was capable of.

After we broke off, I sat and considered it. I had no doubt that Pete Lotz, senility and all, could get to Reno if his unsettled mind somehow set itself.

I punched my machine again.

Flora seemed tired, seemed, speaking to a machine, a bit uncertain of who she was. "I—this is . . . Flora. Baker. I . . . Glory called. She says she's all right. She says for you not to try to find her. I . . . thank you."

I called Sun Valley. Glory Dahlman's daughter told me that Gramma was sleeping.

I punched the machine.

Hayes George's voice lost some of its resonance on the phone: "I brought Tracy home, jerk, and Bobby. Now, if you're through with my sister's ass, tell her to get it out here."

I punched the machine again, smiled at the sound of Frank Calvetti's complaining voice.

"Do you know how tired I get talking to these damn machines? If you don't start returning my calls, I'm going to walk across the street and dismantle that contraption and feed it to you. And thanks for the Dahlman girl's address. Next time why don't you give it to us *before* you toss the place. Give me a call."

I gave him a call. "What can I do for you, Frank?"

"You can tell me the whereabouts of our favorite lady of the evening."

"I don't know where she is."

"What's this? The renowned tracker admits to failure?" He laughed without humor. "What have you been doing?"

I intended to tell Frank everything I'd been doing. But not then. "Do me a favor, and I'll tell you later."

Frank knew what that meant. He tried to escape it. "I've got my own work to do, you lazy—"

"What have you come up with?"

"Zip. As far as we can tell, Haskell Dan had no enemies, no problems, no nothing. He was just an old Shoshone who liked to play cards and fish the Truckee."

"Are you sure he was the target?"

He paused. "Meaning it might have been the girl they were after. No, we're not sure. *Was* she the target?"

"She thinks so." I told him what I'd learned from Leon Whipple.

"Whipple, huh? If he's in this, anything's possible. You dug up any more slimy creatures?"

"Cal Blass."

"Delightful company she keeps."

"What do you have on her?"

"Not much more." He sounded embarrassed. "She's a free-lancer, seems to have a steady run of high-rollers, but she's either very careful or very smart. If her UNR grades aren't just more inflation, she's smart enough. What a way to work your way through school, huh?"

The tone of his voice told me more than his words. "You sound like a man reading yesterday's paper, Frank."

"You know how it is," he said unhappily.

I knew how it was. In a killing like Haskell Dan's, the police work took place in the first forty-eight hours. Statistics argued that if a suspect hadn't been identified by then, the solution, if it came, would be a matter of luck. And socio-political reality argued that the murder of an old Shoshone would not create the pressure needed to keep troops on the job. Frank would plug away, while working other cases, but he'd receive neither help nor encouragement.

"About the favor, Frank. Glory's parents, Stuart and Rose Dahlman, died twenty years ago in Sun Valley. Can you get me the details?"

"Why? What's that got to do with this?"

"I'll explain it later. When you're through, come on over and I'll buy you a drink. We need to talk."

"About what?"

"Me."

"Your favorite topic." But Frank was my friend. He was also my daughter's uncle and godfather. "I'll be over."

I sat looking at the phone. Guiltily. I was about to use it to do something that seemed a violation of the obscure and ambiguous laws of love. But I had to do it.

Nearly four hours later I put the phone down for good. I went into the apartment, put on a tape of Mozart, then filled a glass with ice and a little scotch and a lot of water and took it back to the desk. I studied my notes.

I heard Frank's footsteps on my stairs. Then he stood in the doorway, silently assessing the mess. "Your housekeeper has the day off, I take it."

In his rumpled old suit he seemed even thinner, more boneless, an emaciated amoeba. Under his neat little mustache, his mouth set in a sardonic scowl. "At least you're listening to decent music."

"Only because I can't find Little Jimmy Dickens."

"Praise the Lord for His beneficence."

Frank avowed to despise country music—all music, in fact, in which human voices mouthed words. He also affected a hatred for drama, fiction, any art that aspired to imitate human actions. He knew more than he wanted to about human actions.

Ambling into the apartment, to the bar, he poured neat scotch. I picked up my notes and followed him.

Frank oozed onto the couch. "So what was I supposed to find in that old Sun Valley soap opera?"

"Whatever's there."

"Well it's not so much what's there as what isn't," he said. "Like an investigation. There's a perfunctory medical examiner's report, and an even more perfunctory Sheriff's Office report, and that's it."

"There should be more?"

He told me why there should have been more.

Stuart and Rose Dahlman had been found shot to death in bed in their Sun Valley trailer. The weapon, a .45 owned by Dahlman, lay on his chest. His hand had fired it. Hers had not. A bullet had entered his mouth and blown off the back of his head. A bullet had entered her temple, angled forward, and blown off half of her forehead and part of her face. The contents of a bourbon bottle thinned their blood. The unsigned note in the typewriter read: "We can't live with each other, and we can't live without each other."

The marriage of Stuart and Rose Dahlman had been fraught with altercations, most resulting from his philandering.

Rose Dahlman was three months pregnant.

The Coroner had listed their deaths as Apparent Suicide.
"What don't you like about it?"

"I don't like the note—no signature. I don't like the booze.
They both had a blood alcohol reading that would leave even a
lush like you comatose. And I especially don't like the
pregnancy. Pregnant women don't kill themselves."

"You're saying they were murdered?"

"No," he said evenly. "I'm saying that there are a lot of
things wrong with suicide—the Sheriff thought so too."

"How did he see it?"

"He saw dope. Dahlman was peddling, strictly small time,
but the word on the street was that he was about to up the
ante. There were a couple folks who didn't want that."

"Who did the Sheriff like?" But I already knew.

"Cal Blass. Couldn't tie him to it, though."

"What did Haskell say?"

"He said he came to see Dahlman, found the bodies and the
little girl crying in her crib, took her over to her grandmother's
and called the Sheriff."

"Is there anything in his statement that might . . . ?"
Frank's scowl answered the question I hadn't asked.

"Now, super-sleuth, you want to tell me why I've been
wasting the taxpayers' money on this?"

I took a swipe at my drink. "Glory asked me to find her
grandfather. I did. Rose Dahlman was his daughter. He'll want
to know what happened to her."

He gave me a long look. "Come on, Jack. Spill it."

"You'll have to take off your badge, Frank."

He stared at me. "This is a matter of public record."

"Some of it."

His mouth tightened, then relaxed. "All right, consider it off.
What kind of shit are you mucking around in now?"

I told him.

# 26

**F**rank was shaking his head long before I finished. "How do you manage to get into these things?"

"Talent."

"For disaster. Everything you touch turns to—" Something skittered across his eyes. He changed course. "How do Leon Whipple and Cal Blass figure into this?"

"I don't know. Whip thinks he's the father of Glory's child. He helped her hide out. Glory works Blass's parties sometimes, and Blass feeds the nose of Bobby George's girl friend. Maybe that's all there is."

"And maybe I'm the prom queen. What else?"

"The fact that everybody but the dog has lied to me."

"It's your face. Nobody would trust you with the truth." He sank back into the couch. "How does it work?"

"Start with the extortion. It looked like an inside job all the way. The note and sketches went to Alice George, not to her husband. Who would know she ran the show? And who would know that she was going to be in Reno then? It had to be someone close to the family—or a member of it."

"If it's that clear, wouldn't Mrs. George and Ripley have seen it too?"

"Maybe she did. Maybe they called me because she figured one of the boys for it but couldn't accept it and wanted to lay it on Glory. Alice George has her own myth of her family—something like this wouldn't fit into it. Ripley might have figured it too. For a while, he tried to talk her out of hiring me, and he makes a big production out of being the family's protector."

"Could it have been himself he was trying to protect?"

"No, unfortunately."

Frank smiled. "A friend of yours, I take it."

"Frederick Ripley is a pompous, posturing asshole. And he's got motive. He makes two hundred grand and perks as president of Hollister, but he's broke. He lives high, and his wife's career seems to be spending money. He's made some bad personal investments, he could use the money. But he didn't steal the sketches from Glory. He doesn't fit the description. But both Bobby and Hayes do."

"And a few thousand other Renoites."

"Who drive little sports cars to Cal Blass's?"

He shrugged his shapeless shoulders. "Okay. Which one?"

"Bobby. He's into the Starlight in Vegas for a quarter of a million—"

"Which he doesn't have to pay. That's not motive."

"They still could contract it out to goons. But he's also a big spender. All three of the George siblings have trust funds that pay about ten grand a quarter, but Bobby doesn't have a sou— he's gambled and lived it away. And from the looks of his fiancée, her coke habit is costing at least that much. So he's got plenty of motive."

"He'd blackmail his own father?"

"Sure. It's a way to get money, and nobody gets hurt. He's capable of it, naïve enough to think it would work."

"And Hayes George?"

Something in his voice checked me. "You know him?"

"We've had him for several assaults—all complaints withdrawn, after an injection of Hollister cash eased the victim's pain, no doubt. One rape. The young lady was suddenly offered a wonderful job in San Francisco and left town and the case petered out. Hayes George is also a frequenter of Cal Blass's gatherings."

I'd learned that an hour before, and something else.

"Hayes George owns a chunk of the Silver Saddle Club."

His eyes widened. "Since when?"

"He's been in it for a year or so."

The Silver Saddle Club was a small casino in Sparks, frequently closed and frequently sold, a marginal operation that depended on the overflow from the hotel-casinos like Karl's Silver Club and John Ascuaga's Nugget for its traffic. Without rooms, it had nothing to recommend it to tourists. Without tourists, it had nothing to recommend it to buyers.

"How?" Frank asked.

"Apparently, Hayes is a very good businessman. He's taken his ten grand a quarter and bought pieces of this and that and turned them over at the right time, sometimes the rather spectacularly right time. Word is he's got something like two million himself in the place."

"So what would five hundred grand do?"

"I don't know."

Mozart ended. "So where does that leave you?"

"I'd still figure Bobby, but it could be both of them, or one in cahoots with Ripley." I hesitated. "There's one other possibility—very remote, but possible. Alice George suggested that Glory might be the blackmailer, that she hired me to get concrete evidence of Gabriel George's identity."

Frank watched me. "And?"

"My instincts say no. But I don't know how trustworthy my instincts are these days. And the fact that her story about the theft of the sketches fits the George boys is too much of a coincidence. So I'd still say no."

"So," he said. "It's either Bobby or Hayes, or both, maybe with Ripley. And whoever it is killed Haskell Dan."

"Maybe," I said. "Maybe not."

Frank got up and went to the bar. "Do I look like a rat? Is that why you've got me in this maze?"

"I've been in it for days." Not Hercules but Theseus, awaiting Ariadne and a piece of thread.

"You've been in a maze all your life. Come on, how does the Haskell Dan killing connect to the extortion? Did he know who Gabriel George is?"

"He was at the Dahlman place when Lawrence Parker came out of the desert. The problem is that Haskell was no threat. Neither was Glory. Haskell had done nothing with that knowledge for forty years. And Glory had no reason to want to expose her grandfather. She just wanted to meet him."

Frank came back to the couch. "Now you're telling me that the extortion had nothing to do with Haskell's murder?"

"No. I'm telling you that the extortionist isn't necessarily the killer."

He shook his head in disgust. "Jack, I don't think you know what you're telling me. You're just thinking out loud, guessing, speculating. Wasting my time."

He was right, of course. But that wasn't going to stop me. "How's this for a guess: Haskell Dan was murdered by whoever killed Stuart and Rose Dahlman."

"Jack, we don't know that they were killed."

I shook my head. "Everything I know about Stuart Dahlman says that he wouldn't kill himself. Stuart Dahlman was a hustler, an exploiter, a user. He found the sketches that Parker had left with Dolores Dahlman. He sold two of them to Pete Lotz, and told Lotz that he'd try to find Parker. First he found Flora Magnusson Baker, knocked up both her and her daughter, and married Rose—probably because she was Parker's daughter. But it was Parker himself he was after."

Frank rubbed his hand over his face. "So that's where you're going with all this. You think Dahlman found Parker."

I slid to the edge of my seat. "That's the only way it makes sense. I found Parker in a day. I had help, and some luck, but I also had the sketches. There's enough similarity between those sketches and Gabriel George's photographs to send anybody who has them in that direction. With the sketches, finding Lawrence Parker is fairly easy."

Frank frowned. "Do you have any evidence that this is the case?"

"No. But it makes sense. If Stuart Dahlman managed to identify Gabriel George as Lawrence Parker, he would see that he could get a lot more by shaking him down than by giving him to Pete Lotz for five grand."

Frank tried his drink. "So what you're hypothesizing here is that there have been two attempts to extort money from Gabriel George, or his family, and that the first ended in the murders of Stuart and Rose Dahlman and the second in the murder of Haskell Dan. The Dahlmans were killed because they knew who Parker was, and Dan was killed because. . . ."

"He knew who had killed Stuart and Rose Dahlman."

Frank shook his head. "If Haskell Dan knew that, he'd known it for twenty years. Why would he be killed now?"

"Because of the extortion attempt. Look: the extortion note comes, and the killer immediately thinks that since Haskell Dan is the only one who knew Parker's identity, he must be involved. If he's involved in the extortion, then he's also a threat to expose the identity of the Dahlmans' killer. So he has to be killed."

Frank's eyes told me I was losing him. "This is silly."

"It's been silly from the start. All this over hiding the identity of a man wanted for murder, when in fact the only witness says that the killing was self-defense. It's always been silly, but it keeps killing people."

He still wasn't buying it. "All right, Jack. Who killed the three of them?"

"Frederick Ripley."

"How convenient, since you don't like him."

I ignored that, partly because it was true.

"From what I've been able to discover, there is no real reason that Ripley is president of the Hollister Corporation. As an executive he's said to be mediocre at best. He's okay as a manager, giving orders, but up against other executives and entrepreneurs, he folds. My sources say that Alice George runs the business, makes all the real decisions. What Ripley seems to have is a sinecure, for services rendered. Except there's no evidence that he's ever rendered anyone any service. He tells a great story about his relationship with old Hayes Hollister, but the truth is he was just a kid who worked in Hollister's office, a glorified gofer. There's a suggestion that he was a procurer of young ladies for a rich old man. Hollister did put him through law school, and then he sent him out here, to oversee the Nevada end of the business—but there is no real Nevada business. It's a nothing sort of job, making sure the right papers have the right postmark on them so that the Nevada tax laws can be used. And suddenly, twenty years ago, Frederick Ripley is a vice president of the Hollister Corporation."

"After the deaths of Dahlman and his wife?"

I'd earned some of his credence. "Almost immediately."

"It's tenuous, Jack."

"Granted. But there's more. Ripley told Alice George and me that old Hollister knew about Stuart Dahlman and that he, Ripley, was charged with keeping an eye on him. Ripley must have also known about Haskell Dan, Flora Baker, even about Glory. And, so far as we know, only Frederick Ripley and Alice George are aware of the extortion attempt."

Frank took a healthy slug of his drink. "Assuming that some of what you're saying is accurate—and even you have to admit that it's an incredible story—it could work that way. But it works another way. Gabriel George himself."

"No. He didn't know there'd been an extortion attempt."

Frank laughed. "Are you kidding me?"

"They didn't tell him. They're a strange outfit, Frank. Everybody runs around protecting everybody else, and nobody talks to anybody about it while they're doing it, so they just keep screwing each other up. Mom's been getting the boys out of scrapes for years, paying Bobby's gambling losses and buying Hayes out of assault charges. Hayes thinks he's the only thing between his family and the poorhouse. Ripley thinks his primary job is to protect Alice George and her husband and kids, that he was commanded to by God—in this case, R. Hayes Hollister."

Frank finished his drink. "So where does this leave us?"

"I've told you what I know, Frank, and what I think. I have no real evidence to support anything. I doubt that you could get any evidence either. It's too old, or too close to powerful people. It's mostly just a dusty web of guess and hunch. Half a sneeze would blow it to smithereens. I don't imagine you'll even pursue it. There's nowhere to start, nothing to start with."

"I'm glad you at least see that. So where do you go from here?"

"I find Glory. Then I'm through."

"And with Flora Baker's statement, everything is finished. Except the murder of Haskell Dan."

"That's your job."

"And the thing with Stuart Dahlman and his wife?"

"That's the Sheriff's."

"That's right." Frank looked at his glass. "You'll excuse me for reminding you, Jack, but the fact that you weren't hired to do something never stopped you from trying—if you thought it needed doing."

"That was in a former life. I find Glory, I'm finished. Not just with this. All of it. I'm quitting."

He looked at me for a while. "You serious?"

"Yes."

# 27

**F**rank got up and went to the bar, and I followed. As he filled our glasses, I slipped out the Mozart tape and put in Jimmie Rodgers, stood and listened to the classically simple guitar introduction to the classically simple opening verse of *The Last Blue Yodel*, to its classically simple and age-old refrain: *The women make a fool out of me.*

Frank did not comment on the music. He handed me my glass. "Here's to an eminently sound decision. Your first in a long time. I'd begun to think you'd lost the capacity for sound decisions."

"I've been thinking about it for a while. Now I've just had it. Someone called me Jack Offal Trades the other day. I laughed, but it wasn't funny, it was too close to the truth. I'm tired of it, Frank. Tired of wading in other people's lives, cleaning up their messes. I'm tired of lies and subterfuge and deception. And I'm very tired of corpses—living or dead. I've had it."

"You'd had it a long time ago, you just didn't know it. You never were right for this kind of thing."

That stung. "I'd say I did all right."

He smiled. "I didn't say you weren't any good at it. I said you weren't *right* for it, that it wasn't good for you. You've never been able to be objective enough, to keep your distance. You always had to get involved, stick your nose—if not more than that—into everybody else's business."

"*Quid nunc.*"

"What's that?"

"A busybody."

He laughed. "More or less. But look around, Jack. Look at this place. It's like an old folks home. Most of the stuff in here belonged to your grandparents. Where are you in all this, where's your life?"

I did look around, seeing it with his eyes, as if for the first time. I had thought of it as my home, of the things in it as my things, but he was right. Most of the furniture, many of the decorative pieces, some of the books and records, had belonged to my grandparents.

"I guess I haven't had much of a life."

"Not since my sister dumped you when you were in 'Nam. I'm glad you're about to start one. What's your first move?"

"I'm going to sell Sierra Bail Bonds, and the building. I'm going to let my license lapse, and my membership in the bar. I'm going to do a bunch of nothing for a while."

"Good," he said. "You getting out of here for a while?"

"Maybe," I said. "I . . . might go to Berkeley."

"You—a Californicator? I don't believe it."

I shrugged, smiled. Frank's smile became a grin, stretching rarely used facial muscles. "What's her name?"

"Whose name?"

"*Her* name. I know there's got to be a woman in this somewhere. For all your peripatetic bed patterns, you're the one-woman-needingest man I know. Who is she?"

"Her name is Dolly. Dolly George."

His grin ebbed. Jimmie Rodgers sang *The Long Tall Momma Blues*. "Are you sure you know what you're doing?"

"No," I said. "But I'm sure I'm going to do it."

It was a while before Frank spoke. "Can you separate them—the girl, and what you've told me of her family?"

"I think so. She's not involved in any of this. And once I've found Glory, my interest in her family ceases."

"You think it will be that simple?"

"No. It will be complicated, tricky. Ultimately, it may not even be possible. But I'm going to try."

"She must be special."

I told him why I thought she was.

"All that, and rich too." His face settled into lugubrious folds. "I've got to ask you this, Jack. For you, and for my own peace of mind. By your own description, the Georges are a fiercely loyal family, all members of it watching out for the others. Are you sure she isn't. . . ."

I wouldn't help him. He had to say it himself. "Are you sure she isn't using you?"

That wasn't specific enough. "How?"

He shook his head. "Look, Jack, I don't want to—"

"Get it out, Frank. Let's have a look at it."

He fortified himself with alcohol. Then he got it out.

"You've been living in a nightmare lately, Jack. And the fact is you're extremely vulnerable. Now you've become emotionally involved with someone connected with a case, and suddenly you're about to walk away from that case—after fabricating a nice little explanation that will let you—a case that includes at least one murder, perhaps two more. You've never done that before. You've always stuck with things, seen them through. You're telling me, in effect, that you're going to let a killer get away with murder."

"And you're telling me," I said quietly, "that I'm being— what? Decoyed? Sidetracked? Bought off?"

"I'm not telling you anything, you know that. I'm just asking if you're sure about what you're doing."

"I told you I wasn't, Frank. All I can tell you is that I have absolutely no indication that Dolly has any part in any of this— before or after the fact. I acknowledge that it's possible. But I believe she's been straight with me. I choose to believe it, it's an act of faith, if you will. I'm tired of suspecting everything and everyone I encounter. I don't think I'm wrong in this, but if I am—well, I'm a big boy. I'll take my chances, and the consequences."

He nodded. "And Haskell Dan?"

"Frank, do you think there's any possibility that anyone will ever be convicted of his murder?"

"Without talking to Glory Dahlman, I can't say. But it is possible. It's always possible. And you always kept going, regardless of how remote the possibility might be."

"And spread my guts all over the landscape, ended up empty and cold and pickling my brain." But that wasn't what I wanted to say. I pickled my brain a little more.

"Frank, I've told you everything I know, everything I suspect. I'm going to find Glory, and I'm going to convince her to tell you everything she knows. Then, unless she has some fantastic revelations—which I doubt—I'm going to leave the case with you. It's your job to find Haskell Dan's killer, not mine. I'm going to walk away from it, with a clear conscience, with my sense of integrity whole and inviolate. I'm going to walk away with Dolly George—if she wants to come with me."

"That's clear enough," Frank said. He gave me another of his rare smiles. "And good enough for me."

We had another drink, and we talked. It was a good talk, in the pattern of thrust and riposte we'd developed over the years of our friendship. We both felt better with everything out in the open.

When he had to leave, I walked Frank to the office door. There he did something he hadn't done in years. He held out his hand. I took it firmly. "Good luck, Jack."

"You think I'll need it?"

"I don't know about that," he said. "I do know you've got some coming."

# 28

The sky was a patchwork of gray-bottomed boils of cloud that threatened rain and shadowed the city. It turned folks surly. In the evening rush hour traffic, they drove their vehicles as if guiding weapons, choosing their targets at random. I joined the stream turning into Clearacre Lane and made my way into Sun Valley, braking for surging and lane-shifting idiots, ignoring the screech of rubber on the pavement and the scowls and fingers directed my way.

In Flora Baker's yard, away from the exhaust and nervous sweat of the city, I could smell the rain. Even before falling it seemed to be dampening the dust, freshening the sage.

Emily Dahlman again answered my knock. But this time, when I asked for her grandmother, she simply stepped aside.

Flora sat in the same chair, in a gloomier dimness. For a moment I thought she was asleep. For another panicky moment I thought she was dead. Then her body stirred.

"We don't need you anymore." Her voice was thin, weak; the words began just behind her lips, ended just beyond them. "Lily's coming for Emmy tomorrow. And for me. I'm going into Washoe Med."

"For treatment?"

"I won't be coming out."

"I—I'm sorry, Flora."

Her shoulders may have shrugged.

"Till then, is there anything I can do?"

"We're fine."

Flora Baker had spent most of her life not needing men. She wasn't going to need one now. But now I needed her. "I have to ask you a few questions, Flora."

"Not about Glory. I wouldn't tell the cops anything. I won't tell you either."

"You're sure she's all right?"

"She's fine."

"Does she still think whoever shot Haskell Dan was after her?"

"I—yes."

"Then she's still in danger. I might be able to help. And I want to tell her about her grandfather."

Her pale face seemed to float, already a specter, in the darkened room. "What?"

"He's alive."

Her mouth formed a strange smile. "Loses a gramma and gets a grampa at the same time. Funny." The smile faded. "Will he . . . take care of her?"

"Yes," I said. "And of Emmy."

"Is he rich and famous like he always said he'd be?"

"Yes."

"Good for him."

I tried to get a clearer view of her through the gloom. I couldn't. "Do you mind, Flora, if I turn on the light?"

"Not on me. Turn it away."

I grabbed one of the oval shades and tilted it toward the wall. I switched it on, and light flooded the faces.

"That's nice," she said. "I like to look at them."

I looked at her. I could see death in her eyes, in the hollows on her face. "You won't help me find Glory?"

"Can't. She didn't tell me where she was."

"I talked to Leon Whipple. He took her wherever she is. He said no one would ever think to look for her there. Does that mean anything to you?"

"No."

"Was the call long distance?"

"No." And no background noises, nothing to provide a clue as to where she might be hiding.

I felt depression settling like a soggy weight on my shoulders and neck. Part of it resulted from the fragrance of death that Flora Baker breathed into the room. Part of it resulted from her inability to give me an easy way to find Glory. The largest part of it resulted from my awareness of how I was going to have to locate her. I didn't want to think about that, so I thought about something else.

"Tell me about Rose, Flora, and Stuart Dahlman. Who killed them?"

Her eyes turned to the wall. "They . . . killed each other."

"No, they didn't. Somebody killed both of them. The same person who killed Haskell Dan, who's after Glory now."

Slowly her eyes closed. "I knew it, the first time I laid eyes on you. I knew you'd bring it all back."

"I didn't bring it back, Flora," I said quietly. "It was always here, waiting. Who killed them?"

"I don't know," she said weakly. "I didn't want to know. She was dead, that's all that mattered." Her eyes slid open. "Leave it alone. Please."

I took what she said as confirmation of my theory. I didn't feel happy that the theory had been confirmed. "I wish I could. But everything goes back to it. Stuart was trying to track down Lawrence Parker. I think he found him. I also think he tried to blackmail Parker and got killed for his trouble."

"He . . . was going to be rolling in dough. That's what he said. But he was always saying that. We didn't pay no attention to it. Until it was too late." She turned from the faces on the wall to my face. "Did Larry kill them?"

"Gabriel George, the photographer I told you about—he's Lawrence Parker. But he's not a killer."

"Are you sure?"

I wasn't as sure as I wanted to be. But I had staked my future on it, so I told her I was. "He certainly wouldn't have killed Rose, his own daughter."

As if to confirm my statement, she looked again at the wall, at her children and grandchildren. I looked too, at the cocky grinning young boys, the lovely young girls.

Then I was staring at one of the lovely young girls. My insides clenched like a fist.

I got to my feet, stepped unsteadily across the room. My hands trembled as I took down the photograph.

The formal portrait had the crude color tinting of twenty years before. The blonde hair was harsh, brassy, the cheeks patchy with rosy blush, the wide mouth nearly brazen with its deep red lips. But the eyes were the same sea-gray shimmer I'd looked into the day before.

I looked into the face of the youthful Ann Ripley and felt all my certitude crumble like a dirt clod beneath a steer's hoof.

I took the picture back to the chair.

Flora Baker's dying eyes were wide and filled with fear.

"Has Ann been to see you, Flora?"

"Ann who?"

"Ann Ripley. Anemone Baker Ripley."

"I . . . haven't seen her in years."

"Does she know you're dying?"

"How . . . could she?"

"Would you like me to tell her?"

The fear in her eyes deepened, nearly enough to drive away the death.

"I talked to her last night, Flora. She's in Reno. She's married to Frederick Ripley, the president of the Hollister Corporation, which happens to be owned by the George family. Lawrence Parker's family."

"Leave her alone." The voice was so weak I had to strain to hear it. It was dry, dusty, scratchy, a desert voice, a voice from the desert within.

"I don't think I can. But I don't want to hurt her. I'll help her if I can. But I won't be able to unless you tell me the truth."

"I . . . can't."

"It's time, Flora. It's gone on too long."

She gazed down at the photograph in my hand. "It was Stuart. Everything. He caused it all."

Gabriel George had said much the same thing. "How?"

"He got to her. He got to every woman he went after. She thought that after his big score, he was going to leave with her, not with Rose."

"Did she know who Stuart was getting the money from?"

"I don't know."

But it was the only way it could have worked.

I looked down again at the photograph of Ann Ripley when she was Anemone Baker. I rose, still shaken. "May I borrow this?"

She didn't answer.

"I—are you sure there's nothing I can do for you, Flora?"

"Please . . . take care of them."

I didn't know who "them" included. Her daughter, granddaughter, great-granddaughter. I didn't know if I could take care of them, or if, except for Emily, they should be taken care of. But I didn't say that. I looked down at her pale, fleshless face, her blue eyes dulled by chemicals and concern and death, and I said: "I'll do the best I can, Flora."

Outside, I stood before the trailer and filled my lungs with clean, rainy air. Rain was not yet falling, but the Sierra was shrouded in gray, and the wind that rushed down the mountains carried the scent of damp and pungent pine.

I found myself wishing that it would rain now, that it would pour, that it would rain until Sun Valley and the Truckee Meadows flooded, filled, and became again Lake Lahontan covering the trailers and junk cars and junk lives of Sun Valley, covering the casinos and neon and nothingness of downtown Reno, covering Nevada and everyone in it. I didn't care that I was in it or that I had no ark.

I drove slowly out of Sun Valley. No one followed me this time, but this time I again stopped in the Little Wal. The afterwork shift was working, male and female drinkers looking at each other, searching for a reasonable reason not to go home. In two hours the reasons would not have to be reasonable.

I searched scotch for reasonable answers. In two hours I wouldn't need answers, I'd need an ambulance. I drank up and left.

# 29

The clouds were lower, darker, the wind a stiff bluster by the time I parked before the big white Hollister house. Like fat ripe fruit, the rain hung above me in gray bunches but would not fall. I slipped the portrait of Anemone Baker into my pocket, got out, and climbed the stairs to the door.

When it opened my depression began to lift. Dolly smiled at me. "Can't stay away, I see. You're early."

"You're irresistible," I said, stepping in. Her hair smelled as clean as rain.

She stepped back. "I'm ready, if you want to go."

"I'd love to go," I said, "but I've got some business to do. Is Ann Ripley here? Or Bobby?"

Her eyes widened. "Bobby? Oh, no, Jack. Don't tell me he's in some kind of trouble?"

"Not from me," I said. "But I need to talk to him."

"He's up with Tracy. But I don't think he'll talk to you, at least right now. He's trying to . . . help her."

I didn't know what that meant, nor did I want to. Bobby George could wait. "Ann?"

"I think she's in the den." As if to lead me there, she turned and started down the hall.

"Is her husband here?"

"He went out a while ago." She stopped at the hallway doors. "Jack, is Ann—" The look on my face silenced her. "I'm sorry. I won't ask. I'll be practicing."

174

A big, comfortable room, the den held a spread of dark old furniture, a huge dark old bar, and a large television set before which Ann Ripley sat as colors flashed over her bright head. On the screen helicopters swirled around bare Southern California mountains, the whop-whop of their blades faint beneath the theme from *MASH*. The lyric rose in my mind. Suicide brings on many changes.

I sat beside her, took the photograph from my pocket, watched her eyes shift from my face to the picture of what once had been her face.

She took the picture and gazed at it with a kind of yearning. Then she turned it over, pushed a button on the TV control. The screen went dark, the room silent.

"I knew this would happen," she said quietly. "I almost told you myself, last night."

"Why didn't you?"

"I got . . . involved in other things. I—would you make me a drink, please?"

I rose and moved behind the bar, stuffed ice into two tall glasses, filled them with Glenlivet until the ice floated, and took them back to the chairs.

She took a swallow. "Why don't you tell me what you already know? Then I'll tell you what you want to know."

"I know you're Anemone Baker, and that you were having an affair with Stuart Dahlman when he and your sister died."

Her face showed no reaction. Now that I'd made the connection, I couldn't escape the shadow of her mother's face in her own.

"And what do you want to know?"

I almost laughed. "Let's start with this: Was Stuart Dahlman blackmailing Gabriel George?"

"Gabe?" She shook her head. "No, no. It was Frederick."

I was confused. "Ripley was blackmailing Gabe?"

"No," she said. "How could anyone blackmail Gabe? Stuart was blackmailing Frederick."

"I—over what?"

"He . . . Frederick had gotten a young girl pregnant. Stuart found out, and he threatened to expose him, to have him charged with statutory rape."

"How did Stuart get this information?"

"From the girl."

I tried to stop trying to think. Instead, I focused on her face, her sea-gray eyes. "Who was she?"

"I don't. . . ." The words ceased, as if her throat had constricted.

"Please, Ann. Don't lie. Not now."

She took another swallow from her drink. In a whisper she said, "Me."

It was coming too fast for me.

She looked up. "I told you last night—he likes young girls. He saw me. He was rich, or what passed for it to me. I thought if I gave him what he wanted, I'd be able to make him take me out of the valley. To be sure, I got pregnant."

"Where's the child?"

"It wasn't born. I . . . lost it."

"And he just married you?"

She shook her head. "Not then. He sent me to San Francisco. I went to school for a while, learned things. Learned what he wanted me to—how to dress, talk, be an executive's wife. Then he made me one."

"Why?"

She smiled sadly. "I'm not that bad, am I?"

"You know that isn't what I meant."

The smile lingered like a ghost on her wide mouth. "I was young then, young enough for him. And I knew what he was, what he wanted, and I wouldn't give him any trouble about it. I was perfect for him. He could have a marriage, seem to live the kind of domestic life expected of the vice president of Hollister, and still be what he was."

"I—" I didn't want the details. I didn't care if Frederick Ripley got off with hydrocephalic ground hogs. But I had to know. "What, exactly, is that?"

She laughed, quietly, at the tone of my voice. "Hardly anything horrible. A case of arrested emotional development.

A fixation. He can't get . . . involved with anyone but young girls. I don't mean little girls, children—he's not a pervert. I mean young girls—fifteen, sixteen, sometimes up to twenty or so, as long as they're immature enough."

"That may not be that horrible," I said, "but with fifteen-year-olds it's against the law."

"I know," she said. "Statutory rape. But that's the only thing about it that's rape. I know from experience that he's a very gentle, kind lover, he's very good to them. In all these years not one of the girls has ever. . . ."

"And all these years you've been his beard, his cover. What do you get out of this trade?"

"I got out of Sun Valley."

It made a sort of sense. But that didn't answer the real question. I asked it.

"Who killed Rose and Stuart?"

Finally, a real reaction. But not the one I expected. Her brows sharpened over her eyes; she leaned toward me, as if she hadn't heard me correctly. "I'm sorry. What?"

"Who killed your sister and her husband?"

"They . . . killed each other. Or Stuart killed her and then himself. Suicide. The sheriff—"

"Do you really expect me to believe that, Ann?"

"That's what they said. There was a note. . . ."

I took a long swallow of my drink, watching her. Now her eyes searched mine.

"You had an affair with Stuart Dahlman. You know he wouldn't kill himself—especially not over a woman."

"He . . . they said he was drunk. When he got drunk, he could get crazy. He used to take out that gun and wave it around and—"

"And then threaten to kill himself with it? Besides that, Rose was pregnant. She'd kill herself, or let Dahlman kill her, while she was carrying a child?"

In the soft light her eyes glittered with tears.

"Who killed them, Ann?"

"I don't. . . ." The tears trembled, then slowly seeped from her eyes, through her mascaraed lower lashes, spread into the hollows beneath her eyes like a desert river into its sink. "Why would anyone want to kill them?"

"To keep them quiet."

"I—" Her eyes widened again, spilling more tears. "You mean Frederick? No. He wouldn't. . . ."

I attended to my drink, giving her time to get herself together, giving myself time. I had learned some things, but I wasn't sure how to apply them—or if they applied at all. Nor did I know how much of what Ann Ripley had told me was the truth. It all had the ring of truth to it, but I couldn't tell anymore when I was being lied to. Everything was beginning to sound like the truth to me.

"You . . . don't really know anything, do you? You're just guessing." She had gotten herself together. Her voice was quiet, calm.

"I'm guessing," I said. "But not wildly. You know—"

"No," she said suddenly. "I only know that you're trying to twist things around so it looks like Frederick killed Stuart and . . . Rose. But he didn't."

"You can protect him from statutory rape charges, Ann. You can't protect him from this."

But her eyes told me she would try. If in fact it was her husband she was protecting.

"The authorities might make other guesses. They might guess you killed them?"

"My own sister?"

"Half-sister, to be exact. And twenty years of the good life in San Francisco is certainly motive enough."

"No. It doesn't matter what you say. It's all guesses. If you could prove this, if you could prove anything, you wouldn't be here trying to get me to admit to things that aren't true. You're wrong, about everything. And I'm not going to tell you anything else."

It was true that I was guessing. It was also true that I could prove nothing. It might very well be true that I was wrong. It was certainly true that I would get no more from Ann Ripley.

So I gave her something. "Have you seen your mother since you've been here?"

"I haven't seen her for years."

"If you want to, you'd better do it soon. She's dying."

She looked up at me, stunned.

"She's going into Washoe Med tomorrow. She told me she wouldn't be coming out. She has cancer."

Tears came again. "Is she . . . in pain?"

"I don't think so. Not a lot."

"I—thank you." Her shoulders slowly squared, her eyes opened. "I'll go to her."

She rose, reached for my now empty glass, took it to the bar. Then she turned, and I again had the sense of *déjà vu*—the conviction that I had seen her stand that way long before. Now I knew what I had seen. She stood as her mother had in the drawing by Lawrence Parker, her body voluptuous and inviting, her features blurred by emotion: her mother's daughter.

"You still haven't found Glory?"

"No," I said, "but I will."

"Please," she said quietly, "take care of her."

I watched her walk from the den, her shoulders stiff, her hips swaying with a sensuousness that she could not have controlled had she wanted to.

# 30

**D**olly was at the piano, playing something I didn't recognize—a disjointed, clamoring piece that was obviously modern and not obviously music. I sat in a big chair out of her line of vision and listened and waited for her to finish.

I didn't enjoy listening, but I did enjoy watching. She played with her entire body, from bobbing, dipping head to pedal-stabbing feet, her shoulders shifting and pushing her arms and hands, her back bent, her hips bouncing and sliding on the bench. Given the piece, I couldn't judge the level of her playing, but she did it with an energy that seemed to fill her with delight.

I thought of other things that filled her with delight.

Then she finished. Or stopped. I couldn't tell. She turned and saw me and smiled. "What do you think?"

"Hard to know what to think."

"You don't appreciate contemporary composition?"

"I appreciate those big silences. He should use more of them. Nothing but, in fact."

"Philistine."

"Just an old Nevada country boy," I said, rising. "Come on, I'll take you to hear some real music."

Dolly got her coat and we stepped outside. Rain still did not fall.

I took the interstate north, then east, to Sparks. At John Ascuaga's Nugget we had dinner. A faint and misty rain dampened our faces as we strolled the block and a half to the Silver Saddle, a square of old brick festooned with new neon. Beside the main entrance, a glass-encased poster announced the engagement of Poor Lil. In a glossy eight-by-ten, a booted, jeaned, and lacy-bloused Lily Baker grinned against a background of three guitar-toting young men.

"You trying to make a country-music girl out of me?"

"This ought to do it."

Dolly studied the poster. "Why do I have the feeling there's something else going on? Do you know her?"

"She's Glory Dahlman's half-sister." Among other things. One of those other things she was was working for Dolly's brother. I hadn't pursued that, hoping it was simply a coincidence. I'd liked Lily Baker.

"Is that why we're here?"

"Partly." I told her why. "But that doesn't mean we can't enjoy it."

The Silver Saddle wasn't busy. A few drinkers lolled over glasses and the poker machines embedded in the bar. The casino floor seemed larger than it really was, dotted with handle-pullers, card-scowlers, dice-rattlers—most of them local. Dealers and runners looked bored, even depressed. This kind of business would put them out of work before too long.

Glass separated the bar from the small lounge. Except for three tables in the front jammed with young men and women in a loud and festive mood, the room was empty. I slipped the doorman a ten, which delighted him, then asked for a table against the wall toward the rear, which mystified him. It wasn't the best place from which to watch the show. It was the best place from which to watch the audience, the door, and the bar.

We ordered our obligatory drinks and waited quietly. I watched. Glory was not among those at the three tables in front—they were obviously friends of the musicians, there to wish them well. A few more people, most alone, drifted in. The doorway stood open, the bar remained mostly empty.

Then the house lights dimmed, a disembodied voice boomed an introduction, and the curtains slid back from the stage.

Lily Baker, dressed as in the photograph, grinned into the darkness. Then she turned to the three guitarists behind her, they began to pick and strum, and she began to sing:

> *Lil, she was a famous beauty*
> *Lived in a house of ill repu-ty*
> *The men folk came from miles around*
> *To see poor Lil in her low cut gown . . .*

Her big voice filled the room. Her face took on color, her big body danced to the up-beat tempo. The audience, when the song ended, exploded into applause. Flushed, Lily nodded once, and then the guitars began again.

She did it all before she stopped. Melancholy Hank Williams wails, Johnny Cash growls, Patsy Cline laments; Crystal Gayle slick and George Jones raunchy; folk, country, blues. She sang the maudlin, the touching, the painful, the hopeful, the joyful. She stomped the stage, filled it with her big body, filled the darkness with her voice, at once simple and multifoliate.

When she finished the set, the audience filled the room with hoots and shouts of delight. Lily's grin got bigger. As the curtain closed, she told us they'd be right back.

"My god," Dolly said into my ear. "She's wonderful. I—why is she here?"

Instead of the Grand Ole Opry, she meant. I shrugged. "There's making music, then there's making it in the music business. It's probably the same in your field. But I'd guess that most of all she needs her own material. And a different band."

They'd tried, the pickers. But she was so superior with her instrument that they seemed stumble-fingered with theirs.

As the lights came up, I rechecked the audience. It was larger now, the room three-quarters full, but Glory Dahlman was not present. Nor was she in the small gathering at the door, nor at the bar.

But Hayes George was.

He leaned over his drink, grinning perversely at us. I felt Dolly stiffen beside me. "What's he doing here?"

"Ask him," I said, as Hayes pushed away from his drink and headed our way.

In a moment he slumped across the small table from us. "*Quel coincidence!* The Lady and the Tramp. Or is it that's why the lady is a tramp. Doin' a little slumming, Doll?"

"Why don't you just leave us alone, Hayes?" It was an old, weary complaint.

"You a country fan, Ross? That figures. You can take the boy out of Nevada, but. . . ."

"Keeping tabs on your investment?"

His grin faded. "What investment?"

"The two mill you tossed into this sinkhole."

Surprisingly, his grin spread. "You know about that?"

"I'm a trained investigator."

"Doin' a number on us? What'd you think of that, D.D.? The boyfriend's checking out the whole family. What are we under suspicion for?"

"You're suspected of being infantile," Dolly said. "And the evidence is overwhelming." Then quickly her tone changed. "Is it true, do you actually own this place?"

His laugh rumbled into the room. "A piece of it."

"How? I mean—"

"Brains. And not throwing my money after cheap thrills like you and Bobby-baby." He laughed again. "So what are you trying to make of it, Ross?"

"Not a thing. I'm sure it will astonish you, but my being here has nothing to do with you."

It didn't astonish him. "You running that big bouncy momma in your herd too? You got the balls of a brass monkey, bringing one of your fillies in to see another one. But you better not spread yourself too thin. There's other studs might want to cut that big 'un out of your herd."

"Like you?"

He grinned. "Might be."

"Leave her alone, Hayes."

"Can't do it. Too much money involved."

"What money?"

"My money. Or it will be." He interpreted my silence as confusion, which it might have been.

"Let me give you a little lesson in the gaming business, Ross. Reno was built on gambling and entertainment. But after the last slowdown, when things got a bit sparse out, all the corporate calculator-carriers who run the big clubs decided that they either had to make entertainment pay for itself or get rid of it. So they priced the shows out of the pocket of the average Joe and Mabel from Sacramento, closed down lounges and show-rooms, and then wondered why business kept slipping. Anybody with any sense would have done just the opposite— had more entertainment at a lower price. That's just what I'm gonna do here. And that Lily lady's gonna get it started for me."

"You're going to show the industry how it's done."

"You got it, Ace."

"And what happens to Lily?"

"Not much. All she has to do is sing and flop those big old whompers of hers around and she gets everything she ever wanted—money, recording contracts, TV, the works. Maybe even me for a while, if she plays her cards right."

Dolly had listened, or not listened, in silence. "Why do you always have to . . . be this way, Hayes?"

"I don't have to, dimwit. I want to. You have your little amusements—like Ross—and I have mine. The difference is that mine amount to something, and all yours ever accomplish is a little clit tickle."

She shook her head. "Is it that important to you, to make money, to put together all your great deals, just to show Mom and Ripley that you're better at it than they are?"

"No, it's not important," he said with a sudden soft serious-ness. "It's not important at all. Nothing is."

He rose, stood looking down at her with something very close to affection. "Maybe one of these days you'll learn that and stop letting the world grind you up."

Perhaps something human did lurk in the miasmic psyche of

Hayes George. The possibility only deepened his sister's distress.

He punched me on the shoulder. "She isn't coming, Ross."

"How do you know?"

He shrugged. "She'd have been here by now." And then I realized that we were there for the same reason.

"You can't find her either, huh?"

He grinned. "Not yet. But I will." He leaned at me. "I can beat you at your game, too."

"Why are you looking for her?"

"Somebody's got to settle the mess you stirred up, Ross. Otherwise the whole outfit's gonna be covered in shit."

When he was gone, Dolly and I didn't speak. I was thinking about Hayes and Lily, Hayes and Glory, trying to understand the connections. I didn't know what Dolly was thinking.

Hayes was right; Glory didn't show. We sat through the next two sets, let Lily's voice carry us beyond our concerns. Then she was finished.

The audience was still expressing its approval when Lily slipped from behind the curtain and joined her friends at the three front tables. Dolly and I watched, until Lily's eyes left her friends to swing and search the room. She found my eyes, smiled faintly, shrugged.

Dolly and I left.

The casino was busier. Maybe it was just the time of night. Or maybe Hayes was right—I didn't disagree with his notion so much as find it oversimplified. But there was action on the floor, which meant money in his pocket. His employees seemed to be feeling better about things.

Dolly didn't. She was silent all the way back to my apartment. I drove through the soft wet, the thick mist and faint rain, watching the smeary glare of lights on the slick street and trying not to think of what I was going to have to do the next day.

Dolly fixed us drinks while I, in a fit of perhaps desperate whimsy, put on The Lovin' Spoonful. We sat listening to the childlike simplicities of the music, the quiet harmonies of a more hopeful time.

"Have you been . . . investigating all of us, Jack?"

"Not all of you. Not you."

"What have you found out?"

"What I needed to know," I said. "I'm sorry, Dolly. I know this must make you feel . . . violated. But it's what I do. I'm doing it in part because your mother has asked me to do something for her. It's—just what I do."

"No wonder you want to quit."

"Yes."

For a while we sat, listening not to the music but to the big silence that had risen up between us. Finally I broke it. "What's the matter, Dolly?"

"I don't know. I—I've just got this bad feeling. I'm afraid that somehow it's all going to fall apart."

"Us?"

"Everything. And us in the process."

I wanted to comfort her. I couldn't. I had a similar feeling.

I went to her, took her hand in both of mine. I tried to find something to say, but everything that came to mind was trite, sentimental. So I said nothing. Then I said the tritest, most sentimental words in the language.

"I love you."

She smiled faintly, leaned against me. "I'm glad."

The music ended. We went to bed. We made love quietly, joining together now as if to ward off the specter of our separation, the awareness of our ultimate separateness.

The dawn was gray and dripping when I awoke. Leaving Dolly in bed, I started the coffee. Then I went to my office, my desk. My machine blinked at me.

Peavine Mountain, its summit cloud-enshrouded, loomed. The city was dark and wet, the streets dark and clean. During the night the rain had fallen hard; litter lay in swirled patterns in gutters and around drains. Now particles of moisture danced in the air, awaiting wind to disperse them, heat to make them rain.

I punched the button on my answering machine, heard: "This is Lily Baker. Emmy's here. I don't know when she got here, or who brought her, and she doesn't either. I've called Mom, but there's no answer. She's not at the hospital. Emmy's sleeping, I can't leave her. Can you . . ."

She hadn't finished. She hadn't had to. The fear in her voice said more than I wanted to hear.

Dolly stirred as I was slipping into a jogging suit and running shoes. I kissed her hair, told her I'd be back in a while. I didn't tell her where I was going. I didn't tell her what I knew I'd find there.

# 31

Sun Valley lay soggy and still in the gray light.

I parked in front of Flora Magnusson Baker's lot. The dead cars gleamed slick in the yard. A red Bronco stood ten yards from the trailer, the door on the driver's side hanging open as if sprung, a big muddy booted foot dangling from it.

The door to the trailer was open.

I sat in the blast of the heater warming myself against the chill of the damp morning air, against the chill that seemed to issue from the molecules of my flesh.

Then I got out, followed the barbed wire fence, stepping carefully on the mat of dead vegetation and papery trash that spread out from the bottom strand.

Near the house I examined the tire tracks, fresh and crisp in the bare earth. One set led to the Bronco. Another had been made by a big, heavy car. A third matched the deep-treaded marks left by Gabriel George's Land Rover.

The story the tracks would tell was not quite coherent. The big car seemed to have come and gone at least twice.

I tight-roped a strip of weedy growth to the Bronco.

Pete Lotz sprawled across the front seat, his chest heaving heavily, the shotgun dangling from his hand.

I turned away, to the trailer. The soft mud before the open door took neatly the imprint of my rippled soles. There were other prints, several, confused.

Flora Magnusson Baker sat in the dimness in the chair before

**188**

the wall of faces. The hole in her chest gaped like a silently screaming mouth. Blood spread over her nightgown, drained down into her lap, settled like a dying glutinous river into the sink between her legs.

Carefully I backed out of the trailer, retraced my steps. In the Wagoneer, I turned up the heater and then drove back to the 7/11 store on Clearacre Lane and a phone.

Refusing to give my name, I told the Sheriff's Office where to go and what they would find. I told them about the tire tracks. I told them they would find the imprint of my shoe in the mud before the door, and that in a few hours I would come in and tell them who I was and what I knew.

I called Jess Harkness and told him what I had to tell him. He told me he'd be there in a few hours.

I got in the Wagoneer and headed for the interstate, south.

Under the scuddy sky I drove through the city and the early morning traffic, through Washoe Valley, along Eastlake Boulevard, up the narrow black strip that climbed through ancient sand.

The wind-blasted house stood damp and still. Pulling in through the gap in the fence, I aimed the Wagoneer at the house and didn't stop it until the front bumper was a yard from the door. I rolled down the window, got out, reached in the window and leaned on the horn until the door jerked open.

Leon Whipple, barefoot, in greasy jeans and a clean black Harley-Davidson tee shirt, glared at me from angry eyes set in his sleep-ridden face. Then he stepped through the doorway and with a two-armed blow smashed the Wagoneer's left headlight with a shiny, new twenty-four inch monkey wrench.

I backed in a slow arc over the damp lumpy sand, drawing him away from the house, and weapons, and help.

That he had no boots on was good; that he had the monkey wrench was not.

He followed me, the wrench standing stiffly in the hand at his side. "What the fuck's with you, Ross."

"I'll ask you once, Whip. Where's Glory?"

"Fuck you."

"Then let's do it."

The veins in his arms swelled under the weight of the wrench. His face thinned to bone. His eyes went cold.

He came in a slow circle, turning me, whipping the damp air easily with the wrench. I edged closer, giving him a target. He crouched, feinted, swung the wrench at my knees. I skipped back, leaned in, threw a right that hit his forehead and snapped his head back, dug a left into his ribs, a knee into his stomach, another right to the center of his face. Bone cracked, blood spurted, but he didn't go down.

Spinning out of range, he wiped at his face, looked at the blood. His lips twisting over his blood-smeared teeth, he crouched, came again, faster, quicker. I took the blow of the wrench on the back of my thigh, hit him in the face fast and hard three times, drove him into the sand.

As I stepped back into kicking range I heard a soft shush of sand, hiss of breath, sensed shadow, tried to dodge, felt sudden searing pain at the base of my skull.

Instinctively pivoting, I brought my leg up in a savage round-kick that had all my weight behind it. My foot caught Veronica Hardesty in the chest and she dropped to the sand, breathless, the spike-heeled silver shoe still in her hand.

I got turned back enough that the wrench slammed into the soft, boneless part of my lower back. Gasping in pain, I stumbled. The silver wrench flashed at my head. I grabbed his wrist in both hands and jerked. As the wrench fell from his hands, a stunning blow drove me into the sand.

I tried to roll, but he was on me, fists banging on my head. I smelled fear, rank. His. Mine.

On my side, I got an elbow free and slammed it into the side of his head. He sagged, I rolled and got to my knees.

Silver flashed toward my head. I dived toward it, crashed into Veronica Hardesty's skinny legs, took the wrench on the back. I drove my fist into the side of her head, rolled with the force of the foot that smashed into my ribs.

Rusted barbs snagged the fabric of my running suit.

With an ugly, animal face, making ugly, animal sounds,

Whip threw himself at me. His weight drove the barbs of the fence into my back. Locking his arms around me, he pulled me back and forth over the fence.

The pain in my back was sharp, his breath in my face foul. Struggling, I got both hands together, drove them up into his stomach. His grip slackened. I drove my hands up into his groin. His grip loosened. I drove my hands again into his stomach, shoving him off me.

Flesh and fabric stayed on the barbs of the fence as I jerked away from it. I made it to my knees, my feet.

He came at me again. I kicked him in the chest, driving my toe under his rib cage, feeling the rip of ligament and tendon. Hurt, he staggered back, and I followed, ducking a flailing fist. I hit him a dozen hard times in the face before he went down. I kicked him until he stopped moving.

Blood from his mouth and nose stained the sand. His arms cradled his ribs as if to protect them. His breathing was short, ragged, noisy. I left him there.

Veronica Hardesty was sitting in the sand, her head tilted sharply to one side, her haggard face bloodless, her mouth open and gasping still for breath. The tattooed fly seemed struggling to escape as her flesh quivered.

"Where's Glory?"

"Is . . . he dead?"

"No. Where's Glory?"

"You'd better kill him while you can. He'll come after you."

"Where's Glory?"

"I can't . . ."

"I'll ruin your face, Veronica, make you ugly. He'll throw you out."

Her eyes filled with fear. "No, he. . . ."

I took a step closer, made a fist. "Where is she?"

It came, finally, with the sharp sough of a bitter wind. "Mustang."

I stepped back. "If you're lying to me, I'll be back."

"No. Mustang." She took a slow deep breath, her face

twisting into ugliness from the pain. "Where she belongs, the whore. She knew nobody'd ever look for her there."

Sand matted her hair, her face was thin and blanched and tight with pain, her small floppy breasts hung under her thin nightgown like the dugs of a bred-out sow, her legs were thin and dirty and veiny. I should have felt something for her, I knew vaguely, but I didn't.

I limped back to the Wagoneer. The door to the house was still open. The older child stood in it, shivering in his undershorts, watching me. I felt nothing for him either.

Showers grayed the Sierra; from gray-gutted clouds virga hung over the city like a dying wish.

I drove back to town, my body stiffening to match my inner empty cold. Blood trickled from the base of my skull, congealed on my neck as if to hold my head in place for the stabs of pain that shot through it with each irregularity in the roadway. Blood matted my back, pasting my shredded suit to my shredded flesh. My thigh ached. Under my stiff lower back my insides felt frozen by a dull pain.

In another of my shirts, Dolly sat at the kitchen table, enjoying coffee and Schubert. Her eyes enlarged. I went into the bedroom and began undressing, and she followed.

"You're hurt."

"I'm all right. You'd better go home."

"Jack . . . what happened?"

Avoiding her big eyes, I told her what I'd found in Sun Valley. She sagged onto the bed. "Pete Lotz, he killed her?"

"No."

"Then who . . .?"

"I don't know. Go home, Dolly."

"Jack, you're bleeding, your back. You need a doctor."

Naked, I turned to face her. "Go home." I went into the bathroom, the shower.

Dolly came into the shower.

"Goddamit, Dolly—"

"Shut up. Let me see." I let her see. "Jesus Christ," she said. She took a wash cloth and cleaned the cuts on my back as the hot water boiled in them, as it soaked her hair, her body, my shirt. Then she left.

When I came out, Dolly sat again on the bed, dry and in another of my shirts, with a fistful of Band-Aids.

"Come here and turn around." I did. "You need a doctor. Maybe stitches. What did this."

"A barbed wire fence."

"Then you need a tetanus shot."

"Later." Her hands felt soft on my back.

"Stupid macho bastard. What are you going to do?"

"I'm going to get Glory."

"Where is she?"

"In a whorehouse."

That silenced her. She finished, and I dressed as quickly as I could. "I want you to go home, Dolly. Tell everyone to stay there. I'll bring Glory to them."

"I . . . shouldn't you call the police?"

"No." I sat beside her. We were miles apart. "Go home."

Her eyes were telling me something. I didn't know what it was. So I told her something.

"Go home, Dolly. I'll be there in a while. And when I get there, I'm going to destroy your family."

"But . . . why?"

"To stop the killing."

She didn't know precisely what that meant. Or she was afraid she did know what it meant.

"And us, Jack? Are you going to destroy us too?"

"How are you going to feel about someone who's destroying the people you love?"

"If it's you, Jack, I'll still love you."

"You told me you'd never lie to me, Dolly."

"I'm not . . . I mean. . . ." She didn't know what she meant. But I did.

I left her sitting there.

# 32

From the interstate, the road bent around a salvage yard, then twisted through small hay fields down to the Truckee River and crossed a narrow bridge to Mustang Ranch.

At ten in the morning, the fast-flesh business boomed. The parking lot was filled with everything from big bikes to muddy four-wheelers to motor homes. The sun flickered through clouds building up to showers. In its light the brothel looked like a pink-stuccoed and tile-roofed concentration camp, complete with high wire fence and watch tower.

From that tower Oscar Buonavena, the Argentinian boxer, had been shot in the heart. I saw no one ready to shoot me.

I pressed the gate bell, at a click pushed through and listened to it click behind me. Just inside the front door, a middle-aging redhead gave me a bright smile and a quick scan: in boots, jeans, and a soft chamois shirt, I shouldn't have looked like trouble, but something in my face gave her pause before she gushed her official greeting.

"Welcome to Mustang. The girls are eager to serve you, if you would like to make your choice."

In the center of a large room edged with the fat couches and chairs you find in dentists' offices, seven young women lined up like a candelabrum. Attired in lingerie and cocktail gowns and bikinis, they came in assorted hues, sizes, and shapes. All the smiles were the same: expectant. All the eyes were the same: bored.

Then one of the smiles, one set of eyes, changed.

She wore black sluttish brocade, a cap of blond wig, and makeup so extravagant—heavy red mouth, thick blush and mascara and silver eyeshadow—that it added several hard years to her face. As I neared, her eyes pleaded.

I made a show of examining the menu. Behind the lineup, men sat at the bar with the girls who'd serviced them. From the juke box came the groveling of Barry Manilow, about wanting to do "it" with an anonymous "you."

I ran the gauntlet of brittle smiles and blank eyes, stepped back, surveyed the line, held out my hand to Glory.

"Enjoy yourself," the redhead smiled, as the other girls quickly moved back to their couches and conversations.

Glory led me silently into a narrow hallway, into a small room containing a bed, a nightstand, a small dresser, and, in the corner, a low stainless steel sink.

When she spoke, it was with both voice and eyes. "My name's Helen, honey. What's yours?" Her eyes said, "Please be very careful."

The rooms were wired. For the protection of the girls, the owners said. No one had ever demonstrated otherwise.

"Menelaus."

"So what did you have in mind?"

It was her show, her theater. "What do you recommend?"

She watched me, uncertain. "For a hundred you can have an hour, we can use the jacuzzi?"

"Fine." I took a bill from my wallet and gave it to her.

"You can get undressed, honey. I'll be right back."

I undressed. Then she was back and out of her dress. Her smooth slim young body mocked the garishly makeup face. "Let's check you out, shall we?"

She was already checking me out. Her gaze skittered over the bruise on my thigh, the bruises on my back. And the Band-Aids. And the ooze of new blood I could feel. Her eyes flashed me messages I couldn't decipher.

At the sink, she took my flaccid penis in her hand. It did not stir. "You've got a nice one there, honey. Nice and clean too. So, you want to come first, or try the jacuzzi?"

"Whatever."

From the dresser she took two large towels, wrapped one around her. "Come on, honey. Let's soak and relax."

We went back down the hall and into a room with a large jacuzzi. She flicked a switch and the water churned. She dropped her towel and eased into the water. I followed her.

The steady pulse of the warm water against my bruises felt wonderful. Against the cuts it felt less wonderful. Glory pressed her breasts against my shoulder, lay her lips next to my ear. "What do you want? Leave me alone."

I whispered back. "The police want to talk to you about Haskell. And your grandfather wants to meet you."

She leaned back. "You found him?"

At my nod, her eyes filled with delight. Then they muddied. She leaned against me. "I can't. He'll kill me."

"Who?"

"Whoever it was—he was shooting at me."

I could indulge her, coax it out of her, spend the morning protecting her cover as I convinced her that she had to come back to town. I didn't want to.

All I wanted was out of there, out of it all.

Pulling myself up out of the water, I took up my towel and announced in a normal tone and for the benefit of microphones: "Whoever killed Haskell killed your grandmother last night. It's time to stop the killing. Let's go."

She stood in the waist deep water, stunned, blank-eyed.

"Is the boss here, or Angela?" At her nod, I said, "I'll be in your room."

I was at the door when I heard a weak croak. "Emmy?"

"She's all right."

As I passed the doorway to the parlor and bar, I saw the redhead in close conversation with a very large man and a small, pleasant-faced blonde. Angela.

I was dressed and slipping into my boots when Glory came

in. Angela was with her. She left the door open. A large body breathed just beyond it.

"Excuse me, sir. Is there some sort of problem?"

"No problem, Angela." I rose.

She was fifty, pretty, well-preserved. In her pale lemon skirt and blouse she might have been a bank teller or real estate agent. She'd been in the life for nearly thirty-five years, had seen it all, could handle it all.

"Have we met?"

I took a business card from my wallet. "No. But if the boss isn't around, you're the person to see."

"About what?"

"About Helen here. Her name is Glory Dahlman and she's wanted for questioning in a murder she witnessed."

The woman turned to Glory. "Is that right?"

Glory didn't answer. She didn't have to. The tears carving channels through her makeup said enough.

"What is it you want?" Angela said, turning back to me.

"I want to take her with me. That's the simplest for all concerned. Otherwise, the authorities will come out."

"How does a private investigator fit into this?"

"I was hired by Miss Dahlman."

Glory's wet eyes confirmed that.

"This doesn't make much sense," Angela said. "Hel—you know this guy? Is he straight?" At Glory's dismal nod, she added, "Then you'd better go with him. This kind of trouble we don't need, honey. Get your things."

Glory dropped the towel, turned to the dresser.

Angela glanced at my card. "Let's go to the bar, Jack. I'll buy you a drink."

Disappointment clotted in the eyes of the big man in the hallway as I passed him.

I drank vodka while Angela pumped me. I evaded her questions, watched the business of the brothel: the unengaged girls leaping up from couches and scurrying in from the kitchen at the sound of the buzzer announcing customers at the gate;

the recently engaged girls linked arm-in-arm with the men they'd just relieved of tension, semen, and cash.

"Pretty good, that one," Angela said. "I must be slipping. She had me convinced she was just another bimbo. You sure she's not in real trouble?"

"Not unless she slipped out of here last night and killed her grandmother."

"Nobody slips out of here. But you probably know that."

Sudden psychic temblors rumbled through the room. Heads, eyes, swiveled to their source.

Glory stood in the hallway door, in jeans and a crisp white blouse, her face clean and fresh, her hair brushed smooth and glossy. She looked lovely, stunning, *real*.

Reality had no place at Mustang. Angela hurried from the bar and nudged Glory out of the doorway. I followed them down the hall, into the huge kitchen. Three empty-eyed young women stared at us over their coffee.

Angela propelled Glory straight to the door. "That address you gave any good? I'll send you your money."

"Send it to her in care of me," I said. We slid through the door and were out.

We negotiated gates and walked to the Wagoneer. As I fired it up and pulled out of the parking lot, Glory spoke.

"Are you sure Emmy's all right?"

"Lily has her."

"I . . . Gramma, what happened?"

I told her about Lily's call and what I'd found.

She was crying softly. "But why would anyone . . .?"

"Why would anyone kill Haskell?"

"I told you. They were shooting at me."

"Tell me what happened. All of it."

As we drove to the interstate and through the Truckee River Canyon under a boiling and scuddy sky, she told me.

After leaving me, Glory had gone back to the Hilton, and she and Haskell had walked to his trailer park. Near his trailer, the old Shoshone suddenly froze, then stepped in front of Glory and pushed her down into the dusty gravel. Glory heard a shot, more flatulent *phhtt!* than bang, heard Haskell's grunt, saw him double over. Then he gave her a small melancholy smile and ran into the night.

The canyon widened, and the city spread before us, sun-patched and cloud-shadowed and ablaze with perpetual neon.

"I thought," Glory sniffed, "I thought he was trying to get away—but he didn't run *from* where the shot came, he ran *at* it. And then he was gone."

"You didn't see who fired the shot?"

"I didn't see anything. Uncle Haskell pushed me down, and it wasn't light yet, and I heard him running, and heard somebody else running. Then I ran. I didn't know what to do, you know, I was scared. I didn't know where Haskell was or anything. I called Whip. Is he how you found me?"

I nodded.

"I didn't think he'd tell. Your back—he did that?"

"Why did you go to Haskell's place with him?"

"I—no reason, really. We were just talking, and he said he'd fix us breakfast."

"What were you talking about?"

"You. How you were going to find my grandfather."

"What did he say about that?"

"He said that you'd take care of me. He. . . ."

"What?"

"It was the way he said it, like he knew he wasn't going to be there, like he knew. . . ."

Taking the 395 South exit, I said, "You're going to have to tell the police all this."

"I . . . know. But I'm scared, Jack. Somebody tried to kill me, and I don't know who."

"No. They couldn't have known you'd be with Haskell. They were waiting for him."

"But why? Why would anyone want to kill Haskell?"

"It's a long story. I'm going to tell it only once, in a few minutes."

Her voice, when she spoke again, had lost its edge of fear, had it blunted by concern. "Where are we going?"

"To see your grandfather."

"It's not him, is it, Jack? He didn't kill Haskell and Gramma?"

I didn't answer. I drove, grimly.

On Del Monte Lane, Glory said, "How did Emmy get to Lily's house?"

"That's a good question."

Glory stared as we pulled up in front of the big white house. "My grandfather, Lawrence Parker, he lives here?"

Again I didn't answer.

"Jack, I . . ."

She didn't finish. She didn't have to. It was too much for her, too risky. The dream she'd conceived and delivered and nurtured like a frail child in the grimness of Sun Valley was about to become real, take on flesh. And vanish.

It evoked little sympathy in me. If it was time that I grew up, became an adult, it was time that Glory grew up too.

"I . . . what did you tell him?"

"The truth." Which was more than Gabriel George, or anyone connected with him, had told me. But this time, in the big white house, I would be doing the talking.

# 33

The arc of the drive was jammed with vehicles—the pickups, the Bentley and the Lincoln, the Land Rover, the fifty-four T-bird. I squeezed the Wagoneer in beside it.

Glory stared at it, then at me. "I don't understand."

"Welcome to the club." Leaving Glory to follow, I got out and climbed the steps.

In the corner of the screened porch, in a wicker couch, Ann Ripley kept her silent vigil. Fashionably mourning, she wore black cashmere. Her legs were sleek and white, her hair shining like polished plate.

She glanced at me, then jerked her gaze from my face as if from some unspeakable ugliness. Her eyes fixed on Glory, who stood hesitantly before the house.

"Did you see your mother last night, Mrs. Ripley?"

"Yes." Her arms folded beneath her breasts as if she were cold. She didn't know what cold was.

"Was she alive?"

"I—" She seemed to look through me now, to Glory.

"You took Emily to Lily's, didn't you?"

"I—" Her throat seemed to constrict. "Is that—"

"Glory," I said, turning to the girl, "come here."

When she stood beside me, I said: "Mrs. Ripley, allow me to present your niece, Glory Dahlman. Glory, this is your Aunt Anemone." My voice sounded strange in my ears, icy.

In the shadows Glory's face seemed ghostly, as her grandmother's had the day before. Her mouth opened and made words, but none came out. She sagged, stumbled. Then Ann Ripley was up and had her niece in her arms, cradling her. Leading the girl to the wicker couch, she eased her down, sat beside her, took her deeper into her arms.

"Go away, Jack." Ann Ripley still did not look at me.

"Glory needs to come in with me. So do you."

She turned on me fiercely. "She's had enough."

"Life is hard," I said. "She has information. So do you. It's got to get out."

"Not now. Not from me. I—" Her eyes flashed. "All right. I found my mother and . . . the man. I took Emmy to Lily's house. Now leave us alone."

"It's going to all come out, Ann."

"So let it. Just leave us alone."

I looked down at them, then turned away. They were as well off out here, in their miserable reunion, as they were inside. I left them to it.

Without knocking I opened the door and stepped inside. My bootheels thumped on the glossy, pitted hardwood floor of the hallway. I went into the den.

Wide-shouldered, wedge-backed, Hayes and Bobby George sat at opposite ends of the bar, like book ends on an empty shelf. I moved around behind it and started fixing a drink.

Bobby nodded his head. His face was stained with a bloody residue of anger. He looked exhausted.

"Move right in, Ross. Take over the place. What's the matter—run out of bodies to dig up?" Hayes's big-featured face was grinning.

"Get your parents, and Ripley."

"What about Dolly Darlin'? Had enough of her, have you?"

"Shut up, Hayes," Bobby said weakly.

Hayes kept grinning. "Up yours, sonny."

Bobby flushed, his shoulders stiffening. But he couldn't work up any more real anger. His head drooped over the thick arms crossed on the top of the bar.

Hayes's big face split in a bigger grin. "Feels good, doesn't it, Ross? Power. Exercising it. You've got a little right now, I'd guess. Enjoy it."

I didn't answer. Hayes continued to smile. Bobby's flush faded. He glanced from his brother to me, then slid from the stool and left the room.

"Got it all figured out?"

I didn't answer. The vodka was cold. I was colder.

Then Dolly was in the doorway. She slipped into the room cautiously, as if I were some long-loved pet that might now be rabid. Settling into a chair, she sat watching me.

I drank more vodka.

Frederick Ripley, more in servility than graciousness, ushered in Alice and Gabriel George, shoved aside Bobby George, and came in himself. Bobby followed wearily.

"Dolly told us about Flora and Pete Lotz, Jack," Gabriel George said, moving quickly toward the bar. "It must have been unpleasant for you. I'm sorry."

"Sorry don't cut it."

He stopped, gave me a look, edged over beside his wife. Her brown eyes watched me steadily.

"Hey, real clever, Ross." Hayes rumbled a laugh as his parents sat on the couch beside their daughter. "Got everybody rounded up like in Agatha Christie. Now you can show us how your wonderful little gray cells solved the puzzle, Hercule."

"What do you want of us, Mr. Ross?" Alice George asked.

"I want to be free of you," I said. "And as soon as I say my piece, I will be. Then the Sheriff and the police will take over."

The only real response came from Dolly. Her mouth opened as if gasping for air.

"Ca'mon, Ross—whodunit? Whatever it was."

"Be quiet, Hayes," his mother snapped.

"Your daughter will tell you that I love to tell stories, Mrs. George. I'm going to tell one now."

"Just a minute, Ross," Ripley said. He stood before a window, in another beautiful and beautifully slimming suit, blocking the light. "We agreed that certain matters would remain private. You will adhere to that agreement."

"Any contract we had was broken a long time ago. Every other word out of your mouth has been a lie, Ripley. And four people have died. But the killing stops here, now."

"Four? How can there be—"

"I'll tell you how." I poured more vodka. Either the vodka or my inner emptiness was numbing me.

"Once upon a time there was a young drifter who killed a boy in a fight over a girl in Winnemucca. That young man's name was Lawrence Parker. He ran into the desert, came out the other side at the ranch of Dolores and Barney Dahlman. There he received a new identity. He became Gabriel George."

Dolly turned to stare at her father. Everyone else looked at me.

Frederick Ripley's blue eyes were pulsing like a quasar. "You'll rue the day, Ross, that you ever presumed to—"

"Be quiet, Frederick." Alice George snapped at the president of Hollister Corporation as she had at her son.

"You, Mr. George, told me that Parker was dead, that Haskell Dan shot him to put him out of his misery. I didn't believe that then and I don't believe it now."

"Surely, Mr. Ross, you can see why Gabe would tell you that, knowing that you were tracking. . . ."

"Yes, I can see it," I said. "What you can't see, Mrs. George, is that it never mattered. Lawrence Parker is wanted for murder, but there was no murder. I repeat: *there was no murder.* The only witness to the killing of Daryl Lotz, Flora Magnusson, said so. It was self-defense, clearly."

"We've been over this, Mr. Ross. It doesn't matter that a murder in fact was not committed."

"Like hell it doesn't. Four people died because of it."

"Come on, Ross," Hayes leaned at me. "What four?"

"Ask your father."

"That's enough." Ripley moved from the window, stood behind the couch. "We don't have to listen to this. To accuse Gabe of murder is insane. Hayes, call the Sheriff."

"Call him yourself, you fat-assed wimp. You think I'm your goddamned errand boy?" Hayes's face darkened with anger.

"I didn't accuse him of anything. I told you to ask him about the four who've been killed." I faced Gabriel George. "You told me so yourself, out at the ranch. It all goes back to him, you said. And you were right."

"Stuart? Stuart Dahlman?"

"And your daughter, Rose. Your daughter."

"My daughter," he said very quietly. "They were killed? Is that what you're saying? By whom?"

"They were killed. Except of course at this point no one can prove it. But they were murdered because Stuart Dahlman was doing what someone is trying now—blackmail."

"Excuse me again, Mr. Ross." Alice George was still calm. "You're suggesting that Stuart Dahlman discovered Gabe's identity and tried to extort—from whom, Gabe?"

"Maybe. Or from your father. Or Ripley—I know he was blackmailing Ripley with other information. Or maybe it was you, Mrs. George. I don't know, but it—"

"You don't know shit, Ross." Hayes spat. "I was hoping for better than this."

"You were hoping I'd tell everyone that Ann Ripley was born Anemone Baker, that she's Flora Baker's daughter, Rose Dahlman's sister, Glory Dahlman's aunt. *Quel coincidence!*"

"That's better," he laughed. "Now we're getting to the good stuff. So tell us, Monsieur Poirot, what does it mean?"

"It means that Ann had something on Ripley, something serious enough to make him marry her to keep her quiet. She says it has to do with rape."

"You son of a bitch!" Ripley came toward the bar. I found myself hoping he'd come around it. His face, a mottle of white and red and purple, looked like the bruise on my back. "You're walking right into a slander suit."

"Be quiet, Frederick." I mimicked Alice George's tone. "I might also tell them about your sexual predilections."

His fleshy mouth sputtered spittle. He stumbled back from the bar as if he'd been struck.

Hayes George's laugh bounced off the walls. "All right, Ross! Now we're getting somewhere."

"I don't know who killed your daughter, Mr. George. Maybe you did. I know it was someone in your family."

But he was gone, behind his eyes, wandering in that gray desert within. Dolly's big eyes were filled with horror.

"That was good, Ross," Hayes said. "Ancient history,

though. You couldn't prove anything if you wanted to. Any other revelations?"

"How about the fact that your father is now being blackmailed by his own son?"

"Sorry, no cigar. I'm not blackmailing anybody."

"I didn't say you were."

For the first time, no one spoke. They all stared at the other George son, who sat alone at the end of the bar.

"Hey," Bobby sheepishly raised his head and tried to grin. "It was no big deal. I mean, I just sort of found it out by accident, you know, and I thought. . . ."

"Bobby," his mother said in a painful whisper. "Why?"

"I needed the money to pay off Vegas. Except I couldn't just make it two hundred thousand or right away you'd know it was me. I . . . the money was sort of mine anyway, I'll get that much and a lot more some day. I just wanted it now."

His mother shook her head. "But those gambling debts aren't collectable. You don't have to pay them."

His eyes pled for understanding. "I *do* have to pay them."

I understood. "Because until you do, you can't play."

His head hung in a nod.

"Oh, Bobby," his mother said. "Is it that bad?"

He didn't answer. He didn't have to.

"Another mystery solved. The Case of the Desperate Deadbeat. Way to go, Perry." Hayes turned to his brother. "Pretty dumb, booby."

"Right," I said. "Dumb. Except that it got two more people killed, Haskell Dan and Flora Baker."

Alice George rose from the couch and came to the bar. "Who killed these people, Mr. Ross?"

"I don't know. But there's a tantalizing tale to be told in the mud outside Flora Baker's trailer. The Sheriff will have had casts made of the tire tracks and footprints by now. When I tell him where he'll find the tires and the shoes that made those tracks, he'll sort it out."

"You think that a member of my family has committed four murders? You're distraught. Dolly says you've had some rather harrowing experiences recently. The events this morning couldn't have helped." The voice was laced with a sort of objective compassion, but her brown eyes didn't waver. "You're not especially rational."

"I'm rational enough to know that you will do whatever you have to to protect your family, even if one of them is a murderer."

"You intend to make these charges to the authorities?"

"I intend to tell the authorities what I know."

"Which, in actual knowledge, is next to nothing."

"But enough. With the tracks, the sheriff will have plenty of questions for you."

"And I will answer them, especially those concerning the tracks. I'd be happy to tell you, but I don't think you want to hear." For a moment she was silent. Her eyes assessed me, but not coldly. "I'm sorry you were brought into this. It's clearly exacerbated an unstable emotional condition. I'm sorry for that, I apologize. Now I think you'd better go."

"I agree. I have one more message to deliver. Glory Dahlman is outside on the porch, with her aunt."

I drained my drink.

"Hey, Ross. You can't leave it like that." Hayes was grinning. This was fun. "Ca'mon, who did the dirty deed?"

"I don't know."

"You're going to leave it that way?"

"Maybe the Sheriff and the cops can sort it out. I doubt it, since the only people who know what's going on aren't going to talk. But even if they learn who shotgunned Flora Baker, nothing's going to happen. You've got too much juice. There might be a little publicity, a few stories in the papers, Hollister Corporation stock might dance a little, but nobody's going to be prosecuted for murder." I tried to force my face into a smile. "Isn't that right, Mrs. George?"

"Yes."

"Thank you for the booze." I looked around the room at them, stopped at Dolly. Her big eyes were full of tears.

There was nothing I could do about that.

I left.

Ann Ripley and Glory Dahlman were still on the porch. I walked past them.

I drove into town. The sky was dark, threatening, but no thunder rumbled, no rain fell.

At the Sheriff's office, I asked that Frank Calvetti be called. I didn't want to have to tell my story twice. When he got there, I told it.

I had to tell it a dozen times. The Sheriff didn't like my story. I didn't blame him. There was nothing he could get his hands on, except the tires. They asked me about the tracks so many times that I finally understood why.

It was twilight when I walked out with Frank. It hadn't rained, and it wouldn't. The sky was big and blue and empty.

Frank said, "You know what happened, don't you?"

"They fucked up the tracks."

"The first cars responding pulled right up to the door."

"Not that it matters," I said.

"I'd hate to think that."

"Think what you want, Frank. It won't matter."

He looked at me for a while. "What now, Jack?"

"I'm going to the desert."

He nodded. "All things considered, that might be a good idea. I'll see you when you get back."

"I'm not coming back."

My old friend looked at me. "What does that mean?"

"I don't know," I said. "But I know it's the truth."

I got in the Wagoneer and fired it up and pulled away from the curb and left him standing there.

At my apartment I called my daughter and told her that I'd be gone for a while. I told my ex-wife where I'd be. I told my ex-wife's husband to put my business and building on the market, and my personal possessions in a mini-warehouse.

Then I loaded some things in the jeep and drove it to the desert.

# 34

A heavy July haze blued the distant ranges. Shimmering scrims of heat hung in the still air over the hard-baked playa. A thin column of dust rose in the distance.

The dust stream grew, neared. The pickup making it sliced across the desert as if homing on me. At the edge of the playa it slowed, eased up onto the sand and gravel and brush of the slope, slowed again, and, four wheels pulling, crept toward the shaded rock I sat on.

Jess Harkness lifted a finger from the steering wheel in greeting as he eased the pickup past me, to the trickle of water that fought its way out of a narrow canyon. He followed it back around a bend.

I followed it back too, through the heat and the still, to my camp.

In the shade of the tarp spread between the roof of the Wagoneer and two poles of twisted pinion, he squatted before my pit of sage coals, pouring coffee from the big can that served as my pot into the small can that served as my cup.

I slipped into the shade and sat beside him in the sand.

"Hope you don't mind."

"Help yourself."

"Thanks." He sipped at the coffee. "Nice layout."

It was functional. The coal bed, the shade, my sleeping bag rolled up on the tailgate, my stores stacked behind it. Ten yards from the nose of the Wagoneer, wisps of steam hovered over the small pool that was the hot spring. Ten yards beyond it, the canyon curved in on itself and ended. Beyond that the range rose in ragged steps.

"How'd you find it?"

"Just wandered around till I came to it. How'd you?"

"It's a big country out here," Jess Harkness said, "but it's empty. Easy for folks to keep tabs on who's in it. You mind company?"

"No."

He screwed the can securely into the sand. "Brought something for you." He handed me a paper sack.

I pulled out my shirt. It was neatly pressed, smelled fresh, showed no sign of blood. From the pocket protruded five one-thousand-dollar bills.

I took out the bills and spread them on the sand between us. Slipping the shirt back into the sack, I said, "She did a nice job on it. Please thank her for me."

"I'll do that."

"I don't want your money."

"It's yours. You found Lawrence Parker."

"Right where you sent me."

He shrugged.

"Give it to charity."

"Ain't mine to give. You can, if you want."

We left the bills in the sand.

For a while we were silent. The still, heavy heat sucked sweat in beads like precious metals from my back and belly.

Finally Jess Harkness tossed the dregs of his coffee into the coal pit. "You still in the detective business?"

"No."

"Too bad. I could use a good detective about now."

"I know a couple I can recommend."

"Wouldn't work. Too much background work to do, too many trails wiped out already."

"Sorry."

"Yeah," he said. "Me too. Jan'll be sorrier than either of us, though. It's driving her crazy, not knowing. The Reno Sheriff doesn't know if Pete killed Flora or not. Probably, he says. Pete fired the shotgun, they know that. That's not enough for Jan."

"What does the Sheriff say about the tire tracks?"

"The way I heard it, both Mrs. George and Mrs. Ripley say they were there. Mrs. George was in the Land Rover. She and her husband were coming in from the desert and it was raining and he didn't want her driving the Bentley. She said she just stopped to have a chat with Flora, to find out what she was willing to swear to."

I grabbed a handful of sand, squeezed it tightly in my fist, and watched it trickle out.

"What does Pete say?"

He shrugged. "Doesn't remember anything. Or if he does he hasn't said. They got him at Lake's Crossing."

"How is he?"

"Hard to tell. Shrinks are as hard to understand as lawyers. They're talking senility, Alzheimer's disease, schizophrenia—I don't think they really know."

I looked across the canyon the water had carved over the centuries. On its wall was the story of more centuries, millennia. Deep time, in neat, sharply demarcated layers.

"Pete didn't kill Flora."

"You know that for a fact?"

"No."

"You know who did?"

"No."

He nodded at his big hard belly. Sitting as I did, cross-legged in the sand, he looked like a cowboy Buddha whose face had been gouged and scarred by the desert.

"Been thinking about it, out here?"

"Some. When I couldn't escape it."

"Come to any conclusions?"

"Not really. Notions, mostly. Questions. Guesses."

After a while he said: "Humboldt D. A. says there's not enough evidence to take Gabriel George to trial on a murder charge, now that Flora's dead."

"There wouldn't be if she were alive. She told me that it was self-defense. She was ready to make a statement."

"The D. A. didn't mention any statement. But it doesn't much matter, I guess."

"You always knew that's what happened, didn't you?"

"I wasn't around then. Up to my ears in Anzio mud. But I knew Daryl, and Pete."

After a while he said: "Talked to Gabe George a while back. Nice fellow."

"Seems to be."

"Kind of surprised me, though."

"How's that?"

"I don't know, exactly. But the thing he went through, crossing the Black Rock and all, it leaves a mark on a man. I didn't see any mark."

"It's in his eyes."

"Something's in them. Maybe that's it."

We sat for a while. Then he said, "Nice out here. I wish I could sneak off once in a while and do this."

"Why don't you?"

"Work to do."

"Get somebody else to do it."

"There isn't anybody else."

"Maybe not," I said.

"You figure there's no way to find out the truth?"

I thought about it. Again. "There might be."

"How much trouble would it be?"

"Some. It'd cause more."

"People get hurt? Innocent people?"

I nodded.

"Tough one to figure, huh?"

"Tough," I said.

"The thing is, Pete was a son of a bitch. . . ."

"One registered son of a bitch, Spoon White says."

"Yeah. He caused lots of pain, lots of problems for folks. It'd take a tombstone the size of the Grand to list them all. But for it to say he killed an old woman that he didn't . . . well, whatever he was, *that* just isn't right."

"Are you sure you know what right is, Jess?"

"About all I know is that a fella's got to decide what needs to be done and then do the best he can to get it done." He looked at me and smiled. "Sounds simple, doesn't it."

"Things tend to get simple out here."

"But not necessarily right?"

"Simple tends to be right."

"Tends to," he repeated. He struggled to his feet. "Best be on my way."

I rose. "I can't let you go with just coffee in you."

Reaching into the jeep, I grabbed the Glenlivit, still in its box, and handed it to Jess Harkness. "Uncork that thing, will you?"

While he removed the bottle and stripped off the thin waxy paper, I got out plastic cups and a jug of water. He half filled the cups, shook his head at the water.

The scotch had a soft smooth peaty bite. Jess Harkness sipped it and smiled. "Been saving this, have you?"

"For the right company."

He again looked around the canyon. Brown rock, tan sand, gray and dusty sage, a stain of green at the edge of the water. "Too bad a man can't just stay out here."

"Some do, Jess."

He tossed off the rest of the scotch. "And go crazy."

"Most of them. Not all."

"Better men than me," he said.

He gave me the plastic cup, and his hand. "Thanks."

In his seamed and scarred and lumpy face, his brown eyes shone with a steady, weary wisdom. "You're welcome."

He trudged through the sand to his pickup, fired it up, gave me a brief wave, and backed out of the canyon.

The five thousand-dollar bills still lay in the sand. I looked down at them for a while. Then I picked them up and put them in my pocket.

I spent another night in the desert. I sat on my rock and watched the darkness come, listened to the big silence, scanned the starry and indifferent sky.

Then I slept, awoke, broke camp, left it as much as I'd found it as I could, and drove out of the desert.

# 35

Reno and Sparks baked brown in the hazy mid-afternoon heat. After dropping off the Wagoneer to get its headlight replaced, I walked through the acrid city air to the Sparks Nugget and checked in and took my first shower in nearly two months. Then I got on the phone.

My daughter was in the mountains at music camp. My ex-wife's husband had sold my business and my building, pending my signature on the papers. My things were in a warehouse.

I went downstairs and got my hair cut. I kept my beard. Then I walked over to Gazin's, bought some clothes, went back to the room and changed, went downstairs and had a leisurely dinner. Then I walked over to the Silver Saddle Club.

A new photograph decorated the wall beside the main entrance. Lily Baker, alone, grinned into the evening, her ruffled blouse replaced by a bit of sequined cloth and a chasm of cleavage.

Inside, business was better. I had to nudge my way to the bar. The help wore their bright brittle working masks.

I nursed a Coke before the show, another through it. There was no group now: just Lily. Three new guitarists and a drummer made up a distant background, much of the time, as the spots focused on Lily, in darkness. But they played well, and Lily took from them and sang even better.

She had developed a patter, a folksy, raunchily good-humored routine consisting mostly of comments on her costume and her body. Her audience—the house was full—loved it.

So did Hayes George.

A half hour into the show, he slid into a chair beside me. The shifting light from the stage softened his features and colored his grin. At the end of each number, his rumble of a voice swelled the hoot and holler of appreciation.

Lily finished her show, took her encores. The applause died, the lights came all the way up. The audience, awash in the hum and crackle of residual energy, emptied.

Hayes George and I stayed. His grin grew bigger. So did the silence, punctuated by the shoe-scuff and glass-clink of the busboys clearing tables, till he broke it: "That fur on your face supposed to be a disguise, Ross?"

I didn't answer.

He shook his heavy head. "Don't be that way. You played the game and you lost. Happens all the time in Nevada."

I didn't answer.

"So what do you want? What are you doing here?"

"I came to see Lily."

"An evening's entertainment. Just another tourist." He started to smile. "So you saw her. You're still here."

"I came to talk to her."

"What for?"

"Because I know where she is."

"What? Oh, I get it. Well, lemme fill you in. The continuing saga. Bobby-boy's back on the tour, properly chastised and repentant, on an allowance, being good. Playing good, too—made four cuts in a row. His momma done paid off Vegas, with the stipulation that he never be allowed a line of credit in Nevada again. An' he's gonna marry his bimbo, once she's finished taking the cure."

His head shook slowly in mock despair. "Gramps must be rolling in his grave. It'd been R. Hayes Hollister, he'd of just beat the shit out of Bobby and put Tracy-baby out on her back till her nose rotted away. Times change, though, an' we gotta change with 'em. Right, Ross?"

"It's your story."

"Yeah. Anyway, the old man's back in the desert and the old lady's in Frisco with Ripley and Ann-of-the-gorgeous-ass's out in the Valley where she belongs."

I didn't say anything.

"All that fuss, Ross, for nothing. Like you said. My killer old man's in the clear. Nobody cares who took out Stuart Dahlman and his wife, if anybody did. Nobody cares who took out the Indian. They figure the old guy for Lily's mother because that's all they've got. All that about tire tracks—an hour of questions, that's all it amounted to."

When I didn't answer, he leaned back in his chair.

"You would be well-advised to abjure the posturing, Ross. Clint Eastwood you ain't, and the glinty-eyed silent stuff never bothered me much anyhow. Why don't you just tell me what you want."

"I want to talk to Lily."

His voice softened. "She's mine, Ross."

I didn't answer.

"That surprise you? Surprises me a little. Finally found a broad who's woman enough to . . . absorb me. Changed me, too. Notice how different I am? Quiet, calm. Friendly." He grinned. "I'm so different, so calm and friendly and responsible, that I'll be the Chief Executive Officer of the Hollister Corporation as of the next board meeting."

"What about Ripley?"

"Out to pasture. He'll keep his stock, and get a going away present. After that, counsulting fees."

"How'd it happen?"

"Hey, it's all your doing, Ross. The mess you made. Somebody had to take care of things. So I did. Calmly. Responsibly. Impressed the hell out of the old lady."

"Congratulations."

"Yeah," he said. "So that's why you been sitting here playing games with me and I haven't even hit you. Power of love, you suppose? I been tamed." He grinned. "The thing is, Ross, she's important to me. Don't fuck with her."

I smiled.

He smiled. "You haven't asked me about my sister."

I didn't say anything.

He grinned. "Ah, you're tough, Ross. A killer. Did a real good job on Dolly, too. Oughta see her, what a mess—"

The stage door opened and Lily Baker, in jeans and a Hank Williams, Jr. sweatshirt, stepped through it. A purse dangling from a shoulder strap bounced against her wide hip as she approached. Her smile flickered as she recognized me.

Moving behind Hayes, she slipped her arms around his neck. "Hi, hon," she said, kissing the top of his head.

"Hi." Hayes clasped her hands in his and leaned his head back against the heavy softness of her breasts. His eyes stayed on me.

She smiled. "How are you, Jack."

"Fine, Lily. I enjoyed the show."

"Yeah." Her smile grew. She eased from Hayes's hands, eased into the chair beside him. "A bunch better, huh? All thanks to Mr. Knight here. Never figured that white horse would be a pickup."

"Did you get a recording contract too?"

She grinned big. "It's in the works. Hayes found this boy, he writes these terrific songs, and we sent the tape off the other day." She turned to Hayes. "Did you hear—"

"He likes it. He's making the rounds with it." His hand found hers in her lap. "We'll hear in a day or so."

Lily glowed. "It's a chance, Jack. A real chance. Glory's getting hers, too. She—hon, did you tell him?"

He smiled. "You do it."

"She's going to Hollywood next week. Hayes talked to this guy he knew who knew this other guy, and we all flew down there and she had this test and she got a part in this movie. It's just a little one, no lines or anything, but . . . it's a chance."

"The fairy tales have all come true. Thanks to Hayes."

"I—" The brightness dimmed a bit in her eyes. "Did I interrupt something?"

"No," Hayes said. "Ross was just leaving."

"After I ask Lily a question."

"Sure. Shoot."

"What happened to Haskell's personal effects?"

"We got everything, Glory and me," she said quietly. "There wasn't that much. It . . . was sad."

"What did you do with it?"

"It's in the Valley, at Mom's place. My sister Anemone, she—do you know about her?"

"Yes. Did you or Glory keep anything you found in Haskell's stuff?"

"Glory took his ring. I kept this." From her purse she took a photograph, cracked and lavender-brown with age.

Three figures stood before the ranch house now owned by Gabriel George. Tall, raw-boned-looking in her overalls and long-sleeved shirt, Dolores Dahlman smiled broadly into the glare of the desert sun. Beside her, not so tall, the Haskell Dan of forty years before stared into the lens. Before them Stuart Dahlman, a dark-haired boy of four or so, smirked.

"It's the only one I have of either of them," Lily said. "I didn't see any harm in taking it."

"I don't either."

"Do you . . . know who killed him?"

"No."

"Then what's the point, Ross? What are you up to?"

"The question is, Hayes, what have you been up to?"

He grinned. "Up to my ears in this lady here, every chance I get."

Lily colored. "Hayes, quit it."

"I mean before. When did you find out your father was Lawrence Parker?"

"When you told us, in your great revelation scene."

"No. You already knew."

"And how does the great detective deduce that?"

"Dolly told me."

It stunned him. "How could she—"

"She was the only one in the room who was surprised," I said. "Everybody else already knew. Including you."

We sat in silence. Lily, confused, watched Hayes's face slowly relax and shape itself into a grin. "So what?"

"How did you find out?"

He was calculating so coldly that I could see it in his eyes. I saw too that he figured he had nothing to lose.

"I've known since I was eighteen. My grandfather told me. He knew he'd made a mistake with Ripley, and that the old man was a killer and tough enough to make it across the desert, but not the right kind of tough. He knew I was the only one of the bunch that could take care of things." His grin hardened again.

"You know everything, don't you, Hayes?"

"You got it, Ace."

I didn't know everything. I didn't know if he cared for Lily or not, if in fact he was capable of really caring about anyone. I was about to find out.

"You know who murdered Lily's father, don't you?"

The grin cracked. "Who? Stuart Dahlman? How could I?"

"And Lily's sister. Hayes Hollister told you that too, didn't he?"

"No."

"Sure he did. He told you everything."

He leaned back in his chair. "Like you, I'm a member of the Nevada bar, Ross, and an Officer of the Court. Had I knowledge of a crime, especially a capital murder, I'd be bound to report it. I've reported no crimes."

"Not even your own."

"Come on, Ross," he grinned. "You're pissing in the wind. I haven't killed anybody."

"I wasn't thinking about murder. I was thinking about things like assault."

He shrugged. "So I got in a few bar fights. Ancient history." He smiled at Lily. "I don't do that anymore."

"I was thinking about the affair with the person who suddenly got the great job in San Francisco."

He understood what I was doing, but it didn't trouble him. "That was a set-up all the way, Ross."

"I was thinking about Tracy. About who gave her cocaine and took her to Cal Blass's and why."

He put his hand on Lily's. "You see what he's doing, don't you, hon? He doesn't know anything, so he's just throwing shit out, trying to. . . ."

Whatever his reasons, Hayes didn't want me to tell Lily about the rape charge, or about how he fed his brother's fiancée coke until he nearly destroyed her. But he was going to have to pay for my silence.

Lily slid her hand from under his. "He's right, isn't he? You always say you know everything. And you always do. You know who killed my father and my sister."

Sudden rage twisted and darkened the face he turned on me. "You're finished. You're history."

"Do yourself some good with the lady, Hayes. She has a right to know. It doesn't matter anyhow. Nobody can prove anything. Even at Harvard they must have explained the laws of evidence to you. In this case, there isn't any. Why don't you tell her?"

As quickly as it had appeared, his rage vanished. He turned solicitously to Lily. He took her hands in his own. "Is it that important to you?"

"Yes."

Again I could see him calculating. He finally shrugged. "Ripley."

Lily sagged, sighed. Something left her eyes.

"You had that part right, Ross. Dahlman figured out who Lawrence Parker was, and he got word to Gramps. Gramps would have taken him out himself, but he was too old, so he had Ripley do it. Said it surprised him, he'd always figured Freddie had balls like BBs, if he had any at all. Turned out that except for that time, he was right."

"Why Rose?"

He shrugged. "She was there. He found them passed out in bed, came up with the suicide bit. It worked."

"And he, Ripley. . . ." Lily's eyes were full of pain. "He killed Haskell, and Mom?"

"Did he, Hayes?"

"That I don't know. It makes sense," he said. "But if he did, you'll never prove it, Ross. It's over."

I slid the chair back from the table and stood up. "You're forgetting the immortal words of Yogi Berra."

"Which words?"

"It ain't over till it's over."

"You think you're going to be the one to finish it?"

I smiled.

"Mind if I ask how?"

I smiled.

"You're going to do it? Alone?"

I smiled.

"You're crazy, Ross."

I grinned.

# 36

I was up at dawn. After a long good run along the river, I cleaned up and climbed into new jeans and blue plaid shirt, my old gray tweed jacket, and boots. After breakfast I left word at the hotel desk that I'd be back by eleven.

A white Ford pickup followed me to the shop where I picked up the Wagoneer, then to the bank building in downtown Reno where my ex-wife's husband had his offices.

I went in and signed papers. I also had him draw up one instructing him to put the proceeds from the sale of my business and building into a trust, the interest to go to my ex-wife for my daughter's care, the principal due my daughter on her eighteenth birthday.

My ex-wife's husband protested. I didn't care. I left. The white Ford pickup followed me back to the Nugget.

I wasn't surprised to find someone waiting for me in the hotel lobby. I wasn't particularly surprised that it was a woman. I was a bit surprised that it was Glory Dahlman.

She wore squaw boots, faded jeans, and a fringed and beaded buckskin shirt cinched at the waist with a belt of silver buckles. From a narrow band of leather around her dark head dangled a plastic-looking feather.

She rose from the couch to greet me. "Hello, Jack."

"Glory." She was bright- and clear-eyed, fresh-faced, smiling. "You're up early for a night person."

"I'm not a night person any more. It's Gloria, now, by the

222

way. Gloria Dahl. I like your beard. It makes you look like a professor, or a cowboy poet maybe, or a Shakespearian king. Macbeth."

"Very like a whale," I said.

"What? Oh, no. That's Hamlet."

"I don't suppose you're still a lady of the evening, either."

"No. That was just. . . ." She stopped to consider what that had been, then ignored it. "How are you?"

"Fine. What can I do for you?"

"I—it's what I can do for you, Jack." The hand she placed on my arm seemed succoring rather than solicitous. "Is there somewhere private we could go?"

"My room. Do you still go to hotel rooms with men?"

She ignored that too.

In the elevator, she chattered, explained her outfit. "I'm playing an Indian maiden in this movie. They said I was a perfect flesh for the part—that's the way they talk, 'a perfect flesh.' I'm trying to get a feel for the role, even though I get sacrificed ten pages into the script."

"So you're going to be a movie star."

"No, an actor. An artist."

She hesitated as I held open the door to my room. Then she swept through it as if walking on stage. Which was pretty much what she was doing.

Ignoring—or at home in—the anonymity of the room, she moved to the small table by the window and slipped into the chair. I sat on the edge of the bed.

"So we have privacy," I said. "What do you want?"

Her handsome face organized itself into an expression of queenly compassion. The queen of hotel rooms. "I want to . . . absolve you."

"How generous. Do I kneel?"

She frowned regally. "Maybe that's not the right word."

"You're a poet. You'll come up with it."

She gave up being queen, became an intimate, an old lover long past passion but not concern. "Are you mad at me?"

"No."

"It's just that you're so—but I want to, I don't know, thank you, I guess. For finding my grandfather. And tell you how much I appreciate all that you've done for me."

"You're welcome."

"And I want to pay you." She raised a hand to stifle the protest I hadn't made. "I know you said you were doing it for Haskell, but you put in a great deal of time and effort, and you should be paid."

"Fine." I stood and slipped out of my jacket. I unbuttoned my shirt. I undid my belt and unzipped my fly.

"What . . . are you doing?"

"The last time you were going to pay me, Glory, it was with your body."

"I—is that what you want?"

"No."

"Then . . . what?"

I zipped and buckled and buttoned up. "I want you to tell me what you really want. I already know, but I want you to tell me."

"I told you. I want. . . ." Her gleaming black head dipped. She stared at her hands. "I want you to go away. I want you to leave us alone."

"Thank you," I said. "But I'm not going to."

She looked up then. "We've finally got a chance to be happy, even halfway normal, me and Emmy and . . . and now you're going to just . . . destroy it, ruin it?"

"That's right."

"Why?"

"You know why."

She shook her head, refusing reality. "They're dead, Jack, you can't bring them back. You'll just make it worse."

"How will I do that, Glory?"

"Gloria," she absently corrected. She was inside herself, searching for another role. She couldn't fine one. "Please, Jack, just let it be."

"So nothing disturbs the fantasy that you happen to be living in at the moment?"

Instead of answering she rose and went to the window. She stared out at the Sierra.

"It's all fantasy," she said quietly. "You, Jack Ross, the person you think you are, you're a fantasy, you're just the stories you tell yourself about yourself. Life is just a movie in your head that you make up as you go along."

She turned to me, eyes flashing, body stiff.

"You think you're different now, you think you're mean, hard, tough, but you're not! You're nothing! You just went out into the desert and told yourself a different story about yourself. Well, I've got a different story now too. I'll leave you yours. Why can't you leave me mine?"

I put on my jacket. "That's the problem with fantasies, isn't it?"

"What?"

"They involve other people."

She stood dumb, numb.

"You must have read *The Great Gatsby* in one of those English courses you took. Remember what happened because he chose to live in a dream?"

"He . . . died."

"What happened to everybody around him?"

She slumped into the chair, confused, angry. "I didn't come here to take a goddam test! You think you're so smart, you think you've got all the answers. But there aren't any—what do you want? Why won't you leave us alone?"

"Listen to me, Glory. Gloria. Listen carefully." I stood over her, stayed silent until her face lifted. "Haskell Dan didn't just ask me to help you find your grandfather. He asked me to protect you, to protect you from the past. You told me yourself that he knew he was going to be killed. The past killed him, the dreams, the lies. He didn't want it to kill you. He loved you. He wanted me to find the truth and to show it to you, in a way that you had to believe it. And that's what I'm going to do."

Her eyes shone with tears. "No matter how many people . . . get hurt?"

"The truth may hurt, but it doesn't kill. Lies kill."

She sat, again staring down at her hands. Then suddenly she was on her feet, pushing me back. "I'm sorry I came here. You . . . I'm leaving."

"No you're not."

"Get the fuck out of my way!"

I smiled. "There's a piece of it."

"Of what?"

"The truth. Your truth. You don't get rid of the Valley by pretending it was something else. You don't get rid of prostitution by telling yourself it was . . . what, research? Improvisational theater? Art? You have a lot of fun at Mustang, did you? What sort of delightful story are you going to make of that for Emily?"

"You bastard."

"That's right, Glory. I am a bastard, literally. I have no idea who my father is."

She stared at me. Slowly she backed to the chair. "What do you want, Jack? Just tell me."

"Who called you last night?"

"Nobody. I mean, I know what you mean. They came out, Lily and Hayes. To the Valley."

"What did she tell you?"

"She told me . . . you know."

"Say it."

She swallowed. Then she said it. "That Frederick Ripley killed my . . . parents."

"And yet here you are, Glory, a few hours after learning this, all bright-eyed and bushy-tailed, trying to buy me off, to get rid of me, to keep me from learning the truth."

"I—"

"No. You're not here for yourself. You're here for someone else, someone you're protecting. Do you expect me to believe that you're protecting Frederick Ripley?"

Her eyes searched the room for help. "He's. . . ."

"You're not protecting Ripley. You're protecting his wife. Your aunt. Ann. Anemone."

"No." Slowly, drawn out, nearly a moan.

"Yes." I sat back down on the bed. "Come on, Glory. Gloria. If it comes out that Ripley killed your mother and father, it also comes out that Ann knew it, that she used that knowledge to force him to marry her and get her out of the Valley. She bought her life in San Francisco with silence. She told you all this. What else did she tell you?"

"She told me . . . about my father."

"She told you that he was a blackmailer and dope dealer and adulterer, and all-around asshole. Did she tell you that that justified his murder?"

She didn't answer. Her eyes focused on nothing. The nothing that was not there and the nothing that was.

"What did she tell you about your mother?"

"She. . . ." Her face began to quiver. The quiver became a jerk, sharp and savage. It spread to her body. Her hands jerked, leapt, danced in her lap. Her chest heaved, her breath came in ragged gasps. "She told me that my mother loved me."

Glory was crying. She had the hiccups. Her nose was red and running.

I got up and went into the bathroom. As I filled a glass with water, I looked in the mirror. I didn't recognize the man behind the beard and the eyes.

I gave her the glass of water, then went back to the bathroom for some tissue.

I sat with her.

After a while she went into the bathroom. I went to the window. A solitary patch of snow glistened near the top of Mount Rose. The rest was dark rock, dark pines. But soon it would be all white again, soon the storms would come and smooth and whiten and cover it all.

Glory's soft squaw boots shushed on the carpet. The bed sighed under her weight. I didn't turn around.

"My father was evil. He lied to my mother. He cheated. He betrayed her. He hurt her, over and over again."

"Yes," I said.

"She was young, not even as old as I am now."

"Yes," I said.

"She couldn't take any more."

"Yes," I said.

"He killed her."

I turned. Her eyes were filled with hope. But her capacity for hope was not infinite. She looked at me and the hope ebbed from her eyes.

"Your aunt told you that?"

"It isn't true, what Hayes told you and Lily! Frederick didn't kill them!"

"Why would Hayes lie?"

"He didn't. I mean, he doesn't—he thinks it's true. But it isn't."

Things swirled. I couldn't sort through them. But I knew who could.

"Tell Ann I'll be out this afternoon."

"What . . . are you going to do?"

"What needs to be done."

She rose. "If I had a gun, I'd shoot you."

"It wouldn't stop me, Glory. Gloria. You can sic Whip on me too, if you want. He won't stop me either."

"I—Whip's in jail."

"Surprise."

"He . . . hit his wife. Veronica. She died. It was an accident."

"Like the sun coming up in the east is an accident."

She moved toward the door. Her feet barely left the carpet. She turned. "She loves you, Jack."

"Who loves me, Gloria?"

"Dolly. She told me so."

"Love is fantasy. *You* told *me* so."

"No. I was wrong. Love is the only thing that isn't."

"Dreams, Glory. All dreams."

She opened the door, but she didn't go through it.

"Tell me, Jack. How do you tell which ones are the dreams?"

"That's the problem, isn't it."

She looked at me for a long time. Then she stepped through the door and closed it.

# 37

After lunch, I called the desk for messages. Frank Calvetti wanted me to call. I didn't.

As I was about to leave, the phone rang. I hesitated, then picked up the receiver.

"Jack?" Electricity crackled the long distance of the line that connected me with Dolly George.

"Hi."

"I . . . how are you?"

"I'm fine, Dolly."

"I wasn't going to call. You made it clear enough that you. . . ." She seemed to struggle. "I wanted to warn you. You need to be careful."

"Why?"

"Frederick was here late last night. He was going to fly to Reno this morning. He wanted me to come with him."

"Why?"

"To talk to you, he said. To dissuade you from . . . what you're doing."

"Why didn't you?"

"I told him you wouldn't be dissuaded from anything, if you were determined to do it, and you especially wouldn't be dissuaded by me. I—that's right, isn't it?"

"The first part. It makes the second part meaningless."

"Meaningless," she echoed, filling the syllables with meaning. "I think he knew that. I think what he really wanted was for me to distract you so that he could. . . ."

"So that he could what, Dolly."

She couldn't say it.

"Is he alone? No Hollister security goons or anyone?"

"I don't know. He was here alone."

I thought about it, about what I thought it meant. "Thanks for the warning, Dolly."

"Why—why is he afraid of you?" she asked. She asked as if she too were afraid of me.

"Is that what he is?"

"I think so. He's afraid of someone."

"I think he's always been afraid."

"Maybe," she said. "I know I am."

"I'm sorry."

Silence. Then in a rush: "Am I going to see you again?"

"When it's finished."

"Are we finished?"

"I don't know."

"Doubt," she said bitterly. "That's all you can give me?"

"I'll come to Berkeley, Dolly. We'll talk."

"Do you know what we'll talk about?"

"Yes."

"Thank God for that." The line went dead.

I left the hotel and drove to a mini-warehouse on East Fourth where my possessions were stored. No white Ford pickup followed me.

Packed tightly in the small metal enclosure, what had been the trappings of my life seemed sadly insubstantial, of no consequence. Neatly labeled and stacked cartons of books, records, clothes, pictures, household ware: things and stuff.

I had to work through several cartons before I found what I wanted.

From the box I took a handful of shells and my grandfather's .38 Smith and Wesson. I wiped the revolver clean of its patina of oil, loaded it, and stuck it in the waist of my jeans and the remaining shells in my jacket pocket.

No white Ford pickup followed me to Sun Valley.

In the yard, oil and rust stains marked where the old junkers had stood, trails of hard-packed dirt where children had roamed among them: a map leading nowhere, to nothing.

Near the door, the brown Bentley and the green T-bird gleamed through a film of dust.

In the door, in a white dress, stood Emily Dahlman. The face she turned to my approach was full of uncertainty.

I stepped from the Wagoneer and heard what confused the little girl: laughter. Shrieks and screeches and hoots of it. Laughter like wails of misery. Mad keening prayers of laughter.

As I moved into the open doorway, the girl slid back from me, out into the yard. The laughter followed her.

The wall of photographs was now a blank of faded white paint surrounding squares and rectangles of unfaded whiter white. Beneath it, on a long couch, Glory lay curled in on herself against the laughter that rose like an animal howl.

Before her Ann Ripley, in the cut and caped black outfit Glory had worn the night I met her, paraded, pantomimed, parodied prurience, to the accompaniment of rhythmic gleeful grunts and squeals.

Glory saw me. Her laughter died. Ann Ripley turned, flushed a dark rose from chest to cheek, her eyes glittering with tears and what seemed a kind of manic happiness.

Despite myself I stared, stunned.

As Glory had seemed a child in the costume, Ann Ripley, the black cloth accentuating breast and waist and thigh, seemed Ur-woman, a creature of the oldest darkness, of the oldest blood, not of fantasy but of myth: the source of life, the tantalizing embodiment of its mysteries.

I saw what Lawrence Parker had seen forty years before in a little town on the Humboldt. What had started it all.

Silence had swallowed the laughter. Ann Ripley spoke and broke the spell. "We were just . . . pretending."

I found my voice. "You do it well."

Something of what had created her laughter remained with

her. It flashed in her eyes, tightened her smile. "You liked it? You don't think I need to . . . practice?"

What she had, like her mother before her, couldn't be practiced. It was a gift. Or a curse.

"Why? Did you get back your taste for it?"

Her smile faded. She turned and walked out of the room.

The room was different, light, airy, furnished with pieces covered in nappy cloth in desert pastels. The scent of rosewater, medicine, and death had been replaced by the ubiquitous lemon.

Glory's other black costumes draped the back of a sage-colored chair. Beside it stood a cardboard box, its flaps open and leaning against each other.

"Is that Haskell's stuff?"

Glory sat up on the couch. "There's nothing more. Just . . . old things."

That's what Haskell Dan had seen: old things, things he had seen before.

I went to the box, knelt beside it, and turned back the flaps. Glory came over and sat in the chair and peered down as I removed its contents.

Old things. A pearl Stetson rarely worn. A hunting knife, its blade honed thin, in a leather scabbard. Two pocket knives. An old gold watch. A large silver belt buckle. A set of silver-and-turquoise cufflinks that matched the ring he'd worn. The silver-and-turquoise clasp he'd worn the last night I saw him. Bits of lacquered desert wood. Agates. An opal. A tooled leather wallet. A hand-carved flute. A handful of small horses and cows carved in soft pine. An ashtray tapped from a coffee can lid and enscripted in drippings of solder: *To Haskell from his pal Stu.* A horsehair quirt. Two small hand-braided rugs.

An old stiff-papered accordion file, its strings quickly and sloppily tied. Retied. In it, papers. Certificates of Haskell Dan's birth, Stuart Dahlman's birth, Stuart Dahlman's death, Dolores Dahlman's death. A paper trail of Stuart Dahlman's passage through the Gerlach grade and high schools, complete with report cards.

And photographs. Two. Dolores Dahlman, her hair brushed

smoothly back from her brow and down over her bare wide shoulders, her wide mouth smiling her granddaughter's smile. And another, obviously taken at the same time as the one Lily Baker had, of Haskell Dan and Dolores Dahlman alone in the desert sun.

Glory sat back as I replaced Haskell Dan's life. "I told you there wasn't anything there."

But of course there was something there. Something I saw the night I met her. "It's there, Glory. Gloria."

"What? What is it? We—"

I rose and stood beside the chair. She suddenly sank back into it, as if she would bury herself.

"We?"

"Lily and I. We—" Her eyes were fixed on my waist.

"Who else went through these things?"

From behind me Ann Ripley answered. "Hayes looked through it last night. Frederick this morning."

She had changed into a chaste blue summer dress. Her face was empty, her eyes as still as desert heat.

I turned to Glory. "Go away. I want to talk to Ann."

"With . . ." She nodded at my waist. "With that."

My grandfather's revolver. "You know better than that. Go. Take Emmy for a ride."

Ann Ripley moved beside the chair and put her hand on Glory's shoulder. "Go ahead, honey. It's all right."

Reluctantly Glory rose. Looking at Ann, her face flooded with an emotion I couldn't fathom.

We watched her leave. Then Ann moved to one end of the couch. With a faint flutter of fingers she motioned me to the other end.

I nodded vaguely at the room. "You're moving in?"

"No. I'm going back to San Francisco soon. I'm divorcing Frederick. But I'm keeping this place as a sort of . . . retreat, haven. For all of us."

I sat, watched her, let the silence deepen.

Finally, she said, "I don't know what you want, Jack. I don't have anything for you."

"Right now I want to stay alive. I also want to keep your husband alive, if I can. And you."

"You think we're in danger? From whom?"

"I don't know. But I think you do."

She folded her hands. "I don't know anything."

"You know who killed Stuart and Rose."

"I know what Hayes told you. But it isn't true. Frederick didn't kill them."

"And I know what you told Glory. That isn't true either. What I don't know is why Hayes would lie about it. Hayes George lies the way a rattlesnake rattles, but he couldn't really expect to get away with one like this."

"He thinks it's true."

"If he thinks it's true, then old R. Hayes Hollister thought it was true."

She nodded toward her hands. "Yes."

"And if he thought it was true, he thought so because Frederick told him so."

"Yes."

"And that's what you had on him, that was your ticket out of here. Not the knowledge that he'd killed Stuart and Rose. The knowledge that he hadn't. Because he'd told his boss he had, he'd proved his, what—toughness? That he'd kill to protect Hollister interests, that sort of thing?"

A tremor stirred the smooth flesh beside her mouth. "He was evil, that old man, evil, evil. . . ."

Yes. And he'd spawned more evil. "So Frederick made his career with a lie, the false admission of a capital crime. And you lied too."

"I didn't lie to anyone."

"You just kept silent."

"Yes."

She looked at me. Her eyes cleared. Her face relaxed, sagged subtly, grew older, real, lovely.

She thought my inquisition was over. It had just begun.

"You killed them, didn't you?"

She sucked up breath sharply, lifting her head and, under the pale blue cloth, the jut of her breasts. "No."

"You were having an affair with Stuart, your sister's husband, you got pregnant by him, not by Ripley, he promised to take you out of the Valley, and then changed his mind—why? Because Rose was pregnant too?"

Slowly her head shook. Her smile was small, faintly melancholy, like Haskell Dan's gaze. "We've done this before, Jack. You know next to nothing, and you understand nothing of what you know. You've got nothing. Nothing."

Nothing.

Nothing abounds.

Nothing signifies.

In Nevada.

I stared over her bright head at the nothing on the wall. The squares and rectangles where the photographs had been. The nothing that was not there.

The nothing that was.

"Where are the pictures?"

"I—shipped them back to San Francisco with the rest of my mother's things. Why?"

"When Glory saw you, she nearly collapsed. Why?"

"What?"

"Frederick didn't kill Stuart and Rose, right, Ann?"

"Yes. I mean no, he didn't."

"Did you see him not kill them, Ann?"

"I—I don't understand."

"How did you know he didn't kill them, Ann—Stuart and . . . Rose?"

"They were dead when he got there."

"How do you know that, Ann?"

Then she understood my hammering repetition of the name. But she didn't give up.

"Haskell found them. He brought Gloria here. Then we went back. We saw Frederick coming out of the trailer."

"Why didn't Haskell call the Sheriff when he brought Glory here? Why did you go back with him?"

"I—she was my sister, I wanted to—"

"It's easy enough to prove. I don't need your mother's photographs. You both went to high school. All I need is a yearbook."

"No," she whispered.

"Yes. It's the only way your story makes sense. And it accounts for everything—your mother's fear, your reaction when you saw Glory."

"No." Fainter.

"Why else would Haskell come here, not to your mother but to you? Why else would he not call the authorities then? Because what he found was all wrong, the woman was the wrong woman. Because Ripley hadn't come to the trailer to kill anyone. He was probably making another extortion payment and he walked in and saw them in bed, her with half her face blown away, and he made a natural assumption. And he saw his chance to convince the murderous old man he worked for that he too was a killer, could take care of problems Nevada-style. He may even have typed the note, or the killer did. But it was the note that got you out of the Valley."

She didn't say no. She didn't say anything.

"Ripley must have had a stroke when he saw you."

She spoke, when she finally spoke, softly, her tone strangely nostalgic.

"I was afraid. I didn't understand what had happened. But I thought I could get money from him, enough to go away. Because I was dead, no one would look for me."

She looked at me, but what she saw was her past. "I called him. We met on Windy Hill. He had a gun. He was going to kill me. He couldn't. He couldn't kill anybody. We were both frightened. But all we had was each other. We . . . were bound to each other."

By murder. Lies. Silence.

But the glow of that past moment offered no warmth now. "At least we were for a while."

Silence settled on us like a shroud. I brushed it away. We weren't finished.

"Who else knows about you?"

"Gloria."

"Hayes and Lily?"

"No."

"Who killed Stuart and your sister?"

"I . . . don't know."

"Yes, you do know. You and Frederick know. Haskell knew. Your mother knew."

"Mom didn't know. Maybe Haskell knew. Frederick and I, we don't know, not really. It's . . . just a guess."

"That's why you went inside that night, at his party?"

"I was curious. I'd never met him, never even seen him. He'd never seen me. I wanted to . . . see what he was like."

I got up. "Your husband was following me this morning. He didn't follow me here, because he knew I was coming."

Her lids dipped like flags of acknowledgement. "He . . . has a gun. The same one he had. . . . He's been drinking."

"Where is he?"

"I don't know."

I was about to find out.

She followed me out into the searing sun, to my rig.

"What did you find in Haskell's things?"

"The truth."

"About Haskell, about who killed him?"

"No." I said, climbing in. "It's about your father."

"My father," she said quietly. "That's been . . . hard. To see Gloria with him, to see him be her grandfather, and not be able to let him be my father. Maybe soon I can."

"Don't."

"I—why?"

"Because, Rose, Gabriel George isn't Lawrence Parker. He isn't your father."

"But . . . then who is he?"

"The forgotten man."

# 38

I wheeled the Wagoneer around the yard to the gate. Then I stopped and stared out at the bunched-up, trail-scarred hills.

Frederick Ripley was close by, with a gut full of panicky fear, a snootful of booze, and a gun. I didn't want to deal with any of them. I just wanted a couple of answers, to confirm what I already knew.

Pulling out of the yard, I took to the dirt.

Slowly I drove toward the heat-shimmering hills, silent and still under a big high sky filled with nothing.

The road, as it began to climb, narrowed to a track of dust and rut and rock, twisted through sage and scattered pinion, meandered like a sandy creek over land bent and buckled by ancient unheavals.

Only dust appeared in my rearview mirror.

I didn't know how well Ripley knew the hills. Some, if he'd cavorted in them with the young Anemone. I didn't know them that well myself, but I knew what I was looking for.

Then I found it.

The road dipped down around a brown bank to the sudden slope of a wide, dry, boulder-strewn wash. For two hundred yards the tracks skirted the bank, gradually dropping to a natural ford at the entrance to a small canyon, where they crossed, climbed, and hairpinned back. The spot directly across the wash from me was a quarter mile by road, a hundred yards as the crow, or the bullet, flies.

I got to it as quickly as I could, jumped out and pulled the pieces of my 30.30 from the trunk, slapped it together and stuffed it with shells. Then I got back in the Wagoneer and sat, waiting.

Sweat beaded on my body. Dust, seemingly stirred by the windless heat, danced in the sunlight. In the silence the cooling engine cracked and sighed.

Then into the silence crept the low faint mutter of another engine. As it grew louder, drew nearer, dust like smoke from a fire of earth boiled up over the hills.

The white Ford pickup rounded the corner and stopped. The windshield was a broad slash of sunglare. Above the pickup, beyond the hump of the hill, another filmy steam of dust rose into the afternoon heat.

The pickup eased forward along the wash, crossed it, and headed toward me. Thirty yards behind me it stopped.

I got out of the jeep, raised the rifle, and put the bead of the sight in the center of Frederick Ripley's forehead.

His face exploded with fear. Then it disappeared.

I waited. His face didn't rise from behind the dash.

A big laboring engine groaned behind the hill as it dragged its burden of rolling dust closer.

I moved behind the Wagoneer, laid my arm on the hot metal of the hood, the stock of the 30.30 on my arm.

A dark blue Cadillac eased around the corner.

I shot out its right front tire. The Caddy shuddered, listed, leaned toward the bank.

The wheels jerked left. I shot out the left tire. Like a weary crustaceous desert creature, the big blue mass of metal waddled to a stop at the edge of the wash.

No one got out.

I shot out the headlights.

Four doors flew open. Four men leaped out and scrambled behind the back of the car.

I waited. Dust settled in the silence.

I shot both outside rearview mirrors.

I waited, listening to the silence deepen, wondering if there was a brain in the bunch.

Finally one man rose slowly, his hands in the air, and stepped away from the car. Then another. Then the other two.

Slowly they backed away from the Cadillac. I put two slugs in the sandy hillside behind them. They stood still. I pulled out my grandfather's revolver and held it up.

I waited. Then one of the men reached in his jacket and carefully took out a pistol and hurled it into the wash. Three other guns followed.

I moved out from behind the Wagoneer and dipped the rifle barrel down.

They backed up the road and around the corner and were gone.

Ripley stood beside the pickup. Pale as desert heat, his face glistened. His suit was wrinkled, open vest buttons exposing the paunch pushing at his gray shirt, open collar exposing his white damp throat and twisting his tie.

The pistol in his hand was small and dark. It wavered, shook, in his hand. It was pointed at me.

I couldn't read his face. It seemed a glutinous mass. His blue eyes stared at me but didn't see me.

I leaned the rifle against the jeep. Then I moved slowly toward him, the .38 hanging loosely in my fingers.

"Give me the gun, Ripley."

He didn't move, didn't speak.

"There are about three places you could hit me with that pop-gun that would kill me. It would take a perfect shot. You don't have the time or the skill for it. And if you pull the trigger and that shot isn't perfect, you're dead."

He looked at me, considering it. Considering his death.

"You don't want to die, Ripley. That's why you're here."

His eyes, red-rimmed, red-veined, closed. I raised the .38. "Drop the gun, Ripley."

His eyes didn't open, but his hand did. The gun dangled on his fingers, slid slowly from them, dropped to the dust at his feet.

As I moved to pick up the gun, I got a whiff of him, rank with alcohol and stale sweat and fear.

The old short-barreled .22 lay light in my hand. Fit for purses, it was useless at any distance, perfect for executions or suicide. I dropped it in my pocket.

His eyes opened. "If you're going to kill me, do it."

He was still trying to play the president of the Hollister Corporation. He still couldn't handle the role.

"That's too easy. Besides," I said, nodding at the Cadillac teetering on the bank of the wash, "they were the ones who were going to kill you. And me."

Sweat smeared his blanched, pasty face. "Who . . . ?"

"Cal Blass's boys."

He looked at me blankly.

"You were supposed to kill me, or die trying. If either of us was left alive, they were supposed to finish it."

"I don't—why?"

"Think about it for a while. You'll figure it out."

Maybe he wouldn't. He seemed incapable of thought.

"Come on," I said. Back at the Wagoneer, I got out scotch and water and two glasses, filled one with scotch and another with water. He grabbed at the scotch, drank deeply.

I sipped water. Color crept back into his damp face.

"What do you intend to do?"

"With you? Nothing."

He didn't know if that was true or, if it was, if it was good.

"Where'd you get the gun?"

"It's mine. Hayes Hollister gave it to me twenty-years ago, to. . . ."

"You carry it around with you?"

"No. I left it here, at the house."

"Where's the silencer?"

"In the pickup. I didn't think I'd need it to. . . ."

"Who called you last night?"

"Hayes. He said that you knew I'd—" He sucked up a lungful of dusty air. "—killed Stuart Dahlman and his wife."

I sipped more water.

Ripley drained his drink, shuddered. "What are you going to do, Ross?" he asked again.

"Nothing."

"You're not going to the Sheriff?"

"And tell him what?"

"That I . . . killed them."

"Why would I want to do that?"

Slowly his body sagged, his shoulders slumped. His gaze lost focus, drifted from my face to the emptiness of the desert hills. "She told you."

"Rose? Yes, she told me."

"That too?"

I finished my water, put everything back, shut the back door.

"I'm curious about something, Ripley. Why would you kill me to keep people from finding out that you hadn't killed?"

"I had to."

"Old man Hollister is long gone. You haven't needed to impress him for years."

He shook his head, stared down at the dust. "No, it wasn't for him, not later, maybe not even then. It was for me. I didn't kill them, but—" He raised his eyes, tried to stiffen his shoulders, his character. "I would have."

I smiled. "You know what I think, Ripley? I think you had to kill me because you couldn't let Hayes George learn that you didn't kill Stuart and Anemone, that the rewards old Hayes Hollister bestowed on you were unearned. I think that lie has kept you around. It kept Hayes from crushing you."

Ripley flushed. "You're ignorant, Ross. You do your sleazy little jobs, tinker with meaningless little lives, and you think you understand reality. But you understand nothing. Real life goes on far above you, through the exercise of a power the immensity of which you can't begin to comprehend. Reality is power. Hayes Hollister had it, and now I have it. And I'm going to keep it."

"Is that what you get from the little girls—power? You feel like a man with children who look like women?"

His flush deepened. "You understand nothing, Ross."

"I understand that the only people who worship power are the impotent."

His bright blue eyes flashed meaninglessly.

I climbed in the Wagoneer. Ripley stood by the door. "Are you going to the authorities?"

"No."

"You know who killed them, don't you?"

"Yes." I started the engine.

Ripley was suddenly confused. "You're just going to leave?"

"Yes."

"And you're not going to do anything . . . about me?"

"I don't have to. You're already finished. All that power you're so thrilled with—it's gone, Ripley. Hayes George is making his move, and his mother's backing him."

"I'll . . . fight him."

"You'll lose. If you're still alive, that is."

"What do you—who would kill me?"

"You've been a walking dead man since last night."

He didn't understand. I didn't feel like explaining.

Ripley buttoned his vest, brushed at the wrinkles of his jacket. "What do you suggest I do, Ross?"

"How should I know?"

"But I—"

"Look, Ripley—you can run and hide. You can get those guns and go try to kill somebody else. You can stick one in your mouth and splatter your brains all over the desert. You can stand here forever. I don't care what you do."

"But. . . ."

"Nobody cares what you do, Ripley. Nobody."

His mouth opened, but no sound issued from it into the still and the heat and the silence.

# 39

The big white Hollister Ranch house sat cool and still in the shade of the poplars. A single white Ford pickup stood before the door. I parked beside it.

I didn't know if I was ready to go inside. As I'd picked my way along twisting trails back to U.S. 395, I'd tried to prepare. Prepared or not, I was going in.

A small old woman I'd never seen before answered the door. Her face was as brown and rough and seamed as a well-used work glove—which, in a way, I supposed was what she was. She told me Hayes George was upstairs in his office.

The hallway had been sanded and refinished, absolving Bobby George's sins. I followed it to the stairs, followed them to the second floor. The first door, behind which I'd listened to so many lies, was closed. The second was open.

Hayes sat at a paper-strewn desk, a pen in his hand, a telephone at his elbow. There was little else in the room: a filing cabinet beside him, a stuffed chair before the desk, a couple of his father's photographs on the plaster walls.

As I stood in the doorway, he looked me over slowly, his grin spreading. He leaned back against the spring in his chair and propped his boots on the corner of the desk. He nodded at the revolver tucked in my jeans. "You come a-gunnin' for me?" His arms and his grin spread wide: "Sorry to disappoint you. I ain't packing."

His left hand drifted to rest in his lap; his right slowly disappeared behind the desk.

"Five'll get somebody ten, Hayes, that if I made a move something very nasty would appear in your hand. But," I continued through his chuckle, "it's not you I'm after."

"Who?"

"Cal Blass."

"Cal? What for?"

I came inside. I settled into the chair across the desk. The .22 I'd taken from Frederick Ripley dug gently into my back. "He killed them."

"Killed who?"

"All of them. The two in the trailer in Sun Valley twenty years ago. The Indian. Lily's mother."

"Come off it, Ross," he said with disgust. "I told you, Ripley did Dahlman and his wife."

"He didn't kill them. He just found them."

"Did he tell you that? He's just trying to get you off his back. Unless you can prove it . . . ?" He let the question hang; something in my face had made it, in that strange savage thing that was his mind, a real question.

"I can prove it. Ask Stuart Dahlman's wife."

I didn't have to explain it to him. After a long moment his eyes slowly brightened with a deep delight. "Goddam. I told you she was cute, Ross. I told you."

Then his fist rose and slammed onto the desktop. "That weasely, sneaking, lying son of a bitch!"

"Give him a little credit, Hayes," I said. "He conned all of you. He pulled it off."

He wasn't going to give Frederick Ripley credit for anything. "When I get a hold of that fat asshole wimp—"

Thoughts rose in his mind like half-disintegrated turds in the acrid solution of a septic tank. For a moment he savored the delectable rankness of his intent. But only for a moment.

"So, can you prove that Blass took them out?"

"No, but I don't have to. We won't be in court."

He dropped his heavy head, seemed to study his crotch. "What do you expect you're going to do about it?"

"I expect to confront him. I expect him to admit he killed

them, because he'll be planning to kill me. Then I expect I'll kill him."

He laughed. "You think you can?"

"Yes."

He laughed again. "I don't know, Ross. If you're right, I mean. Dahlman and his—the girl, I can see that, maybe. What was it, dope?"

"Dahlman was bleeding Ripley and putting the cash into more and better drugs, moving out of the three-joints-to-a-lid market and into Cal's. And bragging about it. Blass couldn't let that pass."

"Yeah, okay. But the Indian and Lily's mom. I'm looking real hard, but I don't see motive."

"I don't either, for sure," I said. "But I keep coming back to the fact that there are only two kinds of human beings who kill with what seems to be logic. The crazy ones, desperate and demon-driven, who get into something they can't get out of. And the cold ones, the sociopaths who don't give a shit one way or the other. There aren't any crazies in this. Mostly what everybody is is scared. The only sociopath around is Blass."

"No cigar," he said. "That's not motive."

"I don't know exactly how it works, Hayes, but I know it works somehow. Haskell and Flora both knew that Blass killed Stuart and Anemone. The day that extortion note arrived, both of them were finished."

He didn't like that. "The only way anything like that could work is if Blass had a pipeline into this house."

I nodded. "For a while I was convinced it was you. But finally, for a bunch of reasons, that didn't wash. There's only one other candidate."

"Ripley?"

"Tracy."

"That's way out there, Ross. In the ozone."

I shrugged. "It makes sense, if you think about it. But it really doesn't matter. Cal will tell us soon enough."

He laughed again. "Us? You think I'm going after Cal Blass with you?"

"The notion appealed to you before."

"Not the same notion," he grinned. "That's what you came here for? To talk me into helping you take out . . . ? How can you walk with testicles that big?"

I grinned back at him.

"Why me, Ross?"

"Who else is there?"

He was incapable of questioning that. "Cal's never alone. We'd have to take on a small army."

"How many?"

"He's got two shadows. Then there's always another half dozen guns if he cocks an eyebrow. Eight to ten."

"Just your kind of odds, Hayes." I grinned at him.

He grinned. "Not quite."

"Let's lower them. Right now, four of Blass's goons are halfway between Sun Valley and nowhere, on foot."

He laughed. "How'd you manage that?"

"Skill and cunning. You know the house. If we don't have to blast our way in, we might be able to take them one at a time. They won't be expecting us. It might be easy."

Again he shook his head, grinning. "You're crazy, Ross."

"Could be."

"What if I say no?"

"I go alone."

"Wacko."

"Maybe. But you won't say no. This is your chance to be a hero. Score more points with Mom. Dazzle Lily and any other lady that strikes your fancy."

"And how do I get to be a hero in this fairy tale?"

"We'd been digging into this, Hayes, these four murders. And we'd done what the authorities couldn't, we discovered the identity of the bad guy. Aware that the authorities had nothing, and could do nothing with what we had, and being responsible attorneys, Officers of the Court, upstanding members of the bar and community and state, we went to see Mr. Blass, armed only for protection and with weapons we are licensed by the state of Nevada to carry, to question said Mr. Blass in the hope of obtaining evidence which, of course, the authorities could never obtain. Unfortunately, said Mr. Blass, upon realizing that we were a genuine threat to expose his murderous activities, panicked and brought deadly force to bear upon us. We of course were compelled to defend our persons. Lead ensued. Mr. Blass died."

"What if one of us died too, Ross? What if you died?"

"Then my daughter buries a hero. But I don't plan to die. You don't either."

He wasn't grinning. "You've got it all worked out."

"But that's not the best part. The best part is, it'll be fun."

He looked at me for a long time. I didn't see him calculating. I didn't need to. He'd been calculating from the moment I stepped under his lintel.

He eased his boots off the desk, squared himself with it, and stood up. He had a gun in his hand. He had it pointed at my chest.

"If my eyes don't deceive me," I said, "that's a Walther PPK. James Bond's weapon of preference."

"Old double-ought seven himself."

"Licensed to kill."

The muscles around his mouth tightened. That might have signaled the beginning of a smile. It might have signaled the end of Jack Ross. "You really think this is a game, don't you, Ross?"

"Of course it's a game. It's all a game, Hayes. You said so yourself. Remember what you told Dolly that night. Nothing's important. Nothing matters. It's all a game."

"Philosophy, Ross? You giving me philosophy now?"

"If I am, Hayes, it's a very old philosophy. One your grandfather understood. You and I understand it too."

"Yeah, a game," he said. Then he stuffed the Walther in his waist. "So let's go play it."

I got up, and Hayes George and I, after the laughter and the grins and the lies, set off, a brace of philosophers, to kill Cal Blass.

# 40

**H**ayes took the pickup. I followed in my own rig.

Reno, the Truckee Meadows, Washoe Valley all unreeled, somehow distant, removed, unreal, like back-projected scenes in a second-rate movie.

I too was distant, removed, unreal. I was deep within myself, in that big still and silence of the self I'd first encountered in the steamy green of Southeast Asia: the emptiness left by the abandonment of what I had been in anticipation of what I was about to become.

I was nothing. Nothing abounding. Nothing signifying.

Franktown Road undulated over the contours of the brief foothills, cool in the shade of the big pines, in the bigger shade of the sheer rock escarpment that was the Sierra.

The pickup pulled off the road a hundred yards from Cal Blass's house and disappeared into the trees. I followed it.

Hayes waited in a piney cove, his gun in his hand. I got out and joined him, my grandfather's gun in my hand.

"Let's check the back first, the pool. If he's got action going, that's where most of it'll be."

I shrugged. Dust and sage and pine perfumed the air. His wide nostrils flared eagerly, as if sucking it in.

He nodded at my gun. "You any good with that?"

"Good enough."

"Good enough ain't gonna be good enough, Ace."

"You said it yourself, Hayes. I'm a killer."

He grinned. "Let's do it."

He moved quickly, silently on the spongy bed of dead needles, through thick Ponderosas, around gray boulders, over a clear creek half as wide as his back, through the dim woods made dimmer by the occasional flash of bright sunlit hillside across the valley.

Then, through the trees, sun glared on glass. Harsh music dulled and died into the air.

Silently we approached the house. A dozen yards from the low brick base of the patio we separated, each picked a tree, slipped behind dark bark, and took a look.

In the shadow of the mountains the pool was sea-gray, its surface a dull shimmer, like Rose Dahlman Ripley's eyes. On the curve of brick closest to us, on a plastic reclining chair beside the hot tub, a young woman in a yellow bikini bottom stretched sweating in the small remaining slab of sunlight. Empty chairs and tables lined the pool. Near the house, at the same table at which Cal Blass had worked his wiles on Rose-then-Ann, a squat burr-headed man in shorts and a red poplin jacket turned cards.

Hayes caught my eye, flicked his gaze toward the girl, and grinned. Then he jerked his head and we moved silently back, deeper into the trees.

"We'll have to deal with Solitaire Sam there, but so far it looks good," he half-whispered. "We'll go in the front."

We stayed in the trees, circling until we had a clear view of the parking lot and the house. The music ended.

The brick of the house was mottled and marbled and veined like the flesh of fat dead animals. Before it stood two Mercedes, a Buick, a Datsun, a Chevy van.

"Not bad," Hayes grinned. His breathing was sibilant in the silence. "I don't know the Datsun, might be a buyer, or a broad. The others belong to Cal. You might be right. This could be real easy."

"Where is he?"

"In his office there," he said, nudging his gun toward a wide window on the second floor. Then the muzzle moved to a wider window just back from a small deck extending from the house. "Or there, his bedroom, if he's having fun. There's another room, sort of a party room, on the floor below it. If there's goons, they'll be there."

"How do you want to play it?"

He jerked his head. "Come on, back to the road."

By the time we got there, he'd worked up a wind. And a slippery sheen on his wide forehead. And a plan.

He leaned heavily against a tree. "Gimme your gun."

I smiled.

"Come on, Ross. I'm gonna march you in, caught you sneaking around out here. It gives us an edge."

"I'm not going in unarmed."

"Goddamit, I'll be armed. I'll be—" He grinned suddenly. "You don't trust me?"

"Like a brother. But I'm not going in unarmed."

"What's going on? You scared, Ross? Come on, this is your fuckin' genius operation!"

"The prisoner bit's okay," I said. "But I keep the gun."

Taking the barrel in my left hand, I shoved and tugged and wedged it butt first into the right sleeve of my jacket. It was a tight fit. I raised my arms in surrender. "Like so."

"They'll see it, for Chrissakes!"

"Doesn't matter. It gets us close. When they see it, we'll know. Then we move."

"Shit." Then he laughed. "Why not?"

"It'll take both hands for me to get it out. That means there'll be a couple of seconds when you're on your own."

"I can handle it," he laughed. "Can you?"

"You're the one who's sweating, Hayes."

He grinned. "Let's do it."

I stepped in front of him, gave his gun my back.

We walked down the short drive and into the parking lot.

The front door swung open. A big man in a blue suit and a pistol waited for us. The hole in the end of the pistol loomed like the maw of the abyss.

"Lookee here what I found," Hayes called quietly as we approached. "Done sniffed out a snoop."

Pleasure seeped into the big man's seamy, fleshy face.

I was close enough to smell the beer and sauerkraut he'd had for lunch when his eyes jumped to the large lump under my sleeve and his face froze.

I kicked at the gun and caught him just above the wrist. He turned under the force of my boot, into a hard hook that hit him with a soft crack on the back of the jaw.

His eyes dulled with pain, but he didn't go down. He stumbled back into the door jamb, the gun still in his hand but dangling like fruit on a dead limb. Then Hayes was around me, and the barrel of his revolver was jabbing into the folded flesh under the man's chin.

"Drop it."

The man dropped his gun.

"Turn around, real slow."

The man turned around slowly.

Hayes raised the barrel of his Walther and brought it down hard on the back of the man's head.

With a soft, almost sexual groan the big man sagged toward the open door.

Hayes grabbed his collar and hit him again with the gun. He lowered him quietly to the ground.

His arm raised again. I grabbed it. "That's enough."

"We gotta be sure."

"He's sure," I said. I tugged and jerked the .38 out of my sleeve. Grabbing a handful of suit, I dragged the man inside. Hayes shut the door carefully.

Into the silence of the big woody room wafted the muted inanities of a television game show. Hayes nodded toward an open door on the right. He leaned close. I could smell the sharp acidity of his excitement. He whispered. "You take the guy at the pool. Anybody in there I'll know."

I nodded and stepped quietly toward the doors leading to the pool stairs as Hayes clumped loudly toward the open door, calling casually, "Hey, where the hell is everybody?"

I stepped out onto the tiny deck at the top of the zig-zag redwood stairs.

The girl in the yellow bikini bottom still lay in the narrowing slash of sunlight. The pool still shimmered dully. The squat man still turned cards.

I started down the stairway, the revolver pressed to my leg. The man heard me, looked up. With my free hand I gave him a friendly wave and a grin.

He started to return the wave. His arm stopped halfway to his shoulder.

He came up fast from the table, digging at the pocket of his jacket. I vaulted over the redwood rail into a small sage as a pistol cracked, dived behind a rock as the pistol cracked again, rolled and rose to a knee and fired.

The squat man spun, fell, grabbing at his shoulder. I leaped over a railroad-tied terrace of desert flowers, stumbled as his gun fired again, tumbled down into the supports of the stairway, raised my head and arm and pistol and shot him twice in the chest.

I got to my feet. The man didn't move. The girl in the yellow bikini bottom was gone. The sound of our firing, the smell of it, the smell of the squat man's death, tinted the sudden afternoon stillness.

I picked my way down to the patio and the body. It was a body, no longer a man. His blood, on the red jacket and the red brick, was black.

I turned back to the house.

Three men with guns were halfway down the stairs. The small man in the lead had a face like an Airedale. I dropped to a squat and fired twice and rolled under the table.

Sighting through white iron legs and crests of sage, I finally found them. The small man was jackknifed over the rail. Cal Blass, in a white jumpsuit, crouched behind him.

Two steps above them, Hayes George loomed like a broad grinning vulture.

He raised the Walther and sighted down its barrel and

squeezed the trigger. A plastic cup a foot from my shoulder spun and skittered away.

His voice boomed louder than his pistol. "Come on out, Ross. We can grind you into hash. Come on out and take it like a man."

I didn't move. I didn't fire.

He did. Brick dust spewed six inches from my face.

"You want to die like a snake, on your belly? Let's see you on your feet. You played the game, and you lost again. Pay up."

I squirmed and slid out from beneath the table. I got to my feet.

Hayes had the Walther trained on the center of my chest. "Into the drink with it."

I tossed the .38 into the pool.

Hayes grinned. Cal Blass rose, caught me in the dark empty gaze of his .45, turned half a head to Hayes and said something I couldn't hear. Hayes grinned.

They descended. Barefoot, Blass padded silently toward me. His aging surfer's face was the color of the brick, his wide eyes nearly blank with rage. He came closer. The hole in the end of his .45 grew darker, larger, emptier.

He raked the pistol across the side of my face.

The pain was bright and dull. I staggered back a step.

"You son of a bitch! It's going to be very slow. In the gut, low. It'll take you a long time to die."

At the end of his sleeve his wrist tensed, cocked.

"You can shoot me, Blass. But you won't hit me again." My words sounded strange in my ears, as if each syllable floated in a briny bubble.

They didn't sound strange to Blass. His wrist uncocked. "I'm going to shoot you all right, you motherfucker. As soon as you tell me what the fuck this is supposed to be."

"You killed Stuart Dahlman twenty years ago."

"So what?"

"So you pay for it."

"Wrong, dead meat. You pay for it."

I turned my eyes to Hayes George. He grinned, pointed the muzzle of the Walther directly at my heart.

I looked into Blass's blue eyes, watched for the moment, the only chance I'd have. No chance.

Hayes George laughed. Cal Blass turned his head toward the sound. Hayes fired and one of Blass's eyes became a small dark bloody hole and the back of his head became a large dark bloody hole.

Blass's body collapsed to the brick as if from inside, like a building under demolition.

With the toe of his boot, Hayes George nudged the .45 from the loose grip of Blass's dead fingers. He switched the Walther to his left hand, bent and picked up the .45.

"Nothin' to it, Ross."

"Piece of cake," I said, watching the .45 barrel swing toward me. "Still a couple of loose ends."

His grin spread. "Only one."

Numbness had spread over the side of my face. At the edge of my jaw I felt an itch. Through my beard I touched gently with my fingers. My fingers felt blood.

"You got a hole in your face, Ross."

"I've also got a .22 pistol in the back of my jeans."

"I know," he said. "What were you thinking of doing with it?"

"I was thinking of putting it in Blass's hand and firing it at the mountains a couple of times."

"Nice touch. Why don't you do that, very carefully."

Slowly I reached around and pinched the butt of the .22 in two fingers. Slowly I pulled it from my jeans and brought it around so that he could see it, took a pen from my shirtpocket and stuck it through the trigger guard, took a small cloth from my jacket and carefully wiped the pistol.

"Nicely executed." He stepped back toward the pool.

I gave him my back and stepped over to Blass's body.

"How did you know I wouldn't shoot you, Ross?"

"I knew you'd have to tell me about it first."

"Why?"

"Who else can you tell? You killed Haskell and Flora. No fun unless you can tell somebody. Especially somebody who can appreciate it. No fun being a killer if nobody knows it."

I knelt and placed the pistol in Blass's death-curled fingers.

"How'd you figure it?"

"Elimination," I said, wrapping the dead bone and flesh around the grip. "You're the only one left. Haskell was easy enough. You thought he was the blackmailer. Or one of them. You thought Glory was the other. That's why you were looking for her."

"If I hadn't had that pea-shooter there, I could've had 'em both at the same time."

"Haskell drew you away from her, didn't he?"

"I thought I'd hit him, but I couldn't be sure. Wasn't even sure when he fell in the drink."

"The one I really can't figure is Flora."

"You can take credit for that. You got her to agree to make a statement. Who knows what she would have said?"

"What were you afraid of, that she'd name Ripley as Dahlman's killer? Why would you care? That'd just give you Hollister Corporation on a platter."

"Ca'mon, Ross. I couldn't let that happen. You know what that'd do to the Hollister image. Shit, if it wasn't for that, I'd of turned him in myself."

"Only Ripley and your mother knew Flora was willing to make a statement."

"Just imagine what a surprise it was, Ross, when I came into my office and heard the three of you on the intercom."

I slipped a finger through the guard and onto the trigger, rearranged the dead hand. "And she was there alone, and old man Lotz was passed out and his shotgun was just begging to be used. It was easy. Do her, go out and put the shotgun in his hand and fire at Peavine Mountain."

"Fish in a barrel."

"You're a real killer, Hayes."

"I come by it honestly, Ross. Both sides of the family."

I placed my fingers over those on the pistol.

"You're too far away, Ross. Can't hold it steady. Gotta jerk it. No way."

"Probably," I said. "You still don't know, do you?"

"What's that, my man?"

"It was all over nothing." I slowly squeezed the dead flesh under my hand. "Your father has never killed anyone."

"Except that kid in Winnemucca. Maybe it wasn't murder, but, hey, nobody's perfect."

The flesh under my hand seemed boneless, oozed. "No."

"Then who did?"

He watched the barrel of the .22 slowly angle upward. His thick finger tightened on the trigger of Cal Blass's .45.

"Lawrence Parker."

"Right."

"Your father isn't Lawrence Parker."

His eyes searched mine for the truth.

I shot him through the heart.

The .45 exploded as he fell, clattered on brick as he hit the edge of the pool, stilled as he slid into the water.

I rose and picked up the .45. Hayes floated face down in the water. Shadows darkened the water and hid his blood.

I stepped around the body of the squat man in the red jacket, around the body of Cal Blass, went to the stairs and climbed them, passed the body dangling over the rail, reached the top and went into the house.

In what Hayes had called the party room I found two men with their heads beaten in, one unconscious and one dead. I found the photograph that Glory and Bobby George had talked about. I found a beer and a phone.

I made a call. Then I wiped the .45 with the rag from my pocket and put the gun and rag in a drawer behind the bar.

Then I sat at the bar and sipped the beer and waited, creating a story, recreating myself.

# 41

In Nevada, anything is possible.

In Nevada, nothing is as it seems.

In Washoe County, nobody believed my story. But most came to like it. It concluded things neatly.

Conclusions are important. Neatness counts.

It had some problems, of course. I didn't try to explain them. I got some help.

The girl in the yellow bikini bottom told the Sheriff that I'd fired only after twice being fired upon. The Sheriff seemed to think that meant something.

One of the best criminal attorneys in Reno came to see me, listened to my story, then disappeared for twenty-four hours and returned with a writ of habeas corpus and the assurance that I would not be charged with a crime.

The attorney told me that a Hollister Corporation check had covered his fee.

I also got a check from the Hollister Corporation, for ten thousand dollars. My bonus. I cashed it.

I lost my beard. The sight of the .45 had torn through my cheek, and the beard had to go before I could be sewn up.

Hayes George received a hero's burial. I didn't attend. As his body slid beside his grandfather's bones in a large mausoleum in San Francisco, I sat in the shade of a tarp in the desert, listening to my daughter's plans for school.

I took her back to Reno when school started. Then I drove to

Berkeley. Dolly George and I talked. I didn't tell her that I had killed her brother. We made love. She taught her classes and I roamed.

She thought everything was over. She thought we could make a life together. She thought she loved me.

After a week she told me she thought I should leave.

I went back to the desert.

One chilly gray scuddy late October day, as I was filling the Wagoneer's gas tanks at Gerlach and watching the ridges for the snow I could smell in the air, the old Land Rover pulled in and Gabriel George rolled down his window and invited me to a cup of coffee.

We met in front of Bruno's Cafe and went inside and took a table by the window where we could see the Sand Creek Desert stretching south toward Pyramid Lake, the Black Rock Desert stretching west, the peaks of the Selenite Range disappearing in the lowering sky.

Steam misted his glasses as he sipped his coffee. He put down the cup. "I know it doesn't mean much, Jack, but I'm sorry."

"I'm sorry too."

"I'd hoped that after everything returned to normal, you and Dolly might be able to. . . ."

"Normal," I said. "Is that how everything is?"

"I guess not," he said to his cup. "Nothing's ever normal in this country. Maybe that's why men like us come and stay in it."

Men like us.

I looked at my cup. "I had hopes too. They didn't come about."

"Do you know why?"

"When I met Dolly, I was a mess. So was she. We tried to use one another to solve our individual problems. It didn't work. It never does. Now we can't go on, and we can't go back and start over."

He nodded. "No."

I drank some coffee. "I have something to tell you."

He nodded again. "Yes."

"Cal Blass didn't kill Hayes. I did."

He didn't look at me. He looked down at his coffee, his cup, his hands. "Why?"

"Because he was going to kill me. And because he killed Haskell and Flora."

"When Alice and Frederick went through his papers," he said slowly, "they learned that he was worth several million dollars. Frederick had an accountant go over everything. Things . . . weren't right."

"Too much money and no way to track the source?"

"Yes."

"Blass's money."

"Was it?"

"I think so. That's the only reason Hayes was with me. To make sure Blass died. Cal used Hayes as a front, to get his coke money into legitimate businesses. Or he thought he was using Hayes. But Hayes was using him, to get the money. He would have killed Cal sooner or later anyhow."

His voice came steadily, but as if from a long distance. "I mourn my son. I've mourned for a long time, long before he died. I saw what he was becoming and that there was no way to prevent him from becoming that. I couldn't change him. All I could do was love him."

I looked out at the desert.

"He didn't kill Stuart and . . . the girl, did he?"

"No, Cal did that himself."

"Do you know why he killed Haskell and Flora?"

I looked at him, at his bent head, bowed shoulders. He was an old man, and he was very tired.

"Because of you."

He looked up slowly.

"They all died because of you. Some of them directly, some indirectly. But you're responsible for it all."

I could see nothing in his expression, nothing in his eyes but that familiar sadness. Yet he was not the same. Something was gone.

"You know."

"Yes."

"Who else?"

"I told Hayes before I shot him. That's what, in a real way, kept him from killing me. Rose knows that you're not Parker."

"I . . . wondered. The way she looked at me when she told me who she really was, as if she were asking me to do the same. How did you . . . find out?"

"The story you told me that day, after taking me to the graves—I didn't believe it. It was preposterous, that Haskell would kill Lawrence Parker, regardless of the shape he was in, and then not claim the reward or notify the authorities. It was unbelievable. But it was true."

"Yes."

"Not all the details, though. And not the motive. I didn't really understand any of this until I went through Haskell's effects and saw the memorabilia from Stuart's childhood. And the family pictures. Haskell's family."

"Yes."

"Someone was missing from those pictures. The same someone who took them. 'The forgotten man,' you called him."

"Yes."

"Parker's in that grave beside Dolores, isn't he?"

"Not Lawrence Parker. Bones. Nothing. We knew no one would be able to identify those bones, no one would know. That's what's in that grave, Jack. Nothing."

"The nothing that had been Lawrence Parker."

He looked at me, nearly smiled. "You haven't quite got it yet, Jack. It—you asked me once about my photographs. That's what you see in them. Nothing. That's what the desert does—strips and scours you down into what you really are: nothing. That's why men go crazy out here."

"Except that some don't. If you're nothing, you have no limits. You can be anything. You can be Gabriel George."

"Yes."

"So Haskell killed Lawrence Parker and left him to rot in the desert until it was time to find the remains of Barney Dahl-man."

He disappeared behind his eyes, said: "Haskell had a hard time with that. Not the shooting—he really thought he was doing the right thing for Parker—but leaving his body. . . ."

"The price he had to pay, to keep his son from growing up a half-breed."

"The price he had to pay for loving Dolores. She's the one who wouldn't allow Stuart to go through that. It may not seem so bad now, but forty years ago, out here. . . . But Haskell paid the price," he said. "We all did."

"That's part of it. But there's more. Your part."

He nodded heavily. "I'd served my purpose. I'd given her son an acceptable name, an acceptable father. But I couldn't stay, couldn't pretend to be Stuart's father, not when he got older. Besides that, Dolores didn't want me around, I was a convenience and I'd served my purpose. She thought it was better that Stuart didn't even know Haskell was his father. When Haskell found Parker, Dolores saw it as the answer to everything."

"So you buried Lawrence Parker as Barney Dahlman and became Gabriel George and left. And Haskell stayed and raised his son, and kept silent too, never telling Stuart that he was his father, never telling Glory and Lily that he was their grand-father. And then you met and married Alice Hollister and fathered a family and never told any of them who you really were, let them believe you were a killer."

The warmth of the room had begun to collect in a damp gray film at the borders of the chilling window. Gabriel George—for that, not Barney Dahlman, was who he was, had made himself into—looked through the misting glass.

"Hayes Hollister found out about Alice and me and came running. It took him about two minutes to discover that Gabriel George had died a day after he was born and that I was a phony. He got to Dolores. She knew what he was, knew how his warped mind worked. Dolores told him I was Parker."

"And you let him believe it. You let all of them believe it."

"Yes."

"And your silence killed nine people."

"Yes."

"Three of them by my hand. One of whom was your son."

"Yes."

My coffee had grown cold. I pushed it from me, pushed my chair from the table. His eyes followed me as I rose.

"What are you going to do, Jack?" He wanted me to do something. He wanted it over.

"Nothing."

I walked out of the cafe into the chill and wind and climbed in my rig and pointed it at the white flakes of snow flurrying in the desert.

The next day the Land Rover was still parked in front of the cafe. Somebody called the Sheriff.

Somebody else recalled seeing a man walking across the highway and down onto the hard-cracked playa of the Black Rock Desert.

The authorities searched.

Hollister Corporation money has some still searching. I see them sometimes, in their white Ford pickups. They know me. We pass. I shake my head. They shake their heads.

Nothing.

## AFTERWORD

Rereading something I wrote—be it in the distant past, the recent past, yesterday, an hour ago—is usually an occasion of intense embarrassment. Almost always the gap between the remembered intention and the actual execution looms like The Abyss. Inconsistencies and infelicities and downright idiocies gambol about the pages in most high mockery of my aspirations toward clarity and effect and coherence. I reread, and I squirm and flush and sweat. Because writers—or at least the kind of writer I am—can't really reread; they can only, as they reread, rewrite. And cringe.

I squirmed and flushed and sweated and cringed at some rereading of *The Big Silence*—at a clunky or stilted phrase, a transparent plot device, a not-quite-nailed character or scene, a not-quite-made thematic connection, a missed opportunity to... make it better. But I didn't squirm and flush and sweat and cringe an awful lot. What I did mostly was enjoy myself, remarking with pleasure at the little details or bits of business or snippets of language I'd forgotten, remarking with surprise how close the novel is to what I wanted it to be.

Were I writing it now, of course, I would do a few things differently. In particular, I would simplify the genealogy of the denizens of Sun Valley; these relationships seem, even to me at this remove, if not confusing at least more complicated than necessary—complicated because in my attempt to present a "realistic" portrait of life in certain Reno environs I forgot that the fiction writer's job is not to *reproduce* reality but rather to *suggest* it. And I would probably handle differently a couple of the characters—do a bit more with Haskell Dan, for instance. But, despite the fact that I know a lot more about writing fiction now than I did when I wrote *The Big Silence*, I wouldn't significantly change much else. The book pretty much does what I wanted it to do and is what I wanted it to be.

What I wanted it to do was to move the figure who used to be called the "hardboiled" detective out of the Chandlerian mean streets of the city and put him back where he was born, in the towns and deserts and mountains of the West. And I wanted the book to use this figure to tell a story that was about something other than simple "detection." That is, I wanted it to use the private eye as the narrator not of a detective story but rather of a novel about a detective.

*The Big Silence* does this.

I wanted this to be a novel about, in a very real if general way, the American West, and about, in a very real and specific way, Nevada. And I wanted it set in the real Nevada, the Nevada of casinos and whorehouses to be sure, but also the Nevada of sagebrush and playa and working ranches and dirt roads—the Nevada that is perhaps most real in its stories and legends, most alive in its history.

*The Big Silence* is this.

Of course, it isn't just the road to Hell that's paved with good intentions. So none of this means very much if *The Big Silence*, as an account of recognizable human beings involved in a significant human action, doesn't engage and affect its readers. It doesn't matter much what a novel is about if it isn't any good.

And the only important opinion about the novel's quality and value is yours. All I can say is that I don't squirm or flush or sweat or cringe when I see my name on it.

# WESTERN LITERATURE SERIES